A GRAVE MATTER

RICK POLAD

**CALUMET
EDITIONS**
Minneapolis

**CALUMET
EDITIONS**

Minneapolis

THIRD EDITION June 2026

10 9 8 7 6 5 4 3

ISBN: 978-1-960250-47-6

Cover photograph: Carol Deleskiewicz
Cover and interior design: Gary Lindberg

To all the poor souls.

A GRAVE MATTER

RICK POLAD

Chapter 1

BECAUSE OF A SURVEILLANCE JOB, I HADN'T BEEN TO THE OFFICE in two weeks. I walked from the deli to the office in a warm drizzle, opened the front door, did a double take and then turned around and let the door close. I looked at the door and saw my name in big black letters. It was the right door but it was the wrong office.

I looked through the glass and again saw the carpet over the linoleum floor, the old bare walls painted a warm shade of blue, furniture that looked modern and attractive rather than functional, and art on the walls.

When I opened the front door a second time, I heard Carol say, "Hang on a second, he just came in." She put the call on hold and told me a woman wanted to talk to me but wouldn't give her name. I set the bag with the subs on her desk, raised my arms as I looked around the room, and headed for my office.

The woman still wouldn't give her name. She just said she wanted me to go look at a place at the Walker State Mental Health Facility in Elgin... a cemetery. I asked why. She just wanted me to look around and see if I noticed anything. I told her I was too busy to play games and was about to hang up when she said *please*. There was something about the way she said it that made me pay attention. I asked what I was supposed to see there and what I was supposed to do after I saw it. She said she would call Monday at noon. She didn't want to tell me anything until after I had been there. I hung up and looked up at Carol who was standing in the doorway with a puzzled look. I just shook my head.

"Tell me about that over lunch," Carol said.

"Not much to tell. She wants me to go look at a cemetery."

"Why?"

I shrugged. "Beats me."

"You going?"

I thought about it for a few seconds and said, "Sure. Sounds intriguing. But not as intriguing as the office. Where did my office go?"

"Well, do you remember saying that I was in charge of the office and you would trust my purchase choices?"

"I do. As I recall that was about a computer."

She looked a bit sheepish. "It was. But the shiny new computer looked so out of place. I may have gotten a bit carried away."

I was trying hard not to laugh and to look as stern as I could. "Well I hope the computer is happy."

"Spencer, I—"

I had to let out the laugh. "It looks wonderful, Carol. I do hope the computer is happy, but more so I hope you are. You're the one who has to be here every day. Do you like it?"

"I do," she said hesitantly. "Do you?"

"Well, I'll take another look, but so far very nice."

"You can take another look while we eat." As she set the subs on paper plates on the new conference table, she said, "By the way, I finished my course and got my—Watson!"

I started laughing. "Whose sandwich is he eating... yours or mine?"

"Yours! Watson, sometimes I could just..."

"He's making a mess on the new carpet," I said.

"I'll clean it up," she said.

I joined her at the new glass table. "They're big subs. Let's just cut one in half."

She took out a Coke for me and a Sprite for her. While we ate, we talked about the call and came up with some pretty bizarre scenarios.

I had finished a case the week before that sent a police detective to jail on murder charges. Two of his fellow officers had also been arrested. I had called Ben, my retired deputy state's attorney, to see if he was interested in spending some time at my cabin in Door County. He was. I'd have to call and postpone.

"If you have to be here Monday, I guess you're not heading north," said Carol between bites.

"I guess not."

"When are you picking up Rosie?"

"Her plane gets in tomorrow morning."

She gave me a playful look. "You anxious to see her?"

Rosie had been gone for almost a month. "I missed her," I said. That didn't really answer the question, but Carol didn't respond.

As I finished my sandwhich I looked around the room again and only had one negative comment as I pointed to the back wall and a painting of a clown holding some balloons. "That painting is pretty close to the dart board."

She smiled. "Billy picked that out, and he hasn't had any trouble."

I shook my head. "Well, if one of my darts happens to pop one of those balloons, I won't be held responsible."

"Deal," she said with a smile.

Chapter 2

I HADN'T BEEN TO THE BLUE NOTE IN ALMOST TWO YEARS. Whenever I had thought about going, something had come up. But it was the perfect spot to spend an evening with Rosie. And I figured with a little alcohol and a lot of great jazz she'd tell me what she'd been doing in California.

Jesse, the parking lot manager who had been there forever, wasn't there. The lot was packed, and the kid who came up to my window was new to me. He gave me a ticket, and Rosie and I made our way into the lounge. The hostess was new too. Things change. But Blue Eyes was behind the bar and the quartet was on the bandstand, so all was right with the world. It was Saturday night, and the place was crowded. The hostess led us to a table in the corner, farthest from the band, so I figured Lemon, the sax player and leader of The Boys, hadn't seen me. But when they finished "Billie's Bounce" he spoke quietly to the other three, and they slowed the tempo down for "Girl Talk," my dad's favorite song. A measure before he started the melody, Lemon looked at me, and we both nodded.

"Did I miss something?" Rosie asked.

I told her about the band playing Dad's favorite song every time we came in and the first time they played it after he and Mom were gone. She reached over and took my hand.

"That's sweet."

I nodded and looked up at the waitress. We ordered draft beers and listened to the rest of the song. The same soft-blue light played on Lemon's sax. Lou Wright on drums and Bones Slattery on bass laid down a steady rhythm while Marty Larkin chorded on the piano. Dad had brought me here before it was legal for me to walk in the door, but I didn't drink, and I guessed Blue Eyes wasn't worried as long as a police chief was sitting with me. The Boys were as good as I remembered. The waitress brought our beers, and I raised my glass to the band when the song ended.

Rosie and I touched glasses.

"Good to have you back, Rosie. Here's to your tan." Rosie was pretty fair-skinned, and she had come back from California with a shade of light brown. Whatever she was doing must have been at least partly outside.

She gave me a look with a squint and said, "Good to be back. But I hear I missed a few things."

I finished a long drink and said, "Things got interesting."

She laughed. "If you call buddying up with the leader of the biggest gang in the city interesting then, yes, I guess they were."

I smiled. "Hardly buddies. Seemed like the thing to do at the time."

"Get help from a known drug dealer?"

"Well, you see, there was this nun."

"Yeah, I heard about the nun. What did she have to do with Williams?"

I drank some beer. "Well… she kept saying the Lord would provide. Williams was the provision."

"I suppose that makes sense somehow, but I'm not going to try and figure it out."

I smiled and said, "You must be dying to tell me all about your trip."

She smiled back and said, "When you join the force and become my boss, I'll fill you in."

"So it's like that is it?"

She took a drink. "If you're going to badger me about this all night, let's go home." Her tone was snotty. But her challenging look was playful.

"It was worth a try. But you can't blame me for being curious."

"No, I can't. And I'm sorry I can't tell you. Just special training that needs to have a lid on it for a while. When I can tell you, I will."

I nodded, finished my beer, and motioned to the waitress for two more.

As the band played the intro to "April in Paris," she said, "Stosh says you're heading up to Door County."

"That was the plan. But I got a strange phone call yesterday from a woman who wants me to look at a cemetery."

Rosie raised an eyebrow. "Look? What for?"

"That's where the strange comes in. She didn't say."

"What cemetery?"

"At the Walker State Mental Health Facility out in Elgin."

She looked surprised. "And you don't know what you're looking for?"

"I do not. She's going to call me Monday at noon. I assume I'll find out then."

The waitress arrived with the beer.

"Perfect," Rosie said. "You'll have this solved in no time with all those clues."

"You wanna come? We could head out after breakfast and find a place for an early dinner. Lots of good restaurants out along the river. A couple were hangouts of Al Capone."

She set down her glass and said, "Sure. Sounds like an adventure."

"And if you'd like to spend the night, I'll make breakfast."

She smiled. "I'll let you know."

Chapter 3

WE WERE HEADING WEST ON GOLF ROAD PAST SCHAUMBURG. I had let Rosie sleep in and started breakfast at ten. She woke up to the smell of bacon cooking. I had watched the sun come up and read the paper on the deck. But by the time we left, the sky had clouded over.

I turned left on Route 25 and made my way through downtown Elgin as it started to drizzle. We cut through town, crossed the Fox River, and headed south on 31. As we climbed a hill, two islands in the river came into view.

As I stopped at a red light at the top of the hill, I asked Rosie, "Do you know how Alan Pinkerton got his start?"

She pulled a leg up under her and said, "Wasn't he a detective with the Chicago Police?"

"He was. But he got his start out here in Kane County. He was a barrel maker back in the forties… eighteen forties. He was out here looking for wood and came across a gang of counterfeiters on one of the islands. He notified the police and helped catch them." The light turned. "Word got out, and he started getting requests from people who needed a detective. He became Chicago's first police detective and an agent for the US Post Office and the railroads. Around 1850 he started the Pinkerton Detective Agency. At one point his agency was bigger than the US Army. He was also part of the Underground Railroad."

"From barrel maker to famous detective. Amazing."

"Yup. He's responsible for the term 'private eye.' His motto was 'We Never Sleep,' under a picture of an open eye."

I pulled away from the light and continued along the river.

"But not everything in his career was wonderful. Lincoln put him in charge of army intelligence at the start of the Civil War. That didn't go so well."

"Stick with what you do best."

Soon after crossing Lake Street, I turned right off of 31 into the grounds of the Walker State Mental Health Facility. At the end of a horseshoe drive was a sprawling, two-story brick building. I figured a cemetery wouldn't be in the front and followed a blacktop service road that curved around the south side of the building.

I drove along a wing of the main building that extended back to the west toward a faded red barn at the rear of the property. As we passed the end of the wing, we looked out over a large, open field with forest at its edges. But there was no cemetery.

As I was turning around, an older man came out of the barn and walked toward the Mustang. As he neared, I rolled down my window.

"Nobody allowed back here," he said suspiciously.

"Sorry," I replied. "We're looking for the cemetery."

He squinted and looked at us like we were crazy. But he pointed out over the field and said, "Other side of those trees."

As he turned to go, I asked how to get there.

"Back to the road. Turn in at the big rock." He turned again and started walking away.

"Does the cemetery belong to this place?" I asked.

He just kept walking.

I looked at Rosie.

"Well, that was odd," she said.

"Yes it was. Let's go find that rock."

I drove slowly back up 31, and in less than a minute we found a rock as big as a Volkswagen. Just past it I turned onto a dirt road that wound to the west a couple hundred feet toward a wooded area. The road became overgrown with weeds as we approached the trees. Fifty feet farther on, wheel ruts branched to the left into the trees. Straight ahead we could see a heavy chain stretched across the road.

"This must be it," Rosie said.

On the other side of the chain, the road turned to a walking path overgrown with weeds. I stopped in front of the chain. As I got out of the car I glanced backward and couldn't see the main road. All I saw was prairie grass under a gray sky. As Rosie closed her door a blackbird flew out of the trees and up the path, causing a spray of droplets from the leaves. There was a smell of wet dirt in the air.

She walked around to my side of the car and said, "Looks like a lovely spot for a walk in the woods."

I nodded. "Except for that phone call."

"Which makes it a little spooky." She smiled. "But hey, what's life without a little adventure?"

"You don't get enough adventure?"

"Not since I've been home. And standing here isn't changing that any."

I took her hand, and we walked around the chain. We had walked about fifty feet when we heard a rustling in the trees. We stopped but didn't hear it again.

"Deer?" she asked.

"Maybe."

"Ghost of Alan Pinkerton?"

"Maybe."

"By the way, Mr. Detective, did you bring your gun?"

I took a deep breath. There were several people who berated me for not carrying a gun all the time, Rosie and Stosh being the two most verbal. She knew I hadn't.

"No, did you?" I already knew the answer. I didn't have to look for the slight bulge under her jacket.

"Yes, but two is better than one."

That was a point I couldn't argue.

In another fifty feet the path narrowed and turned to the left. I could see part of a clearing ahead and the top of a tower over trees on the other side. As we neared the end of the path a breeze started, and we got a sprinkling from the arch of trees above us.

We came to the end of the path and looked out over a grassy area about the size of half a football field. About half of it was filled with rows of worn concrete markers. It was surrounded on all sides by mature trees that hid whatever was beyond. If you didn't know the cemetery was there, you wouldn't know it was there… like a secret garden. I felt like I was in a different world.

"Wow," Rosie said.

"Indeed."

Ten feet ahead of us in the clearing was a solitary oak tree. Next to the tree was a large granite boulder with a plaque attached. The plaque read: "Here lie the poor souls of the Walker State Mental Health Facility."

We stood silently and looked out over the rows of markers. The sound of birds chirping was louder than the sporadic muffled rumble of cars on Route 31. It was idyllic… and sad.

"What do you think we're supposed to be looking for, Spencer?"

"No idea. But we're not going to find it standing here. Let's walk the rows and meet in the middle."

"Okay."

"Holler if you find something," I said.

"Holler? Boy, you PIs know all the fancy words."

I headed to the left and stood in front of the first marker. I couldn't read the name or the month, but the year read 1887. I figured they hadn't known a birthdate. I walked down the row. All the markers were basically the same—rectangular, about a foot wide, and about eight inches high. The date of death got later as I walked up the row, and the names and dates became more legible. Some were cracked, and some were partially buried and at odd angles. Some had birth dates as well as a date of death. Each one had a number as well as a name, and the numbers weren't always consecutive. And about halfway up the row there was one that had no name, just a number and a date.

Rosie and I met on my side of the center. She looked like she had lost her best friend.

"This has to be one of the saddest places on Earth," she said.

"Yeah, I can't imagine what these people's lives were like."

"Spencer, there are some markers with just numbers."

"Yes."

She took my hand.

"You live your life... and you end up as a number."

We stood for a few minutes listening to the birds.

"Did you see the top of that tower on the other side of the trees?" she asked.

"Yes. Must be the mental health center."

"I didn't see anything out of the ordinary," she said. "Did you?"

"Nothing worth hollering about. But there was something... see what you think. Let's change places and do it again. Meet you back here."

We met close to the middle and compared notes. We both thought the grass looked disturbed on one of the graves. It was a bit unnaturally mounded. We wondered why the grass would be disturbed on a grave dated 1914. I told her I thought there was another one, dated 1911. We walked back to it. She said if it had been disturbed, it was longer ago than the 1914 grave. The mound wasn't as noticeable.

Rosie knelt and touched one of the markers as I looked around the clearing. The only path I saw was the one we had walked in on.

***

AS WE WALKED OUT, the wind picked up and rustled spring through the trees.

"Do you believe in ghosts, Spencer?"

I thought about that for a bit. I had never experienced a ghost, but friends had, and their stories were credible. But...

"I don't know, Rosie. Seems a bit far-fetched."

"Well, if there are such things, here is where they are. And Einstein predicted them."

It took a few seconds for that to register. "What?"

"Einstein."

"Yeah, I heard. But what does he have to do with ghosts?"

"E equals M C squared."

I let go of her hand and just stared at her. She explained.

"Energy and mass are related and interchangeable. If you die, something has to happen to your mass to keep the equation the same. You turn into energy. And that energy is ghosts."

I smiled. "I know I'm not supposed to talk about it, but you keep giving me hints about what you did in California."

She smiled back. "And how did I do that?"

"Well, I know you spent time running on the beach and probably working out."

"And how do you know that?"

"I detect things. You came back with a summer tan and with a body tone you didn't have when you left."

She laughed. "How do you know it was a beach?"

"Lots of them out there. If there is a beach nearby, why not run on it? And now I know you were taking a course that had something to do with physics. But I'm not quite sure how you can mix physics with metaphysics."

"Wow. Sometimes it's pretty scary how your mind works."

"*My* mind? I'm not the one talking about Einstein and ghosts."

"So, do you think there's some logical explanation about the graves?"

"Probably."

"Like Capone's bank money is buried there?"

"Yeah, like that."

"What do you *really* think?" she asked.

A squirrel ran across the path as we came to the chain.

"I think it will be an interesting phone call."

"Monday at noon?"

"Yup."

"I've got some vacation coming," she said. Mind if I join you?"

"Not at all." I looked at her as I opened the door. "Didn't you just *have* a vacation?"

As she got in she said, "Did I hear someone say lunch?"

"Sounds good, but I'd like another look at the facility."

***

I TURNED RIGHT ONTO 31 and then pulled into the long, sweeping drive of the facility. I stopped in the parking lot in front of the building. It looked dreary under the gray sky. I noticed the top of the tower we had seen from the cemetery.

"Big place," Rosie said.

"Yup. Kinda place a person could get lost in."

"And end up just a number."

I sighed. "Yeah."

"Probably a lot of sad stories in there," she said.

"Yup," I agreed. "One for every patient they've ever had."

I drove around the horseshoe driveway and headed north on 31. Twenty minutes later I turned left into a drive that had no markings. It wound through the trees and opened into a small parking lot next to a cedar-sided building that also had no markings. Rosie looked like a kid on Christmas morning.

The front door was solid wood, and there were no windows in the walls. I knocked on the door, and a small rectangle of wood at eye level slid sideways.

A voice that sounded like it didn't care whether we got in or not said, "Password?"

"Mustang," I said.

The door opened, and we were led down a dimly lit hall and into a room with all windows overlooking the Fox River. The host said our waiter would be right with us.

A very confused Rosie was staring out the window. It was hard not to laugh.

She finally looked at me and said, "You want to explain all this?"

"All what?"

"Sure. Well, let's start with how you know about this place."

"Dad."

A waiter dressed in clothes out of the twenties brought menus and took our drink order.

"And the password? How did you know that?"

I laughed. "I didn't. There isn't a password. It's just a game."

"So everyone gets in? You just make up a word?"

I nodded. "You just make up a word. But not everyone gets in. It's about an attitude. If you're sure of yourself and come up with some password, you get in. If you have no idea what's going on you don't."

"So they turn away customers?"

"I would think not. Remember the entrance? You need to know about this place. And if you know about it you know about the password."

"Does it have a name?"

I pointed at the menu. Embossed on the leather front was "The Hideaway," written in fancy script.

Chapter 4

WHEN YOU'RE WAITING FOR SOMETHING TO HAPPEN, TIME GOES very slowly. I had been at the office since ten, just in case the woman called early, and I was on my third cup of coffee. Carol was at her desk staring at the phone. The only one who wasn't anxiously waiting for the phone to ring was Watson… he was curled up on his bed, sound asleep. Rosie arrived at eleven, just as curious as Carol and I.

When the phone rang at ten to twelve Rosie and I were in my office chatting about the Cubs. Hopes were high… but not as high as usual. When the seventy-fifth year went by without a world series, attitudes had changed. Fans didn't hope as much as they used to.

Carol answered, and Rosie and I looked at each other as we listened. Whatever they were selling, Carol didn't want any. At twelve thirty Rosie went to the deli for sandwiches. We were done eating by one.

"So what now?" Rosie asked.

I shrugged. "I'll give it until one thirty. Then I'm going back to smelling a steak on the grill."

"Dinner tonight?" she asked.

I laughed. "Not quite. The grill is up on Moonlight Bay."

"Can't you do something?" asked Carol from her desk in the other room. "This is driving me crazy!"

Rosie looked at me, and we both laughed. Carol walked into the office.

"I've only got one thing to go on, Carol. And we already did that."

"So now what?"

"If something's gonna happen, it has to come to me."

It did, but not until Wednesday, an hour before I was going to leave to pick up Ben.

***

I HAD JUST CLOSED A SMALL SUITCASE and was going to go through my checklist of shutting down the house when the phone rang.

"Spencer, there's a man in the office. Says his mother's missing."

Carol has a list of referrals for any number of tasks... friends and friends of friends who could take care of the jobs I didn't want. *Missing* I'd usually want, but not when there was a steak sizzling without me there. I told her to use the list.

There were a few seconds of silence.

"Spencer, he says he found a note on his mother's nightstand. It says to call you at noon on Monday."

"I'll be there in twenty minutes. Please call Ben and tell him I'll call."

***

I DIDN'T RUN ANY RED LIGHTS, but I got there in fifteen. When I came in the back door, I saw Watson sitting outside my office looking into the room. Carol leaned around the corner and nodded at my office.

"What's with Watson?" I asked.

"He's guarding the kingdom. He got tired of hearing you say all he does is eat and sleep."

I looked at her with my best frown. Watson wagged his tail once and headed back to his bed.

Sitting in front of my desk was a man in his middle thirties, a bit overweight, the start of a bald spot on the back of a head of black hair and wearing a gray suit that looked like he had slept in it. He turned around nervously as I offered a *good morning.*

"Thank goodness," he said. "That dog has been making me nervous... like he thought I was going to steal something."

That thought had never entered my mind, but perhaps it had entered Watson's. So, I wondered if that was because he once *had* stolen something.

As I walked to my chair we introduced ourselves. He was Gregory Janice. He filled up the chair. A moustache that needed trimming, coal black eyes, and shoulders too large for his body made him look a bit odd.

I said, "I understand you think your mother is missing, and you found a note." I assumed it was the piece of paper he was fidgeting with. He handed it to me.

His nervousness was quickly replaced by anger. "I don't *think* she's missing... she *is* missing."

I turned my chair toward him and sat. "Have you called the police?"

"No. When I found the note and heard you were a PI, I came here first."

"What's your mother's name?"

"Susan."

"And why... how long has she been missing?"

"Did she call you Monday?"

"No."

"Well then at least since then."

"And you found this note on her nightstand?"

"Yes. I was supposed to pick her up this morning for a doctor appointment. She didn't answer, so I used my key."

"Where does she live?"

He gave me the address of her apartment building in Oak Park.

"You found nothing else there?"

He shook his head. "I met the lady across the hall on my way out. She had last seen her on Saturday when they chatted in the hall. Nothing seemed wrong."

I read the note again and told him about my trip to the cemetery.

"Do you have any idea what she was concerned about and why she mentioned a cemetery?"

"No clue." He shifted in the chair and looked back at the doorway... probably checking on Watson.

He had no idea about the cemetery. But he did say his mother had a vivid imagination and had bizarre theories about every crime she heard about on the radio. She called them her *little mysteries*.

She had even called the police a few times to tell them she had a case solved. I could imagine what the response was.

I leaned back in my chair and sighed. "There's not much to go on here, Mr. Janice. I suggest you call the police and report it. They have a wide network of options for finding people."

"Okay. But I'd like to hire you to see what you can do."

"I'm not sure I can do anything with what we have so far."

He took a deep breath. "There must be something. I admit the cemetery bit is odd, but it's even more odd that she would be missing after talking to you. Don't you think that's strange?"

I did, and I told him so.

He nodded and looked lost in thought.

"Wait a minute," he said. "She had a journal. Do you think that would help?"

"What kind of journal? Do you mean a diary?"

He shook his head. "No. It was her notes about her *little mysteries* as she called them."

Nero Wolfe came to mind… solving crimes without ever leaving the comfort of his oversized chair. But there was something about this case that had bothered her enough to call me. It wouldn't hurt to look… I owed her that much.

"Okay, let's go take a look through her apartment. Hopefully we can find the journal. But after we look, you're calling the police."

He agreed, reached into his pocket, and handed me a check for five hundred dollars.

"Is this enough for a retainer?" he asked.

I handed it back to him. "I'm not sure there's anything to retain me for. Let's look at the apartment first."

He put the check back in his pocket.

I gave Susan's address to Carol and told Gregory I'd meet him at the apartment building.

Watson opened his eyes long enough to make sure Gregory had left and then got up, turned twice in a circle, and settled back on his bed. It was tough duty being a sidekick.

Chapter 5

HIS MOTHER'S NAME WAS SUSAN. SHE WAS FIFTY-SEVEN YEARS old. I got that fact from Gregory while climbing the stairs to the third floor. Her apartment was in an old stone building six blocks east of the section of large homes in Oak Park that included the Frank Lloyd Wright houses. The neighborhoods got more rundown as you went east toward the west side of Chicago. Oak Park was a study in social strata.

We turned left at the top of the stairs.

"It's halfway down the hall," Gregory said.

As we neared apartment 3D, the door across the hall quietly closed. I glanced at Gregory, and he rolled his eyes.

"I imagine even the mice don't have any privacy," he said.

Gregory opened the door and flicked a light switch.

"My mother kept the shades down. She was sure someone from one of her mysteries was spying on her."

He opened the shades and let in the day as I wondered why I was spending my time on someone who needed help of the kind I couldn't give. His mother obviously had problems that weren't in my line of work. But I was there, and she had called me, and she did appear to be missing. So I resolved to stop thinking about steak and see if there was anything meaningful in her apartment.

"I'm just going to look around," I said. "See if you can find the journal, but don't touch anything. If you need to open drawers use a towel or napkin and touch as little as possible."

The apartment looked like nobody lived in it. It was spotless, and all the surfaces were bare. I was in the living room. To my left was a hall that led to a kitchen and, I assumed, a bathroom. Ahead of me was another door that I assumed led to a bedroom. Gregory opened that door and went in. There were no bills or pens on the desk, no pictures on the two tables, nothing personal anywhere. It didn't bode well for finding anything meaningful.

As my thoughts drifted back to steak, Gregory came out of the bedroom and said he had found the journal.

The bedroom was just as bare as the living room except for two pictures on the dresser. One was a recent photo of Gregory and a woman I assumed to be his mother. The other was a much younger version of the same two.

He pointed to the nightstand. "It's in there."

The drawer was open far enough to see a small book with the words "My Journal" on a gray cover. He handed me a hand towel, and I opened the drawer far enough to see the whole journal. I tossed the towel back to Gregory and went to the kitchen in search of something less bulky. A stack of paper napkins provided the answer.

I used a napkin to lift the journal out of the drawer and turned to the last entry, dated April 20. It was her call to me on Friday with a note that said she would call back at noon on Monday. I was hoping for some explanation, but it said nothing more than she had told me about the cemetery. I checked a few other pages and read her notes on two other mysteries. Dates and times were followed by short, factual reports on what the problem was. One was a car accident. Following the report of the facts was a fantastic timeline of events that started with an illegal adoption. If nothing else, she had quite an imagination. Then she noted that she had shared her ideas with the police and was told a detective would call her back. No one had. I wasn't surprised.

The second was a robbery of a local jewelry store and a note that said she didn't have enough data to form a conclusion. I decided I *did* have enough data. At the very least, Susan Janice had way too much time on her hands. At the most, she could use some professional help. I kept those conclusions to myself. I put the journal back in the drawer, looked through the rest of the apartment and, seeing nothing out of the ordinary, told Gregory he needed to call the police.

"There's nothing else you can do?"

"Like what?" I said.

He shrugged. "Check the bus station, call her friends, check with people in the building... anything."

"You already talked to the lady across the hall. Do you know her friends?"

He thought for a few seconds. "No."

"Might be listed in an address book, and I haven't seen one."

"It might be in a drawer. Everybody has an address book."

"Might be. But I'm done looking in any more drawers until after the police have been here."

He just stared at me.

"Is there some reason you don't want the police involved?" I asked.

He shook his head slowly. "No. It just seems so... final. You call them when there's no hope left."

"You call them when you need help. They'll talk to people in the building and check the neighborhood. They have a lot more resources than I do. I'll stay and see what they have to say if you call. If not, I'm done here."

He took ten seconds to agree.

***

TWO PATROL OFFICERS ARRIVED twenty minutes later and spent a half hour looking through the apartment and taking our information. Neither one of us told them about the journal. I figured her name was already part of station lore, and I could guess how she was referred to. The journal would only add flames to the stories about the crazy lady in 3D.

After the officers left, I asked Gregory if I could borrow the journal. He smiled.

"So you *are* going to do something."

"I'm going to read the journal. I'll get it back to you."

He was still smiling as he handed me his check.

Chapter 6

IT WASN'T MY DECK ON MOONLIGHT BAY, BUT A STEAK AT McGoon's was just as good, and I didn't have to drive six hours to get there. Ben and I were on our second beer as I explained the call from Mrs. Janice and the events that followed.

Ben savored his Guinness and listened without interrupting. But I knew his mind was racing as he listened, and he was moving the pieces around trying to make them fit. When I finished he said, "Curious."

I raised my glass to him. "Yes. Do you know anything about the facility?"

He nodded slowly. "More than I'd like to. Since it's run by the state, a lot of the paperwork goes through the State's Attorney's Office... anyone who is legally committed, criminal cases that have a mental aspect, or John and Jane Does."

"What *doesn't* go through your office?"

"There is a private portion... someone who voluntarily enters for treatment."

"Like a health spa?"

He sighed. "It's not a pretty place no matter which part you're looking at. So not a health spa... no."

"Abuse?"

He took a longer drink. "There were some cases... hard not to have trouble dealing with violent patients. But mostly it's people working in less than desirable conditions because the budget doesn't pay for fancy rooms and high pedigree doctors."

"Were you ever there?"

"I only handled the more extreme problems so not much, but enough to not want to go back. It's a sad place." He finished his beer. "I can deal with complaints, just like all the rest. You talk to people and straighten things out. But what got me were the people sitting in wheelchairs just staring into space. And when I walked by, their eyes followed me like a portrait on a wall. It was worse than any jail I'd ever been in."

"They were in their own private jail," I said.

He just looked at me and then turned as the steaks arrived. They were sizzling on the platter.

As I was cutting into mine, I said, "You always avoided my question about why you retired early. Is that part of it?"

He took his first bite and took a deep breath and smiled. "A steak cooked to perfection. One of life's little pleasures."

"No argument here. Are you changing the subject?"

He took another bite and spread sour cream on his baked potato.

"It was just part of the job... not an easy part, but none of it was easy. We didn't see the people who lived on the north shore and drove Mercedes. Not that they were any better than anybody else. They just had the connections and the money to make their crimes go away."

Ben wasn't telling me anything I didn't already know. I just never knew how much it bothered him.

The waiter set two more glasses of Guinness on the table and took our empty glasses.

"Dad's solution was to do something about the things he could and let the rest go."

Ben nodded. "But it bothered him."

"Sure. But he came home every day knowing he'd done his job as best he could, and he had the support of the people around him."

"That would make a difference."

"Are you saying you didn't?"

He cut another piece of steak and let it sit on his plate. He looked up at me and said, "I'm saying the current AG and I didn't agree on how some things should be handled. He pushed hard for convictions, and he got them."

"So what's wrong with that?"

"It's how he got them. The game is all about politics and money, and he thrives on playing the game."

The current attorney general was Rodney Lansing. He dressed well and made a point of being seen with important people, people with money... people on the right political side of the street. "Are you saying he's crooked?"

"I've already said too much. Let's just leave it at I quit because the game was too big a part of the job. Those who played it moved up the ladder. I didn't want to play."

"But you had a good career... made a good name for yourself."

He set his glass down and wiped his mouth. "To an extent... because I was fair and worked hard."

"So what changed?"

"A case a couple years back. I was told what was going to happen and how I was going to handle it. I didn't agree."

"Which case was that?"

He shook his head.

"What happened?"

"I was replaced by someone who would do as he was told." He took a bite of potato and picked up his knife. "That's when I knew my career was over. I'd spend the next ten years pushing misdemeanors through the courts and doing paperwork."

I chewed slowly. "I never knew, Ben. I always thought it was the lure of the links."

He laughed. "I do love golf. But I loved the challenge of a good case more."

The waiter cleared the table, and we sipped our beer. I knew there was more. I also knew he didn't want to talk about it, at least not now.

"So, you think you're just dealing with a lady with a vivid imagination?" Ben asked.

"Her journal is proof of that. But the cemetery angle is odd, maybe too odd not to be true."

"Got a plan?"

"I'm going to read her journal tonight and go from there."

He laughed. "Not much of a plan."

"Every puzzle starts with one piece. And I'll check with the police in a few days and see if they come up with anything."

"And I'll go home and unpack my bag," he said with a sigh.

The waiter asked if there was anything else we would like. When we declined he set the check on the table. Ben reached for it, but I got it first.

"Why don't you leave your bag packed," I said. "If nothing comes of this, we'll leave Friday."

"Sounds good. Thanks for dinner, Spencer."

"Always a pleasure, Ben."

***

I GOT HOME A LITTLE AFTER TEN, turned on the news, and stretched out on the couch with Mrs. Janice's journal. By ten thirty I was halfway through. All the cases were things she had heard on the radio. Facts were followed by her theory. The most interesting was a professor at the University of Chicago who had been accused of propositioning a female student in his office. He had been suspended with pay pending an investigation. Several of his fellow professors vouched for his character and said there was no way he would have done that. The professor was divorced. Mrs. Janice's theory was that the ex-wife was angry and had hired a student to make a false claim. I had to admit that was an interesting possibility, one I'd like to look into. I turned off the TV and thought about stopping... I was getting drowsy. But I continued reading.

Ten minutes later I read something that caught my attention. On April 6 she had tried to call a Martin Rentel. There had been no answer. Same thing on the seventh and eighth. That was odd for two reasons... she had never tried to contact any of her cases. And I remembered that name.

Chapter 7

I SCANNED BACK THROUGH THE ENTRIES AND FOUND MARTIN
Rentel on February 6. He had been brought in for questioning by the
Chicago Police in connection with the stabbing murder of an eighty-
two-year-old man, Amos Grant, in an alley behind a drugstore on
north Cicero. He had lived in the neighborhood all his life, and the
neighbors were angrily demanding the police do something. Mayor
Cronley had been elected two years ago mostly on a campaign based
on cleaning up the neighborhoods. Everyone knew that wasn't going to happen, but he had to make an effort, had to show outrage
when something like this happened, rally the troops and get results.
Because if he didn't get results, someone else would have his job in
two years, someone else with new promises.

One of the neighbors had said Amos went to the corner bar every
night for a beer and then cut through the alley back to his house.
Martin Rentel matched the description of a man who was seen getting into a car on Cicero at the time of the killing, a few minutes
after eleven. A witness had picked his picture out of a mug book. But
after questioning, the police had let him go. He had an alibi, but they
also didn't have any evidence other than the ID.

I hadn't noticed the first time around that Susan had no theory.
All she wrote was that they had the wrong man.

Martin's name showed up again on April 3. The neighbors had
kept up their pressure on the police who had found some evidence.
They weren't saying what it was, but Martin was brought in again.

An entry on April 5 said Martin was arrested. And then, on April 6, Susan had tried to get information from the police about Martin and wasn't getting any answers except that he was in custody. She had called several more times wanting to know about bail and charges. She kept getting the runaround. On April 9 she had written that she couldn't even get information on where Rentel was being held.

Then, on April 18, Susan had received a call from a woman who told her that if she knew Martin Rentel she'd find answers at the cemetery at the Walker State Mental Health Facility. Her entry also said she had heard a Beach Boys song, "Surfin' Safari," in the background.

The last entry in Susan's journal was dated April 20, her call to me saying she would call again on Monday.

I wondered about calling her son Gregory this late. I had lots of questions, and he would be the first place to look for answers. I usually didn't make calls after ten but decided he was the one who was concerned about his mother.

I called and asked if he knew of a Martin Rentel. He did. Martin Rentel was his cousin. He asked why I asked, and I told him his name was mentioned in the journal. He wanted details, but I wanted to do some thinking before talking to him. He agreed to meet at my office at ten in the morning.

I was tired but made one more call, to Rosie. After bringing her up to date, she volunteered to come along on the next field trip.

Chapter 8

I WOKE AT A LITTLE AFTER SIX AND TOOK THE JOURNAL AND A notepad out onto the deck. But as I sat on one of the cedar chairs the smell brought back a childhood memory. My folks had friends who lived on the south side near the Union Stock Yards. Until the early twenties more meat was processed in Chicago than anywhere in the country. The arched entry gate had recently been declared a national historic landmark. Their friends were the first people I knew who were White Sox fans. I had friends who wondered how anyone could be a Sox fan, but I had wondered more how anyone could stand the smell of the stock yards. And they had a rain barrel that I would drink from even though, or maybe because, I was told not to. The water had a slight taste of cedar. I could still taste the water as I sat in the chair.

I reread the entries as the sky lightened under a thick blanket of clouds and made a list of the dates and the entries. I wanted to make sure I had the facts straight.

***

GREGORY ARRIVED RIGHT ON TIME, looking worried. He nodded and said black when I offered coffee, and I poured him a cup. We settled in my office, and I told him about the entries with the anonymous caller and the cemetery.

"I told her to stay away from him," Gregory said.

"Her nephew? Why would you do that?"

"He was no good. As a kid he was no good. Always in trouble. He had a record as a juvenile that had been sealed, and as an adult it got worse."

"Anything serious?" I asked.

"Everything. Stolen cars, robbery, home invasion." He shook his head. "I told her to stay away from him, but she kept trying to help him."

I took a sip of coffee. "Why your mother? What about his parents?"

He sighed. "His father left when he was ten. His mother, my mother's sister, died in a car accident when he was fifteen. That's when the problems started. My mother wanted to take him in, but Martin was close to his father's brother, and he went to live with him. That guy wasn't worth two cents. He should have been in jail too."

"Too?"

He gave me an angry look. "Yeah. Along with Martin."

"He didn't break the law?"

"He never got caught. I guess Martin wasn't as smart as he was."

"Or as lucky." I heard the front door open. "So how does your mother fit in?"

He took a drink and set his cup on the desk. "She always felt sorry for the kid. Sent him money. Not much… a few bucks when she had some to spare. She never stopped trying to get him to move in with her. She figured she could make a good man out of him." He shook his head.

"You didn't agree?"

"Waste of time… and money. And she didn't have any to waste."

"Did you talk to your mother about the murder?"

"Nope. She knew how I felt about him and never brought him up."

"Did you know about Martin being questioned?"

"Heard it on the news."

"Your mother wrote in her journal that they had the wrong man."

He stared straight at me. "She was wrong."

"You think he did it?"

He laughed… not the funny kind. "That and twenty other things they hadn't caught on to yet."

Carol appeared in the doorway and pulled my door closed. Whoever came in evidently was staying awhile.

He pulled a pack of cigarettes out of his coat pocket and said, "Mind if I smoke?"

"Yes," I answered.

He looked shocked. That was just a rhetorical question that doesn't usually even get an answer. *No, I don't mind* is assumed. But in my office, especially with the door closed, I minded.

"Let's talk about the cemetery. Still means nothing to you?"

It took another ten seconds for the shocked look to wear away and for him to put the pack back in his pocket before he shook his head and said, "Not a thing."

"And she hadn't said anything to you about the anonymous caller?"

"Nope."

"Seems like something she would talk to you about."

"Not if it had to do with Martin. She knew how I felt."

I finished my coffee and wondered about their relationship. I didn't think he was lying, but they didn't seem very close.

I picked up a pencil and rolled it between my fingers. "She asked me to go look at the cemetery. I'm wondering if she went and looked herself."

"She didn't."

"I would think she would. You seem pretty sure."

"Positive. She had no way of getting there. She didn't have a car, never even had a driver's license. She either walked or took the bus, and she didn't do that much. She hardly left that apartment."

I thought about that for a bit. "Friend who could have driven her?"

"No. She only had one lady you might call a friend, and she doesn't have a car either."

"But she might have called there."

He shrugged. "Maybe."

"Perhaps Martin is involved somehow," I said.

"How so?"

"Maybe he tried to rob her, and it got out of hand."

He shook his head. "She didn't have any money besides a few spare dollars."

I set the pencil down. "But maybe he thought she did… she gave him money."

"Maybe. I wouldn't put anything past him."

"So, we have two missing people."

"I hired you to find my mother. Martin I couldn't care less about."

"Okay. Do you know any of Martin's friends?"

He shrugged. "I know some people who had some dealings with him. Wouldn't call them friends."

"Get ahold of whoever you can think of and see if anybody knows of his whereabouts."

"I just told you I don't care about Martin."

"I know, but he's the only link we have at the moment to your mother."

"Okay."

Gregory left, and Carol leaned around the corner and told me there was a woman waiting to see me. The woman, dressed very expensively, wanted me to follow her husband. She handed me a blank check. Life didn't want me sitting on my deck on the bay. I didn't take it. I referred her to a friendly competitor and wished her well.

I took Carol's lunch order and was back in ten minutes with subs. Watson managed to stay awake until the sandwiches were gone. I rewarded him with a piece of roast beef, and he went back to sleep.

Chapter 9

I CHATTED FOR A MINUTE WITH THE DESK SERGEANT AND THEN took the steps two at a time up to Stosh's office. Since I was going to Door County, I had canceled last night's Wednesday Gin game. When I looked in his door he was on the phone. He waved me in. I sat and closed my eyes, pretending I was looking at the peaceful water of Moonlight Bay. He didn't say goodbye before he hung up.

"Just when I thought my day couldn't get worse," he said, looking at me.

"Nice to see you too."

"You're not in Door County."

"Eyes of an eagle. Something came up. I won't be in Door County Saturday either, so lunch and cards?"

"Sure. So what came up that you want my help with?"

I smiled. "Doesn't it feel good to be needed?"

"Depends." He opened a file folder.

"What do you know about Martin Rentel?"

He looked up from the file and squinted. "Not my precinct."

"And if you know that much you know more."

"And why would you be asking?"

I told him about Susan and her journal and the cemetery and Gregory and the connection to Martin.

"Rentel was brought in for questioning. They didn't have any evidence and he had an alibi, so he was released. I don't know everything about it, but there was reason to look at him again. Detectives found the dead man's watch in his apartment, and he was arrested."

"They were getting a lot of heat from the public," I said.

"And the chief," he added.

"Susan called several times wanting information," I said. "She didn't get any. They wouldn't even tell her where he was being held. She wrote that it was like he had disappeared."

"So?"

"So, don't you find that odd?"

Someone looked in his office, and he held up a finger. "Not necessarily. We don't give out information to the public. Cases are handled through lawyers."

"What about the cemetery?" I asked.

"Hah. You gotta admit, all that journal stuff is pretty nuts."

"I admit it's imaginative. But no different than the way most people spend their spare time. Everybody has a hobby. But the cemetery wasn't something she heard on the news. It was something the anonymous caller told her about."

"Told her she would find answers," he said. "Answers to what?"

"I'm assuming—"

"Yes, you're assuming. We can't arrest somebody on an assumption."

"The only thing she had questions about was where Martin was."

He leaned back in his chair. "Okay, I'll play along. How does the woman on the phone know she's looking for Martin?"

"Wondered that myself. I'd like a look at his sheet."

"You would, eh."

I nodded.

"And you think you can just walk into a police station and it will magically appear."

I shrugged. "It's worked in the past."

He rolled his eyes, let out a sigh, picked up his phone, and punched a button. "Kate, please call the Fourth and have them fax over the file sheet on a Martin Rentel." He paused. "Thanks."

As he stood, he said, "I need to chat with the captain for a few minutes. Make yourself at home."

I walked across the hall into Kate's office and helped her wait for the fax. Stosh wasn't back when the fax came in fifteen minutes later. She handed it to me, and I walked back across the hall.

It was four pages of history... theft, assault, robbery, drugs, possession, and selling. Gregory was certainly right about his cousin, and I wasn't surprised about any of that. But I did find what I was looking for. Susan Janice, aunt, was listed as the contact person. I went back to envisioning the bay and waited for Stosh.

"You have any revelations?" he asked as he walked in.

"Susan Janice is listed as the contact person."

"So?"

"So, if the anonymous caller had access to this sheet, she would have Susan's number. And she obviously knew something about Martin Rentel that the rest of us don't."

"You've outdone yourself, kid. Assuming and jumping to conclusions in the same visit."

"Makes sense."

"So do ten other scenarios I could come up with."

"That involve that cemetery?"

He stared over my head at the wall, then looked down to me. "Did you and Rosie find anything at the cemetery?"

I told him about the graves with the disturbed grass.

He shrugged. "Again, several scenarios come to mind. That's what they do in cemeteries... they disturb grass when they dig holes."

"Yeah, *new* holes. These two are more than seventy years old."

"A bit odd, but, again, probably several valid reasons. I need a bit more than some disturbed grass after you waste Rosie's afternoon by dragging her out to a cemetery in the middle of nowhere."

"But followed by a steak dinner at the Hideaway."

He laughed. "I do have to admit, hanging around with you has fringe benefits."

I stood. "If I need anything else, I'll let you know."

"I can hardly wait."

***

I CALLED CAROL FROM THE CAR and asked her to get me an appointment with someone at Walker, as high up the food chain as possible. She called back an hour later none too happy about getting the run-around for ten minutes. But she is nothing if not persistent, and I had an appointment Friday morning at ten with a Mr. Quark, the director of public relations. My next call was to Rosie to see if she wanted to go along… she did.

Chapter 10

FRIDAY DAWNED WITH A CLEAR SKY AND A CHILL IN THE AIR.

As Rosie and I drove west, she asked, "So what do you plan on saying? Tell him you know about the stolen jewels that are buried in the graves? What a great spot to hide stolen merchandise until the statute of limitations has run out and the heat is off. Or is it money from the bank heist?"

"Hey. One Susan Janice is enough." I caught a smirk out of the corner of my eye.

"What *do* you plan on saying?"

"Might just be a curious citizen."

She laughed. "Sure. You just happened to be taking a leisurely stroll in his cemetery hidden in the woods pretty far from the main road."

I didn't really have a plan, and she knew it. "You have a better idea?"

"Nope."

We drove in silence, and I tried to think of something better than my usual plan when I didn't have a plan which was to shake the trees. It wasn't much, but my usual plan usually worked... something valuable usually fell out. As we were crossing the river, Rosie mentioned the sunlight sparkling on the water, and as I pulled onto the grounds of the facility, even *it* looked less dreary in the sunlight. Rosie stayed in the car and said she'd come in after me if I wasn't back in an hour. She also said that a mental health facility probably had several good places to hide a body. I thanked her for her concern.

***

A MAN WITH GRAY HAIR that needed trimming and wearing a white coat was sitting at a wooden desk inside the front doors. He looked to be in his seventies. He watched me walk to the desk without saying a word or changing his dead-pan expression. I waited for him to say something. When he didn't, I handed him my card and told him who I was there to see. Without looking at the card, he pushed a button on top of the desk and handed my card back. As he had reached for the button with his left hand, his coat had slid up his arm, and I saw a two-inch scar just above his wrist. He pointed to a worn, green couch on the wall to the left of the door. I stared at him for a few seconds and then decided he was a mute. I sat and looked around. I was in a center vestibule. There was a hallway to the left and one to the right. In the center, behind the desk, was a glass double door.

Ten minutes later a big, brawny kid in jeans and a white coat came out of the double doors behind the desk. He wasn't much older than early twenties and looked like he was no stranger to physical labor. A deep tan suggested most of that was outdoors.

"Mr. Manning?"

I stood. "That would be me."

"Please come with me."

On the other side of the doors were brightly lit halls, one straight ahead and two leading off to each side. We walked straight ahead down a long hallway with offices on both sides and no windows. Each door had a nameplate and a title. The floor was twelve-inch green vinyl tile, and the walls were bare and painted white. Halfway down he opened a door with the nameplate Robert Quark, Director of Public Relations. I had a feeling I wouldn't be calling him Bob. The sunlight was bright inside the office, but that was the only thing different from the hall. It was a typical spartan office with metal file cabinets, a metal desk, a thin, sold-gray carpet, and a few pieces of modern art on the white walls.

A rather prim looking woman sat at a desk in a small outer room. My guide handed her my card, introduced her as Mrs. Starley, and left, closing the door behind him. She looked at the card longer than needed. While she was admiring my card, I took in what I could see above the desk. She looked to be about forty and was about as plain as a woman could be, with short brown hair and eyes, little makeup, no jewelry, and a white blouse buttoned up to her neck. I had the feeling she was all business and tough as nails. She wasn't about to take any crap from anybody. But that didn't fit with what was on her desk… a ball of red yarn, two knitting needles and about a two-foot length of scarf.

She looked warily up at me and said, "I wonder why a private investigator has an appointment with Mr. Quark."

I had several things I was wondering, too, like why his secretary would be wondering that and why it was any of her business, but I kept them to myself.

"Perhaps Mr. Quark will let you know," I said.

She glared at me, stood, and handed my card back. Her black skirt was just as plain as her blouse. She knocked on Quark's door, and he said to come in. She opened the door for me and then left it ajar. His office was pretty much the same as hers but bigger and with an extra window and a wooden desk that served as a surface for a mess of papers that made it look like he was busy. He was standing at a cabinet behind and to the left of his desk.

Quark was an odd-looking fellow. He was a head shorter than me and had sunken cheeks, eyes that were a little too large for his face, and a high forehead. There was a hint of a brown moustache. He wore a cheap suit that was a bit big for him. He extended his hand as he introduced himself. I handed him my card, and he waved toward a wooden chair. He didn't need as much time with the card as Mrs. Starley.

With raised eyebrows, he said, "A private investigator. Whoever it was who made the appointment didn't mention that. You have me curious about what needs investigating here."

I gave him my best smile and said, "It's just what I do, like pastry chef or race car driver. But the occupation on the card doesn't necessarily have anything to do with why I'm here."

"Necessarily? Meaning it *might* have something to do with it?"

"Not necessarily."

He shook his head. "I'm not a psychologist, Mr. Manning. I'm in PR, so how about you just tell me why you're here."

"Curiosity."

His eyebrows went back up, but he didn't respond.

"I'd like to know something about your cemetery."

"Our cemetery?"

"Yes. I happened to be in the area and came across it."

He laughed. "Pardon me, but it's not an area people just happen to come across. Given that it's pretty well hidden, you have to make some effort."

"Let's say I made some effort. I have some questions."

"Which are?"

"Seems odd that a place like this would have its own cemetery."

He folded his hands on the desk. "Well, that's not a question, but the cemetery was started in the late eighteen hundreds when there wasn't much control over things like that. They needed some place to um... bury the people who died here." He shrugged. "It just continued through the years."

"Is it still used?" I heard a typewriter from the outer office.

"As needed."

"When was the last time someone was buried?"

He leaned back and placed both palms flat on the desk. "These are rather odd questions, Mr. Manning. Why are you asking?"

"Still curiosity. Is there some reason you don't want to answer my question?"

His body tensed, and he grabbed onto the edge of the desk. "First of all, I don't know. Second, I find your manner confrontational."

"Yeah, I get that a lot. Be different if I was a pastry chef."

He just glared at me for a moment and then said, "I'm afraid I have no more time to give you, Mr. Manning. If you have any further questions, please make an appointment with our director, Mr. Bridgewater."

"I may do that." I stood. "Thanks for your time."

He stood but didn't respond. Not taking his eyes off me, he said, "Mrs. Starley, please have someone escort Mr. Manning out."

Mrs. Starley gave me a stern look and told me to wait for the escort. With just a few steps she reached out and closed Quark's door. I glanced at my watch as I was waiting. I'd make it back with time to spare. The same kid who had brought me in arrived in half a minute. We walked back down the hall, and, saying nothing, he frowned, opened the door and nodded toward the lobby, like I was lucky to be leaving.

***

"SLIM HERE," a man said, answering his phone.

"It's Mrs. Starley. Mr. Quark just had a visitor, a private investigator named Manning." She switched the phone to her other ear. "He's asking questions about the cemetery."

"What sort of questions?"

"How old is it? Is it still used? When was the last person buried?"

"How did Quark respond?"

"Told him he had to talk to Bridgewater."

"Good. Let me know if he comes back."

The line clicked, and Mrs. Starley hung up.

***

I WALKED QUIETLY UP TO MY MUSTANG and looked at Rosie napping. I was glad she was back. I had been standing there for more than a minute when she said, "I know you're there."

I laughed. "Must be the force field of my charming personality."

She smiled. "Right. We'll go with that."

We were back on the main road when she asked what had happened. I filled her in.

"You do meet some odd people."

"Yes, not exactly what I'd expect from the PR department."

"You didn't ask about the graves?"

"No. Don't ask questions you know you're not going to get answers to. That would have given them some idea about why I was there. Now they're just wondering."

"So what's next?"

"Lunch and another chat with Stosh tomorrow. And I imagine at some point I'll be back to see Mr. Bridgewater."

"I imagine you will."

Chapter 11

ROSIE AND I STOPPED FOR LUNCH AND DISCUSSED QUARK. I drove her home and then headed to the office and sat with my thoughts.

There was no reason to think that Susan Janice had met with foul play. I had found nothing in her apartment to make me think so. I called Gregory when I got into the office, and he had no new information. I had Carol call the Oak Park Police, and they also had nothing. There was also no reason to think anything untoward had happened to Martin Rentel. He was somewhere in the system, and it was a big system. But both Martin and Susan seemed to be missing. And I would think Martin would have called his aunt, the only person who had shown any interest in him.

I sat back in my chair and thought about two people, the anonymous caller and Robert Quark. Why had the anonymous caller only told Susan she would find answers at the cemetery? If you want to lead someone to something you give them specifics. But maybe she didn't know the specifics for whatever reason. And Robert Quark's behavior was certainly odd. I wanted to know more about him. I reached out to punch the intercom button and then decided I needed some exercise.

Carol was typing up notes when I sat on the corner of her desk. I handed her a sheet of paper with Robert's name on it.

"I need you to work your magic and get background on this fellow."

She looked at me with raised brows. "When do you need it?"

"Monday morning is fine."

"Okay. It'll be on your desk first thing. But as the person assigned to keep track of your bank book, I must point out that, even without the rush, this will use up the rest of Mr. Janice's retainer and then some."

I smiled and crossed my arms over my Cubs T-shirt. "I greatly appreciate your attention to my welfare, Madame Accountant."

She made a sound very much like a humph. "It's my welfare I'm concerned with. If you go out of business where else will I find a job with all these perks?"

My smile turned into a laugh. "I'll do my best not to let that happen. In the meantime, get out your magic wand."

"You think this guy is hiding something?"

"Everyone is hiding *some*thing. But he just rubbed me the wrong way. For a PR guy he wasn't very PR."

As she thumbed through her flip file, she asked what the rest of my day was like.

"Nothing much. I have that PI dinner tonight, so I'll go over my notes for my talk."

"You nervous?"

"Just a little. Peers are always a tough crowd."

She picked up the phone and punched in a number. I scratched Watson behind his left ear and went back to my office.

***

ONE OF MY RULES WAS TO AVOID official functions. The bi-annual meeting of the Chicago Private Investigator Association was one of those. I usually went but tried to blend in with the scenery. This time they had asked me to give a talk on how what we did differed from the police. I assumed that was because of my department connections. I had called the president, Josh McLean, whom I knew from work-related issues, and tried to politely decline. He said the topic was hot, and my name had immediately been brought up by the board, and I would be letting down the CPIA if I didn't accept. I accepted... but I wasn't happy about it. After a bit of thought, I realized Stosh had often given me the perfect topic—Crossing the Line, How Far Should We Go?

***

THE DINNER WAS ALWAYS GOOD, prime rib with all the trimmings. I sat at a table with people I didn't know and tried to ignore the *wait'll you hear about this one* conversation while I went through my talk. After dinner, Josh introduced the guests who were seated at one of the first-row tables. They included Jackson Grimes, the sheriff of Cook County. I had seen him on TV but never in person. He was bigger than he looked on TV, had a crew cut, and was wearing a casual brown sport coat with no tie. His broad, pug nose looked like someone had helped to flatten it. I was introduced as the guest speaker. There was a polite round of applause as I walked to the lectern.

The theme of my talk was based on the gray areas of the law and whether or not we as PIs had leeway that the police didn't. Stosh had always told me I could be arrested just as well as the next guy if I stepped over the line. But in talks with Ben, mostly involving alcohol, it was evident that in many areas the line was wavy. He had given me several instances where interpretation could lead to either side being able to make an argument that might hold up in court. Which side won depended on the skill of the attorney. I proposed that we had a bit of leeway and could use that wavy line to our advantage. And it helped that, while the laws applied to us too, we didn't wear a badge and weren't held to the scrutiny that went with it.

I gave several examples where the law was fuzzy and left our actions open to interpretation. Then I talked about a few of my cases, especially the one involving kids at Riverview. I made it clear that I wasn't proposing criminal activity, but to get criminals off the streets, especially where kids were involved, I'd be willing to cross into that gray area.

When I was done, the president asked for questions, and several hands went up. The first in the air was Sheriff Grimes. I was pretty sure what his question would be and hoped McLean would ignore him until we ran out of time. He didn't. He introduced himself as Cook County Sheriff Grimes.

"So, Mr. Manning, if I heard you correctly, you are saying you would break the law to apprehend a criminal."

I smiled to hide my discomfort and said, "While that doesn't sound like a question, I'll answer it this way. No, that's not what I said." I took a drink of water. "I have a friend in the Coast Guard. They're trained to rescue someone in the water using their equipment and skill rather than jumping in after them. As a matter of fact, that is frowned upon. But this friend told me if there was a child in the water drowning, he'd go in."

"So you are saying?"

"If the means serve the end…"

"And doesn't that make you judge and jury and jailer?"

I really didn't want to get into a verbal boxing match, and I did realize the vulnerability of my position, but there I was. I was starting to sweat.

"Sheriff, wouldn't you admit that your hands are tied at times by the system?"

"If you mean the laws that protect *all* of our rights, yup. But I realize those rights need to be protected, even for the criminals. We who wear badges work within the system you don't respect."

He was baiting me, and I needed to stay calm. "I have great respect for the system. I'd also like to see criminals in jail."

He started to say something else when McLean came to my rescue and said we were out of time and thanked everyone for coming. After McLean wrapped it up, I left in a hurry and drove home wishing I had declined the talk. I also hoped there weren't any reporters in the room.

Chapter 12

I ALWAYS LOOKED FORWARD TO SATURDAY CARDS WITH STOSH. I could smell the hot pastrami as soon as I walked in the front door, and as I walked across the living room past the card table I heard the oven door squeak. If I wasn't hungry before, I was now. As I walked by his chair my eye caught a book on the end table... *Forensic Science Handbook*, by Richard Saferstein.

As we made our sandwiches, I asked him about the book.

"Should be required reading for everyone in this business," he said as he added mayo to the rye bread.

"How so?" I asked.

"Basic principles. A lot of information on a wide range of investigative subjects, not the least of which is Locard's exchange principle."

"Whose what?" I asked.

He shook his head. "Kids. Don't know how you've managed to do what you do. Edmund Locard, one of the fathers of forensic science. His exchange principle is the cornerstone of forensic science." He took a bite of pastrami and continued. "Whenever two objects come into contact there is always an exchange of material. If you enter a room you leave some evidence behind and take some with you. Soil on your shoes. A fiber of clothing."

"Makes sense," I said. "Can I borrow it when you're done?"

He laughed. "I've read it several times. That's volume two. There are three. You can take the first home with you."

We settled in front of the TV. The Cubs were on WGN at one. Stosh was ever the optimist about the Cubs. I tended a bit toward realism. But no matter what happened, an afternoon in the bleachers with a dog and a beer was always a good time. We had made it through another winter, and it was time for baseball.

He waited until I was about to take the first bite of my sandwich before saying, "So, I hear you don't give a damn about the law."

I put down the sandwich and sighed as I let out a deep breath. "Where'd you hear that?"

He laughed. "Got a call from somebody who heard it from somebody who was at your little party last night. That makes it at least second-hand knowledge, so maybe the story has been twisted a bit."

On the way home last night I realized what I said could have been taken that way, but it wasn't what I meant. And I had thought of ten ways I could have said it better.

"I may have misspoken." I explained what I had said while we ate.

He took some beer and said, "Well, if it makes you feel any better, you were doomed from the start. No way you could not look bad with that topic. How did you come up with that idea?"

"From you."

He about choked on a bite of pastrami. "Me?"

"Well, sorta. You're always telling me not to cross the line. So *where's the line and where does it break?* seemed like a good talking point."

"How does it seem now?"

"Not so good." I picked up my sandwich and took a bite.

He shook his head. "Think before you open your mouth and you'll keep it closed more often."

"Would have been okay if it wasn't for that damned Grimes."

"I don't know about that, but Grimes *can* be a pain in the ass."

We both ate in silence for a minute before Stosh continued about Grimes.

"This is just scuttlebutt, so treat it accordingly. Word going around is that Grimes wants the chief of police job."

"Really? Is Swalee in trouble?"

"Not that I know of, but you never know who's pulling whose strings. Rumor also has it that Grimes and Lansing are buddies."

"And Lansing is up for reelection as AG," I said.

"Yup. So both have some skin in seeing convictions go up."

"Interesting. One controls jails, and the other controls the courts."

Stosh picked up his bottle of Schlitz. "Lots of power there."

We switched to baseball, and when we were done with lunch Stosh asked, "So, any more on your secret cemetery?"

I told him about my visit with Robert Quark.

"I'd be surprised if the guy *wasn't* a bit odd," he said. "How can you work in a place like that and not be?"

I considered that his job wasn't much different, but I thought before I opened my mouth.

I took a long drink of Schlitz and asked him again if he had heard any more about the Martin Rentel case.

"Not much more than what you read in the paper."

"But *some*thing more?"

He took a drink, wiped his mouth on his sleeve and rolled his eyes. "Things I share with the guys wearing blue uniforms."

I set down my bottle and nodded. "Okay. We'll just overlook the cases I've solved over the last four years, including two in your precinct. I'll just—"

"Okay, okay. Point taken."

"How about this? I'd like to talk to someone in the Fourth. Who can I talk to over there and get straight answers?"

He nodded at my plate. "You want another sandwich?"

"Not right now."

He picked up the plates and said, "I'll make a call."

I turned up the volume on the TV, moved to the table, and got out the cards. Steve Stone was interviewing Andre Dawson on the Lead Off Man. Stosh was gone longer than I would have expected. I was playing solitaire when he came back with a concerned look on his face. He sat and leaned back in the chair.

"This is a bit odd," he said slowly.

I raised my eyebrows and waited patiently.

He stared out the window for a few seconds and then turned back to me. "The arresting detectives were Barker and Yancy. They also questioned Rentel the first time." He looked out the window again. "I asked if they were on duty. I was told they are both on vacation."

I was confused. "Why is that odd? People go on vacation."

He nodded. "Yeah. Then I asked who the desk sergeant was when Rentel was brought in. Both times it was Malone. He's on vacation too."

I shrugged. "Okay, a little coincidental, but still not odd."

"I asked if Captain Meyer would be in on Monday."

"He on vacation too?"

"Out-of-town conference."

"For how long?"

"My guy didn't know. Indefinitely."

"And the vacations?"

"Same answer."

Now I had to agree with the *odd*. "Who's your guy?"

"Somebody who wants to be nameless. And somebody who wouldn't answer any more questions."

I scooped up the cards and shuffled them. "Maybe someone else needs to ask the questions."

He shook his head. "I guarantee you, if I didn't get answers you won't either."

I smiled. "I have ways."

He didn't return my smile. "And one of these days your luck is going to run out. I'd like you to live to say something nice at my funeral."

I smiled again. "I already did."

"I mean the one where I'm dead."

I went back to shuffling the cards. "What do you know about Barker, Yancy, and Malone?"

"They're cops. They do their jobs."

"Do you know any of them?"

He leaned forward in his chair. "You're going to wear out those cards."

I squared the deck and set it down.

"I've had cases with Yancy. Barker must be new… haven't heard the name. Malone has been around forever."

"Tell me about Yancy."

"I already did. Let this go, kid."

I finished my beer and asked, "Can you get me addresses?"

"Addresses?"

"Barker, Yancy, Malone."

He just stared at me.

"Okay. How about this? Mrs. Janice's anonymous caller… how did she know to call her?"

He looked confused.

"How did the caller know who to call?"

"She knew Janice was Rentel's aunt."

"My point exactly. And the only way that could have happened was if someone read it off of Rentel's police sheet."

He looked skeptical. "Well, there may have been other ways."

"Tell me one."

I got a stare.

"Exactly. So who in the Fourth would have access to that?"

He sighed. "I hope you're not right."

I waited.

"A whole lot of people," he said. "But if it was a woman, that narrows it down."

"Can you narrow it down to some names?"

He didn't look happy. "Maybe. I'll let you know. Let's play some Gin."

Chapter 13

I BEAT CAROL INTO THE OFFICE MONDAY MORNING AND FIRED up the coffee maker. The file on Robert Quark was waiting on my desk. It didn't take long to read the two pages. And while I was reading, Carol came in the back door.

"You get Billy to school okay?"

"I did. I was surprised to see the Mustang. What brings you in this early?"

"I wanted to see the report on Quark."

"Anything interesting?"

"Not really." I poured coffee and handed her a cup. "Grew up in small town Wisconsin. Got a Bachelor's degree from U of Wisconsin in Public Relations and Advertising and worked for four years for a PR firm in Madison. At the age of twenty-eight he became the PR Director at Walker. Been there a little more than a year. Lives in St. Charles."

Carol sat at her desk and sipped her coffee. "How does someone go from a small PR firm in Madison to PR Director at Walker?"

"Good question."

"And why does Walker need a PR Director?"

I sat on the corner of her desk. "Yeah. But I guess good PR is important no matter what you do, especially when people are involved." I took a drink.

"And?" she asked.

"And what?"

"Just *and*. You look like you're thinking."

I took another drink while I thought a bit more. "Quark just doesn't strike me as a PR guy."

"How should a PR guy strike you?"

"Slick. Forceful. On his toes. Life of the party. This guy is someone who'd hide in a corner at a party and talk about you behind your back."

She laughed. "Maybe PR for a mental health facility isn't the same as for a used car dealer."

I finished my coffee and set the cup on the side table. "I wouldn't think so. And there's no need for advertising."

"So back to why a PR director."

"Indeed."

"So what next?"

"I need some addresses." I gave her the names Stosh had given me from the Fourth. "And see if you can get photos."

"Can't you get the addresses from Stosh?"

"He was hesitant to provide those."

She looked confused. "Odd."

I sighed. "He was getting some resistance from whoever he was talking to in the Fourth. The guy stopped answering questions."

She looked at me with concern. "That's odd too. Maybe *you* should stop asking questions."

"When I get the right answers, I will."

She sighed. "I already knew that."

Watson raised his head and looked toward the front door as it opened. When he saw it was the mailman, Watson roused himself enough to meet him halfway. He sat and waited, with tail wagging, as the mailman dug in his pocket for a biscuit. He knelt and rubbed Watson behind the ears with one hand and held out a biscuit with the other. Watson gently took it.

"Good morning, Charles," said Carol with a smile. "I don't know why we have that mail slot."

Charles gave her a big smile. "I gotta come in and see my favorite customer. Good morning to you both."

"Good morning," I said. "Beautiful day to be out in the world."

"It is that, Mr. Manning. You all enjoy it."

The door gently closed, and I watched Watson resettle himself.

"That's all you want is addresses and photos?" Carol asked.

"For now, please."

"You staying for a bit? I'll have them within the hour."

"I think I'll take a walk. Why should Charles have all the fun?"

"Why don't you take the attack dog with you? Billy will be late today, so Watson won't get his walk."

I got the file from my desk and handed it to Carol to file. When I pulled Watson's leash off the hook he eyed me warily. It wasn't afternoon, and I wasn't Billy. But when I walked toward him, he grudgingly got up.

We walked down Diversey toward the lake, and I thought about the case. Everything about it was odd. And I had discovered in the past that when I poked at odd things people got nervous. And when people got nervous I got answers. I wanted to have a chat with the director of the mental health facility, but first on my list was having a chat with the detectives. When someone is missing, check the last place they were known to be.

Watson and I got back a little after eleven. Carol held up a folder. "Got 'em."

"Thanks." I took it and walked back to my office.

Barker lived in Sauganash. It wasn't luxurious, but you needed money to live there. It was well known for Christmas decorations… almost every house in the neighborhood went all out. Yancy had an apartment on the far west side near Oak Park, and Malone lived in Stosh's precinct where most houses were bungalows.

I walked back out into the main office. "One more thing, please. I'd like twenty-four-hour surveillance on Malone. Get two of our people on it. Have them stop by for a phone and let them figure out their schedule. As soon as they spot him have them call me… I don't care what time it is."

"Will do. Do you want to know who's on it?" She reached for her copy of the report.

"Nope."

If I left now, I'd get to Sauganash by noon and see what Detective Barker was having for lunch. I picked up two of the portable phones and headed for Sauganash.

Chapter 14

I TURNED OFF OF CALDWELL ONTO NOKOMIS AND PARKED IN front of 260. There were no cars in the driveway. The lady next door was working in the garden in front of her house. As I walked up the front walk, she said, "If you're looking for the Barkers, they're not home."

I smiled and walked across the grass. "They're not?"

She kept pulling weeds with her trowel. "No, they left three days ago. Just packed up and left. Weren't even going to say good-bye. Are you a friend of theirs?"

"I used to work with Detective Barker. Was in the neighborhood and thought I'd stop and say hi."

She put down her trowel and stood up. "Oh, that's a shame. I know how much old friends mean to a person."

"Why do you say they weren't going to say goodbye?"

"The strangest thing. I was working out here Friday afternoon when the station wagon came backing out of the driveway. I waved, but Emily didn't wave back. I know she saw me. So I ran over to the car to see if they needed me to watch the dog. I'd do that when they went on trips. They stopped, but Mr. Barker didn't look too happy. Emily rolled down the window and said they decided to take a last-minute trip. I saw Sparky, that's the dog, in the back. I said I'd be glad to watch him, but she said they were taking him this time."

I was hoping she'd stop for a breath. "Did they say where they were going?"

She shook her head. "I asked, but she said they really didn't know. Seemed odd to me... does that seem odd to you?"

I told her it did... from her point of view. But from another it didn't. Barker had been told to disappear. But by whom? Or was he running?

"Say... what's your name, young man?"

I handed her a card. "Did they say how long they'd be?"

"Nope. She just said they didn't know where or for how long. Then Rob said they had to go, and he backed onto the street. It's an odd time to take a trip. The kids have school, you know." She looked at my card. "I'll tell them you were here, Mr. Manning."

"I'd appreciate that."

She smiled. "Then that's what I'll do."

"How many kids do they have now?"

"Just the two. Boy and a girl."

I nodded. "And he still has that old station wagon?"

She laughed. "Yup. Old Brown Bessie he calls it. Says he'll drive it till it rusts out."

I laughed. "Yup. Same old Barker. I'll let you get back to your garden. It looks beautiful."

She beamed. "Thanks. I try."

I turned around in the driveway, and she waved as I drove by. I figured not much happened in that neighborhood she didn't know about. And she loved to talk. I was always amazed at how easy it was to get information from some people... just give them someone to talk to. I didn't know if any of that information about Barker would be useful, but information is always a good thing. If I needed to find him, I had something to start with—family of four with two kids and a dog in a brown Ford station wagon. And I doubted they had gone far.

My stomach was telling me it was lunchtime, and as long as I was in the neighborhood a hot dog at Superdawg, one of the best hot dog joints in town, was the obvious choice. I headed west on Devon to Milwaukee and turned into the drive-in.

***

I TOOK HARLEM SOUTH to north avenue and turned left. North Avenue was crowded no matter what time of day, and today was no different. It was a warm spring day, and people on the sidewalks were moving faster than traffic. Twenty minutes later I turned south onto Austin and took it to Huron where I found a three-story apartment building at 5847. I turned around and parked across the street and watched the building. In the next half hour, two women came out, and one returned with an armful of groceries. At two thirty I walked across the street and into the vestibule of the old building. The faded green carpet was frayed, and the walls were plaster, grayed with layers of smoke and dust.

Mail slots lined the wall to the left. Yancy was in 3a. The inner door wasn't closed all the way, so I let myself in and climbed the stairs to the third floor. Yancy was in the front apartment on the left side of the hallway. I listened at his door and heard nothing. I knocked and got no answer.

I sat in my Mustang and watched for another hour. After that, I called the pool hall and surprisingly didn't have to wait for Ralph.

"Hey, Ralph. Not in the middle of a game?"

"Just finished one. Gotta let somebody else win once in a while. What's up?"

"Surveillance job. You free tonight?"

"Sure. Tell me when and where."

Ralph had never said no. The money was a lot better than what he made playing pool. I explained the situation and asked him to relieve me around seven. Several people came and went before then, but none of them were Yancy. When Ralph arrived, I gave him the photo and told him to call me at home if Yancy showed up. I gave him one of the portable phones.

***

A BURGER WAS ON THE GRILL, and I was reading the Trib when my home phone rang.

"Spencer, Yancy just came home."

"Okay. I'll head out in about ten minutes. Call me if anything changes."

"Sure."

I shut down the grill and ate and headed back to Yancy's. I had only been driving for ten minutes when the car phone rang.

"He's on the move, Spencer. In his car heading south on Austin."

"Okay, Ralph. I'll keep coming to the apartment. Call me when he lands somewhere. If I haven't heard from you, I'll wait at the apartment."

"Right."

I dropped the phone on the seat and turned onto North Avenue. Fifteen minutes later, as I was turning onto Austin, the phone rang again. I picked it up and answered.

"He's in a bar on Cicero. Mike's. Half a block south of Madison, west side."

"Thanks, Ralph. Where are you?"

"Parked on Cicero across from it. You want me to go in?"

"No, just let me know if he comes out. I'll be there in fifteen."

I parked two cars behind Ralph and got in his car.

"He alone?" I asked.

"He went *in* alone."

I had several operatives. Ralph was the best. He never asked questions, and he always dropped whatever he was doing, which was playing pool. I think he liked the work, but my paying for eight hours minimum probably had something to do with it. All he wanted to know was what he needed to know to do the job… just the how. Why didn't matter. So I didn't have to tell him that my plan was to let Yancy get enough drinks in him to lose his inhibitions before I went in and had a chat with him.

"You need me anymore?" Ralph asked.

"That'll do… thanks. Carol will have your check ready by ten." But he already knew that.

He nodded, and I got out of the car. He'd be back playing pool on my dollar in thirty minutes.

It was a warm evening, so I sat in the car and people-watched with the windows rolled down. I listened to the traffic, music from second-floor apartments, barking dogs, and a siren once in a while, and thought about the peace and quiet of my cabin on Moonlight Bay. Every so often I wondered why I chose to be in places like this when I didn't have to. I wasn't quite sure what it was that kept luring me in. Mike was doing a good business. There were more going in than coming out.

At eleven I rolled up the windows and walked across the street. The bartender was the only one who looked at me when I went in.

Chapter 15

YANCY WAS SITTING AT THE BAR... ALONE. TWO EMPTY STOOLS on either side of him. I stood for a minute to let my eyes adjust to the dim light and then sat at the bar with a stool between us.

"What'll it be, bud?" the bartender asked. I could barely hear him over the music from the jukebox.

I looked at the tap handles and asked for an Old Style. I put a ten on the bar and took a drink. Then I spun on the stool and looked over the people in the booths.

"Looking for somebody?" the tender asked.

"Gotta friend said he might stop in here, but I don't see him."

Yancy glanced at me. He looked like he was well past any in-hibitions. He reached for his glass and had trouble picking it up. I took a drink.

"Whoosh your friend?" he asked, his head nodding slightly.

"Guy named Ray. Big guy, bald. You know him?"

He thought about that for a bit and finished his drink. "Know a big guy, but he ain't bald."

"Wrong guy then."

"Never seen a big bald guy." He squinted at me. "Never seen you either."

"First time in here," I said.

He looked down the bar. "Sammy... nuther drink."

Sammy pulled a bottle of bar scotch off the shelf, added a few ice cubes to the glass, and poured.

I slid over a stool and moved my ten-spot over next to Yancy's glass. "On me," I said.

Yancy nodded. "Thanks."

I raised my glass and we clinked.

"You new in here?" he asked.

I was planning on questioning him, but if he couldn't even remember something from a few minutes ago... Maybe I had given him too much time at the bar.

"Yup. You come here often, Yancy?"

"Often enough." He drained half of his glass and stared at the bar like he was thinking. He turned to me and squinted. "Hey, how'd you know my name?"

"You told me."

He looked confused and said, "Yeah, guess I musta." He took another sip.

I drank some beer and said, "Hey, you're not that detective, are you?"

He had left sobriety behind quite a while ago, but he had enough sense left to know he should at least try to be wary. He looked at me with very little trust and like he wasn't at all sure what he had told me and what he hadn't. He finally made up his mind. "I didn't tell you I was a detective."

"No, you didn't. But I've been working on a case that involves a Detective Yancy. Thought you might be him."

He fingered his glass. "A case. You on the job?"

"Private."

He took that in. "Private." He finished his drink and held up the glass. "Sammy! Fill 'er up!"

Sammy shook his head. "You've had enough, Yancy."

Yancy didn't argue. He set the glass down and pushed it away. Sammy picked it up and set it on a tray.

Yancy's forehead furrowed, and he squinted at the bar. "What case would that be?"

"What's his tab?" I asked.

Sammy told me. I added a twenty to the ten and told Sammy to keep the change.

I turned to Yancy and took a deep breath. I had no idea how he would react. There was every possibility that he'd fall off the stool. "I'm looking for information about Martin Rentel."

His eyes were glazed over, and he was holding onto the edge of the bar. He didn't respond at all to the name.

I leaned closer to him. "He was brought in by you back in February for questioning."

He turned and gave me a blank look.

I continued. "Martin Rentel. He was released and then brought in under arrest on April third."

His eyes were glazed over.

He needed some reminding. "A man had been murdered behind a drugstore on north Cicero?"

There was a new look in his eyes… fear.

"I gotta go," he said. He started to get off the stool and almost fell.

Sammy had come over in front of us. "I can't let him drive. I'll call him a cab. Not the first time."

"It's okay, Sammy." I said. "I'll get him home." He gave me the address, and I thanked him.

I let Yancy lean on my shoulder, and we slowly made our way to the Mustang. I helped him in and hoped he stayed awake long enough for me to get around the car. I rolled the windows down to get in some fresh, cool air and continued.

"You remember?" I asked.

"What's it to you?"

"His aunt says he's missing."

He tried to look angry but just looked confused. "Kid is worthless. Shoulda been in jail for ten other things."

"Not arguing that. Just trying to find him."

He shook his head. "Not my problem."

"I agree." A horn honked as someone was too slow at the green light. "The problem is mine. Just trying to piece together the puzzle, and I was hoping you could help."

He squirmed in the seat. "What'd you say your name is?"

"Spencer."

"Got a last name?"

"Manning." I handed him my card.

He looked at it and looked like he sobered up a bit. "Manning. I knew a Manning. Police chief."

"My father."

He hung his head and then nodded. "Your father." He was staring out the window and trying to think. He rubbed his head with both hands and then slowly lowered his arms and turned toward me. "Chief Manning... Chief Manning was your father."

I nodded.

"Jesus. Give me a minute." He took a few deep breaths and shook his head a few times, maybe trying to shake out the saturated cobwebs. He took another deep breath and then said, "Chief Manning is the only reason I'm still on the force. He was... Those were different times. By the book."

That was a story I wanted to hear, and I was feeling increasingly uneasy about being parked on Cicero Avenue at one in the morning.

"Detective, I'd like to hear about that, but I think you need some sleep first."

He nodded. "Yeah. Help me find my car, and I'll be okay."

I laughed. "Odds are you wouldn't be even close to okay."

"Hey, my car knows its way home from here by itself."

"That may be, but I have a better idea. I've got a comfy spare bed at my place, and I make great eggs and bacon. You can bunk there, and you won't be endangering any citizens along the way."

He pressed his forehead with the palm of his hand. "I'm not in much of a position to argue."

He was asleep before I pulled away from the curb.

Chapter 16

I HAD BEEN AWAKE FOR TWO HOURS BEFORE YANCY WANDERED into the kitchen, probably awakened by bacon cooking. The sun was up, the birds were chirping, and he looked like he had been resurrected from the dead. He looked at me and then looked at the card he was holding. Then back at me.

"I found this card in my pocket. You?"

I raised my coffee cup.

"I thought maybe it was all a bad dream, but then it wasn't my bed I woke up in. You brought me here?"

"I did."

"Your house?"

"Yup."

"You had asked some questions, but I'm pretty fuzzy on what."

"I don't doubt it. Coffee's hot."

He took the cup next to the maker, filled it, took a sip, and sat down across from me at the table. He took another sip and shook his head.

"You always drink like that?" I asked.

He stared across the room and then looked back at me. "I drink, but not like that."

I got up, turned the bacon, and cracked four eggs into a pan.

"You drove me here?"

"Yup."

"My car?"

"Still wherever you parked it. We'll get it after breakfast."

"Well, I thank you for your efforts."

"My pleasure."

"You wanna tie together the loose threads I got floating around in my head?"

"How much do you remember?"

He took a deep breath and more coffee. "You were looking for information about somebody, but I don't remember who."

I repeated my story. He closed his eyes and supported his head with the palm of his left hand. The right was still holding the cup.

"You said the kid was worthless, so you do remember who he is."

He nodded.

"You also said my father was the reason you were still on the force. I'd like to hear about that."

As he talked, I turned the eggs and thirty seconds later slid them onto plates. I moved the bacon to paper towels and dabbed away the grease. It was a short story. He had done something stupid, and Dad had given him a second chance.

"Your father was a good man."

"He was. And he must have seen something good in you too."

He laughed. "I guess. Glad he wasn't there last night."

We started in on the food.

"Didn't I see your name associated with a case a few years back at the Fourth?" he asked.

I finished my bite of eggs. "Yes, Macek. Drug deal, and he killed one of your detectives. But all I did was provide information about where he was."

"Yeah, that was bad. He's in County now."

"Yes, on The Wing." The Wing was Cook County Jail's death row.

"But he got lucky," Yancy said.

"Yup, he was looking at the chair when he was convicted. Now it's lethal injection."

"Either way…" Jerry said.

We finished eating in silence.

"Thanks for the grub," Jerry said. "Hits the spot."

"Sure. So what do you know about Martin Rentel?"

He slowly shook his head. "Nothing more than we brought him in twice. The first time he was let go. There was no evidence other than a lady who picked him out of a mug book."

"Rentel didn't admit anything?"

"Nope. He had an alibi, another upstanding citizen with a sheet as long as your arm. So you tell me what that's worth. Said he knew nothing about it. The second time we had reason to believe he had evidence in his possession, so we went back to his apartment and found it."

"Where did that *reason to believe* come from?" I remembered the watch.

"We got a tip. Who are you working for?"

"His aunt reported him missing."

"Missing? He was under arrest."

"But she couldn't talk to him or discover where he was being held."

"She reported this to you?"

"Well, sort of."

He smiled. "There's a story in that answer."

"Yes, and maybe at some point I'll tell it."

He accepted that answer and nodded. "You in touch with her?"

"Never really was. Just a phone conversation a week ago."

"Haven't talked to her lately?"

"Nope. She's missing too."

He leaned forward. "Reported to the police?"

"Oak Park. So far, nothing."

"Why do I have a feeling there's more to it?" he asked.

I laughed. "Cuz you're a good cop. Is there any more you can tell me about Rentel? What happened that second time he was brought in?"

He sighed. "Your dad... you gotta understand. Times are different. There's a lotta pressure from city hall to close cases, especially in the case of innocent civilians."

"Like Amos Grant," I said.

He looked up from his plate. "Like Amos Grant."

"Martin was let go the first time," I said.

"Yeah. All we had was that positive ID, and he did have an alibi."

"And it was dark," I added.

He nodded.

"And she wanted to ID somebody," I said.

"They all do," he replied. "They look at those books and want to find the guy."

"And maybe it's the wrong guy," I said.

"Maybe."

"And maybe he's got a friend who'll lie for him."

"Sure," he said with a shrug.

I finished my coffee. "So the alibi got him released. Why was he picked up again?"

"Evidence."

"Which was?"

He hesitated and shook his head. "I don't know."

He was obviously lying. There was something he was afraid of. "Would Barker know?"

His eyebrows went up. "You know a lot about this for somebody who shouldn't know this much."

I didn't respond.

"How do you know about Barker?" he asked.

"Same way I knew about you."

He laughed. "And you're keeping that to yourself?"

"For the moment. More coffee?"

"Please."

I refilled the cups and sat back down.

He took a drink.

"And you have no idea what happened to Rentel?"

He looked down and swirled his coffee.

"Something did happen," I said.

When he finally looked up, he said, "Maybe Barker knows."

"You have a guess what happened?"

"Your father saved my ass."

I let that sit and waited for him to make a decision. I hoped it would be the right one.

He took a deep breath and let it out. "When they know they've got the right guy but they are lacking... well, evidence, they bring in someone to... well, persuade him to see it their way."

"Persuade? Questioning?"

"To start with."

"What are you saying, Jerry?"

"When talk doesn't work there are other ways."

I was pretty sure he wasn't going to say what the other ways were. "Who is this someone?"

He shook his head. "I don't know."

"Would Barker know?"

"No. We get taken off the case before the next... step."

"You make it sound like this has happened before."

He didn't answer.

I took a shot in the dark. "Who told you to disappear?"

His look of shock was obvious. "How did you know that?"

I ignored the question. It was a guess. "Barker was told to disappear too. He did. You didn't. How come?"

He shrugged. "I had no place to disappear to. I figured I'd just stay home."

"Except for the bar."

"Yeah."

"Who told you?"

"The chief of detectives. McElroy."

"When did he tell you?"

"Last Friday as I was checking out."

So that happened after my meeting with Quark. "And what did he tell you exactly?"

"To take some time off... just disappear for a while. With pay."

I picked up the plates, ran some hot water, and set them in the sink. "Here's what I think, Jerry. I think everything was going okay until I started asking questions. And then somebody got nervous."

He nodded.

"The problem is, I'm not going to stop asking questions. And I'm thinking you'd be a lot safer if you *had* disappeared."

He thought about that as his eyes squinted. "I don't know anything about Rentel."

"Sometimes you don't have to know anything. Someone just has to think you might. The gangsters that ran the city back fifty years ago killed a lot of innocent people based on that *might*." I turned off the water.

"What about you?" he asked.

"Wouldn't be the first time I ignored my own safety."

"Why?" he asked.

"Why what?"

"Why put yourself at risk for someone you don't know?"

"It was how I was raised. Doing what's right means a lot."

He met my eyes. "I don't know who the someone is, but we call him the goon squad."

"Goon squad? One man?"

"I think so. Rumor is he's good at… persuasion."

"And what do you think happened to Rentel?"

He was quiet for almost a minute. "Maybe he was over-persuaded."

"When did these rumors start?"

"Don't hold me to anything, but I'd say about a year ago."

I gave all that some thought. "I think you *should* disappear, Jerry. Your chief wanted you to disappear because you knew something, and if you disappeared no one could ask questions. But what if the guys who wanted you to disappear *really* want you to disappear?"

"What do you mean?"

"At some point you become a liability."

He thought about that and shook his head. "Like I said, I got no place to go."

"Here's as good a place as any."

"You wanna put me up?"

"I'm gonna keep asking questions, and I don't want you caught in the crossfire."

"I got no clothes, and there's my car."

"I'll take care of all that. You game?"

He shrugged. "Sure."

"Good. Give me your keys. Make a list. I'll have someone get things from your apartment, and I'll take care of your car. What is it, and where is it parked?"

"Blue Chevy sedan. It's in a lot south side of the bar."

As I started to clean up the dishes he said, "I'll clean up. Least I can do."

"Thanks. Make yourself at home and stay inside. I don't want anyone knowing you're here, including the neighbors."

By the time I got myself ready, he was done in the kitchen and reading the paper on the couch. He handed me a list of items.

"My gun is on the list," he said. "It's in a locked metal box in the bottom right drawer of the desk."

I thought about that for a few seconds and decided it wasn't a bad idea. He was a cop after all. "I'll have him bring the box. What kind of gun?"

"Glock… nine millimeter."

I turned to go and then remembered the phone. "Don't answer the phone either. If I want you I'll ring it once then once again. Answer it the third time."

He laughed. "You're pretty careful."

"And pretty alive. Like to stay that way." I wrote my car phone number on the notepad by the phone and told him to call me if anything happened. "See you this afternoon sometime."

"Okay. Thanks, Spencer."

I gave him a two-finger salute. As I was backing out of the driveway, I wondered if I should have locked up the liquor.

Chapter 17

THE POOL HALL WAS MY FIRST STOP. THEY OPENED AT TEN, AND
Ralph was usually first on one of the tables. He nodded to me as I
walked to the bar and then proceeded to run the table. He was wearing his black, pork pie hat that he only wore in the pool hall. Said it
was good luck, not that he needed good luck. He would have given
Minnesota Fats a run for his money.

"Somebody take on the kid. I gotta take a break," he said to the
three men sitting along the wall watching. One of them got up.

"How's our boy?" he asked.

"Recovering." I handed him the list and gave him instructions.
"There's a suitcase in one of the closets. Keep it in your trunk, and I'll
pick it up here later this afternoon. Shouldn't be a problem, but watch
for a tail." I knew I didn't have to tell him that... he always did. "And
don't let anyone see you at the apartment." As usual, he didn't ask questions. He tucked the list in his shirt pocket and picked up his stick.

***

WHEN I CAME OUT OF THE DIMLY LIT HALL, I had to squint at the
bright sun reflecting off the windows across the street. But rain was
in the forecast, and I could see the dark clouds over the roofs to the
west. I headed north to the station.

The desk sergeant waved as I went by, and I headed up the stairs.
Rosie was talking to a patrol officer in the break room. I leaned
against the door jamb and waited.

"Morning, Spencer."

"Hey, Rosie. Slow day?"

"No such thing, but slower than most. What brings you here?"

"The cemetery case. Need to see Stosh."

"Wanna share?"

"I do, but not now. And I want to include Ben. Dinner?"

She smiled. "Do I ever get a dinner with just you?"

I smiled back. "We'll put him at the next table."

"What the hell. A free dinner is a free dinner."

"You do know how to make a guy feel wanted. Pick you up at six thirty."

Stosh was in his office with a pile of folders on his desk. Without looking up, he said, "I was just thinking the day was pretty good so far. And I said to myself… wonder how that's gonna get screwed up."

"Good morning to you too." I sat in the wooden chair on the wall. The cushioned chair in front of the desk was reserved for those with badges. It was an unwritten rule that I had learned after a harsh look.

He still didn't look up. "Spit it out if you got something. There's this pile." He waved his hand over his desk.

"What do you know about a goon squad over at the Fourth?"

Now he looked up… kinda like the look when I sat in the cushioned chair. "Jesus, Spencer. Where'd you hear that? Close the damned door."

I did and sat back down. "Rather not say."

"Then don't say those words in this office again, and forget you ever heard 'em."

"So you know about it?"

He laid down his pen and sat back. "I know it's one of those dumb rumors that gets started for whatever fool reason by morons with too much time on their hands."

"I have reason to believe it's more than just a rumor."

He sighed, audibly. "Tell me."

After I told him everything Yancy had told me, he sat forward in his chair and leaned both arms on the desk. "Your source is one of the names I gave you and not likely to be the desk sergeant. So that leaves Barker and Yancy. I don't know about Barker, but if it's Yancy, I'd be skeptical. The guy's got history."

"History doesn't make someone a liar."

"It tends to cloud judgement." He picked up a pencil and tapped it on the desk. "So it's Yancy?"

"I'm not saying."

He just nodded. I didn't have to say.

"Let's say it's Yancy just for conversation sake," I said. "If any of this is true and he's talking about it, people are going to find out, and he becomes a liability."

He laughed. "Your imagination is running wild, kid. This ain't the Mafia. It's the Chicago Police Department."

"Wouldn't be the first time the police took it upon themselves to be the judge and jury. Look at Boss Tweed and Tammany Hall and several mayoral regimes right in this city."

"Different times, Spencer."

I shook my head. "Power and greed know no times."

He rolled the pencil on the blotter. "And why would that be happening? Why would anyone put their career on the line?"

"Yancy mentioned there was a lot of pressure to solve crimes."

He shrugged. "Always is. That's our job."

"Maybe something else."

He gave me that Stosh look of fatherly concern for a kid that needed to learn a few things. "You find something else, let me know."

"I—"

He put up his hand. "But in the meantime, keep your crazy ideas to yourself. I don't need to be worrying about what hornet's nest you're stepping into."

I said I would, but I figured that didn't include Rosie and Ben.

Chapter 18

I GOT BACK TO THE OFFICE A LITTLE BEFORE NOON AND TOLD Carol I'd go next door for sandwiches. Before I left she had me sign three checks. I had stopped looking at what I was signing not long after she started working for me. I trusted her. As I was signing the last check it dawned on me that I shouldn't even be wasting time signing checks. I called Ben and left a message to meet Rosie and me at McGoon's at seven.

"After lunch," I said, "do whatever you need to do to add your name to the checkbook so we can cut out the middleman here."

She laughed and accused me of being lazy. "That will require a trip to the bank... with you."

"Okay, let's go after lunch. But before we go, please order a full detailed report on Quark, rush."

"Will do. He a suspect?"

"No. Just one of the trees to shake." I headed for the deli and then turned back. "Oh, and see how soon you can get me an appointment with the director out there... Bridgewater."

"Okay."

By the time I came out of the deli, the rain had started... big drops splattering on the sidewalk. People picked up their pace. Luckily the office was only two doors from the deli, because when I opened the door the heavens opened.

***

THE CROWD IN THE CUE BALL WAS TIMELESS... it was the same no matter when I was there. Ralph was sitting turned away from the bar, watching the games, his left arm cradling his custom stick and his right hand holding a whiskey glass. As I made my way to him, he said to the kid at the table, "Hey, Chris, lower it a bit like I showed you." This was one source of income for him. I was another. And I never knew him to lose at pool. One would think he wouldn't get any takers, but the bets weren't big, and he shared his skills, made them better players. When the rest of the crowd played each other it was an even bet. I sat down next to Ralph.

"Get everything?" I asked.

"Almost," he said.

"Almost?"

"Everything but the gun."

I'm sure my surprise showed. "You didn't find the box?"

"Oh, I found the box. What I didn't find was the gun."

"You opened it?"

"I did find the key, but I didn't open it."

I nodded. Empty boxes weighed less. "Where was the key?"

"Taped to the bottom. This guy is a cop?"

"Well... Tell me about the apartment."

"Functional. Looks like nobody lives there. No pictures, nothing personal lying around. It'd take five minutes to move out."

"Any sign somebody else had been in there?" I already knew there was none. Ralph would have already told me.

"Nope. Either the guy had a key or it was picked."

"Easy lock?"

"The easiest."

He finished his drink and reached behind him to put the glass on the bar. A minute later the bartender took it below the bartop and refilled it. I couldn't see the glass, but it seemed he was putting in more water than whiskey.

"You see a tail?"

"Nope."

"You're not seeing what the bartender is doing to your drink either."

He laughed. "You mean my water with just enough whiskey to give it the right color?"

I laughed and shook my head. "My apologies for underestimating you. The more you drink the easier you'll be to beat?"

"I'm never easy to beat. But the bets do go up with the number of refills. And the drinks are on the house. I bring in business… everybody wants to beat me. So far they haven't figured out that when I want a real drink I keep my hand on the glass."

"I'm glad you're on my side."

He raised his glass to me. "Let's take a walk."

The rain had turned into a spring drizzle. Ralph put gloves on and moved the suitcase to my trunk. I knew he had worn gloves in the apartment too.

"Think you'll need me again?" He asked.

"Could be."

"Tell Carol to run a tab till this is over. Rather have one check."

"You got it. Thanks."

He took off the gloves and nodded and walked back to the hall. I had planned on going straight home to get ready for dinner, but it was only a few minutes after four, and I figured I should have a chat with Stosh about the missing gun.

* * *

STOSH WASN'T IN HIS OFFICE, but Kate was at her desk across the hall. After telling me how much I brightened up her day, she said the lieutenant was in with the captain and would be back shortly and I should make myself at home. I set the gun box on his desk and was in the middle of a catnap when I heard his chair squeak and opened my eyes.

"Twice in one day," he said. "I am truly blessed."

I brought him up to speed.

"So why are you here?" He ignored the box.

"The detective's gun is missing."

"Missing? Missing how?"

"The box he keeps it in is empty."

He looked at the box and shrugged. "So report it."

"Well, remember the *disappear* part?"

He sighed. "Your life is like a bad soap opera."

"Personal comments aside, hard to report something when you are supposed to be off the grid."

"Do you know where he is?"

"Yes."

"Good. Where?"

I didn't even have to think about it. Stosh was by the book. If he knew where Yancy was and someone asked, he would say. So, until I knew more, better that he didn't know. I told him that.

He took in a deep breath, held it for ten seconds, and then let it out.

"I assume this box has something to do with this."

"Used to contain his service weapon that someone removed. Would you check it for prints?"

"That would be best done where he works."

"Yes, but we've already been down that street."

"I'll see. What about reporting it?"

"I thought I just did. You now have a record of his gun being stolen."

"Stolen according to him. What if he threw it in a sewer?"

"For what reason?" I asked.

"Who the hell knows?"

"He didn't act like he knew his gun was gone."

"You trust this guy… a total stranger who, if you're right that something is going on, might be part of it."

"So far I'll trust him, until I find out that I shouldn't."

"I gotta admit your instincts are good, but there will come a time…" His phone rang, and he ignored it. "Get him in here to file a report."

"Where he'd probably be recognized by somebody."

"I can't break *all* the rules, Spencer."

"I'm gonna do some more poking. I think he could be in danger. I don't even want him looking out the window. Keep it unofficial. Just remember that as of today, Yancy's gun is missing."

He shook his head and sighed. "Glock nine?"

"Yup."

"I'll let you know about the box."

I stood and then remembered the car. "I need a favor."

He pointed at the box. "What do you call this?"

I ignored him. "Yancy's car is in a lot by Mike's Bar on Cicero and Jackson. I need it towed. Would you get that done?"

He shook his head. "Not my precinct."

"If it was in your precinct could you get that done?"

"And what would be the reason?"

"I want Yancy to disappear. It'd look good if his car was found abandoned."

He didn't respond.

"So, would you?"

"You wouldn't have to ask. That's what we do. We sticker and then if they're still there a couple days later we tow abandoned cars. But it's a moot point… it's not in my precinct."

I smiled. "It will be by tomorrow. I'll let you know when and where. And I'd like to skip the couple days part. Just tow it."

I didn't wait for him to respond. "See you tomorrow night."

"Maybe *I'll* disappear," he said with a scowl.

"If you do, leave some food in the fridge."

***

THERE WASN'T ENOUGH TIME to make it home before dinner, so I stopped at the office. The report on Quark was on my desk. Nothing rang any bells, but I made copies for Ben and Rosie to read. Also on my desk were two notes from Carol. I had an appointment tomorrow with Bridgewater at eleven. I had no reason to think he would be any more helpful than Quark, but one could always hope. The second said she had called Oak Park, and there was nothing new on Susan. This case had been odd from the beginning. This just added to it. The average person didn't just disappear without a trace.

Chapter 19

NATHAN GREETED ROSIE AND I AT THE DOOR AND TOLD US BEN had already been seated at our usual table toward the back of the room.

"So much for a separate table," Rosie said.

"Now, now." I waved to Jack behind the bar and held up two fingers. He saluted.

Ben stood and pulled out a chair for Rosie. Jane brought our Guinness a minute later and told us about the special, Irish Stew, which Rosie and I ordered. Ben said he wasn't wasting a free meal on anything but steak.

By the time the food arrived I had brought both of them up to speed.

"I'm having a problem seeing how these people are connected," I said. "How does a mental health facility in Elgin connect to the Chicago police? Doesn't make a whole lotta sense."

While we ate, I listened to their thoughts. Other than agreeing about the strangeness, they didn't have anything new to offer. As Jane cleared the table, I handed each of them the info sheet on Quark. As he read, Ben nodded twice. He finished the sheet and his beer at the same time.

"I hope those were meaningful nods," I said.

"I knew when you first mentioned it that there was another reason Quark sounded familiar."

"Another reason?" Rosie said. "What's the first?"

"Either of you read *Finnegan's Wake*?" he asked.

I thought for a second. "If you mean the Joyce book, I had a friend in college who said I should read either *Ulysses* or *Finnegan's Wake*. He flipped a coin to see which."

"So which did you read?" Ben asked.

I laughed. "Luckily the coin rolled under the couch. I took that as a sign I shouldn't read either one."

Ben rolled his eyes. "That charming story aside, in the book Joyce penned the sentence *Three quarks for Muster Mark*."

"What's that mean?" I asked.

He shrugged. "Who knows?"

"So what's the other one?" Rosie asked.

"This report says your Quark is first cousin to Robin Beech."

"So?" I said.

"So, Robin Beech is married to my ex-boss, Rodney Lansing, the Illinois attorney general."

"Oh yeah," said Rosie. "Now the name rings a bell. Why the name difference?"

"They got married my second year with the state. In addition to family money, she already had a thriving law practice and didn't want to lose the recognition, so she kept her name."

"A career woman," Rosie said.

Ben laughed. "Only for the power. She brought a bundle of family money into the marriage."

"So she got her cousin a job," Rosie said.

Ben raised his glass. "Springfield is nothing if not a bed of nepotism."

Rosie and I laughed.

"And I guarantee you Lansing is even more concerned than the chief of police about convictions, especially in this election year."

"Nothing wrong with convictions," Rosie said.

"Convictions as a result of good police work are different from convictions as a result of a goon squad, whatever the hell that is," I said.

Jane asked if we wanted dessert. We didn't.

"Perhaps you're giving too much credibility to an alcoholic," Ben said.

"Perhaps."

"And one other thing," he said. "Yancy said they were being pushed to close more cases. He arrests them… the attorney general prosecutes them. The AG is concerned with numbers, especially in high-profile cases when his job is on the line. You always see a push in an election year."

"To the extent of bending the rules?" I asked.

Ben shrugged.

"What do you think, Rosie?" I asked.

She just stared at me for a long ten seconds. "The rules are bent all the time. This job can be rewarding, but it can also be frustrating. We get a good arrest and then watch the guy plead to a lesser charge or skate on some technicality loophole that his lawyer slid him through. Then we arrest him again. So don't expect me to be a great fan of the system… and that system is run by Lansing."

Ben and I glanced at each other.

"How far are the rules bent?" I asked.

She didn't respond.

"Fabricating evidence?"

She set her jaw and looked angry. "Not in the Third."

"Somewhere else?"

"I don't work somewhere else."

I took that as a tactical sidestep. "You ever hear of this goon squad?"

"Like Stosh told you… there are as many rumors in the police department as anywhere else. Our office water cooler is the same as any other office."

"So you have?"

"Show me some evidence, and we'll talk."

Jane stopped by to see if we wanted refills. We didn't.

"Ben, you worked for Lansing. How far would he go?"

"He's power hungry. That's one of the reasons I quit."

"That doesn't answer my question."

He looked at Rosie and then at me. "As far as he has to."

"I get the feeling you're not a fan."

He glared at me. "He's pompous and sanctimonious and downright stupid. If it wasn't for his wife's money and political connections he'd be asking if you want fries with that... and that only if they were desperate."

"Okay. Well, thanks for clearing that up!"

***

WHEN I GOT HOME, Yancy was sitting on the couch watching the news. I set the suitcase down in front of him, and he shook his head.

"Pretty damned sad when your whole life fits in a suitcase," he said.

"Except for one thing," I said. "Your gun is missing."

"Missing? What does that mean? The box wasn't there?"

"The box was there. The gun wasn't in it."

He looked duly shocked. I didn't know the man well enough to know whether he already knew that or not. Seemed like not.

"What the hell? This just keeps getting better." He hung his head and then looked up at me with anger. He slammed down the suitcase and started to open it.

"The box isn't in there."

"Where the hell is it?"

"Being dusted for prints. I don't expect to find any, but worth a try."

He sat back on the couch and didn't ask who was doing the dusting.

"Anyone else have a key to your apartment?"

He shook his head.

"Then it's someone who can pick a lock. Anyone come to mind?"

More head shaking. "Could've broken in."

"Nope," I said. "It was a pro job. An easy one, but still gotta know what you're doing. No signs of forced entry."

"Who says?"

"My best man." He didn't question that. "Anyone who might want to set you up for something?"

"Not that I know of. But I have no idea…"

He let that drift off, and I didn't push it. He needed to put the pieces together himself and decide what he wanted to share. He picked up the suitcase and said goodnight.

I showered and went to bed with the *Forensic Science Handbook* until I lost the battle to keep my eyes open.

CHAPTER 20

WEDNESDAY MORNING YANCY WAS SITTING IN THE KITCHEN reading the paper when I got up. He still looked a bit worn, but he had come a long way from Monday night.

"It's a nasty world out there," he said.

"Yeah, you're not going to be out of a job anytime soon."

"Seems like I'm out of a job now."

"Only temporarily. You settling in okay?"

"Don't think I'm not grateful, but I'm kinda stir crazy. How long you think this will take?"

I laughed. "Good question. If I knew what this *was* I might be able to answer that."

"What about my car?"

"It'll be taken care of."

He raised his eyebrows. "How?"

"The less you know the better."

He sighed. "And there's the gun." He drank some coffee. "Knowing more about that would be good."

"I'm pretty sure we're going to find out. Someone took it for a reason. The trick is to control the situation."

"How you going to do that?"

"Don't know yet. You still have no idea what that reason might be?"

"No."

"Who knew you were in that apartment?"

"Everybody on the job. I didn't hide my anger at where my life had ended up."

We made some breakfast to go with the coffee he had made. I fried eggs, and he handled the toast. I thought about how to ask about his drinking. Most men wouldn't admit a problem, or didn't know they had one, or wouldn't admit what they were trying to forget, or didn't know they were trying to forget. I decided just to ask. If he didn't want to answer that was up to him.

"When I found you Monday night, you were barely coherent. You said you drank but not like that. What was different about Monday night?"

He leaned against the counter, shook his head slowly, and took some coffee. "Just got to me is all."

"What did?"

"Everything. Wife left me three months ago. Had to sell our house, and I ended up in that apartment. The job. Life."

"Sorry to hear that, Jerry. What about the job?"

He pulled out a chair and sat. "Been doing this for fifteen years. Never been like this."

"Like what? What's different?"

He took a sip of coffee, set the cup down, and stared at it. If he was wrestling with demons, my badgering him wasn't going to help. I picked up the dishes and opened the dishwasher.

"Leave 'em, Spencer. I'll clean up."

I nodded. "Thanks."

"What's on your schedule?" he asked.

I was conflicted about whether or not to share details with him. It might help to have him involved, but at the moment I decided to keep the rest to myself. "I've got an appointment at eleven. I'll be back after lunch. There's sandwich meat in the fridge. Help yourself."

He shrugged. "Two heads might be better than one."

"They might. If I get a foothold on this."

"I'm going crazy here. I gotta be doing something... I feel helpless sitting here waiting for something to happen."

"You *are* doing something… you're not making things more complicated. Let me do my job." And then I remembered a dream I had as a kid, and I realized how he felt. It was sometime around first grade. I slept on the upper bunk bed in a room with my sister. I woke up in the middle of the night and saw a grotesque face staring in the window. I screamed, but nobody came. I woke up, sweating, afraid to look out the window. In the morning, I told my folks about it, and they assured me they would have come if they had heard a scream. I had to believe it was a dream. I lost track of how many times I had the dream, more than ten. And, looking back on it, what I remember most is not being able to do anything… just lying frozen in bed, letting out screams that no one heard. So, I knew how Jerry felt, but he had it a lot better than me and my dream.

I got dressed and grabbed my keys and then had a thought. I stopped in the study on the way to the back door.

Jerry was looking out the kitchen window. I walked up to him and handed him Susan's journal.

"What's this?" he asked.

"Susan's journal. You want to do something? Read it. Give me another set of eyes."

He took it and nodded.

As I reached for the door he said, "Spencer." I turned and watched him wrestle with something.

"Your father…" He sighed, and what he was wrestling with left him with the sigh. He was still looking out the window. "Me and Barker were told to go back to Rentel's place." He paused. "We were also told to look for a watch… Amos Grant's watch." He took in a deep breath and let it out. "And we were told where to look for it… under a cushion of the couch. And we were told to then arrest Rentel for suspicion of murder."

"Who told you?"

He didn't answer. He just stared out the window. I knew I wasn't going to get an answer… at least not then. He was too deep in wrestling with memories… memories of what had happened and memories of what he imagined. I pulled the door quietly closed.

As I backed out of the drive, I saw my neighbor, Ann, across the street working on the plantings in front of her house. We waved as I pulled away.

Chapter 21

I GOT TO THE FACILITY FIFTEEN MINUTES EARLY AND SAT IN the car for ten minutes hoping proximity to the cemetery might give me some insight. It didn't.

The same gray-haired man was at the front desk. I told him who I was there to see, but this time didn't give him my card. Without taking his eyes off of me, he pushed the button. The same kid came to escort me down the same hall. As we walked, I asked what his name was.

"Howie Egan," he replied.

"How long you been working here, Howie?"

"About a year. But I just got a promotion. I'm a supervisor. My boss just quit, so I'm doing a lot more things. I started out working the grounds. I could drive the tractor, so I was cutting the grass, digging the graves, things like that. Now they made me a supervisor, so I'm doing a lot of the things my boss was doing, but I still mow the lawn too. They're looking for someone who can drive a tractor. You know anybody?"

"Not off the top of my head. How many people do you supervise?"

He laughed. "Well, no one. There are two other supervisors. Only one of them has anybody he supervises." He shrugged. "I got a raise, but it's a lot of work."

"What did you do before this?"

"Worked at a sod farm. Man, that was hard work."

We walked past Quark's office, and a man wearing a white coat passed us going the other way. He ignored us. "You get many visitors?"

He laughed. "Nope. Only been one since the last time you were here." After a few more steps he said, "I know what you're thinking. So what do I do the rest of the time? Well, I do lots of different things. Whatever the boss says. Just so I stay where I can get to the front quick-like if someone comes."

Ten feet ahead, the door to the ladies' room opened, and Quark's secretary came out. She stopped and gave me a stern look as we went by. Reminded me of my second-grade teacher who never had appreciated my antics. We turned into a hallway to the left.

"You know her?" I asked.

"Old lady Starley? Sure. Mr. Quark's secretary. Gotta watch yourself around her. She's already complained about me twice, once when I left a mop in the hall when I went to the can."

She wasn't old, but I didn't doubt the complaints. People with little power liked to throw it around the most. I didn't tell him that when the day came when his boss called him in and told him he was fired it would be because of her. We stopped near the end of the hall, and he ushered me into Bridgewater's office. It was the same arrangement as Quark's except bigger. There was no one at the desk in the outer office, so Howie knocked on the inner door.

"Come."

Howie opened the door and said, "Sir, Mrs. Cook isn't here. I have a Mr. Manning to see you."

I thought Howie handled that perfectly. When Starley got him fired, they'd be losing a good man.

"Ah yes, please come in."

Howie winked at me and waved me in.

Bridgewater was my height and build and had a full head of wavy brown hair. I had given some thought to what I would say to him and decided to give him the basics. I had beat around the bush with Quark, and that hadn't turned out so well. I walked across a fairly plush beige carpet and held out my hand. He took it.

"Spencer Manning. Thanks for seeing me, Director."

"Certainly, Mr. Manning." He gestured toward the upholstered chair in front of his desk, which was not the mess that Quark's was.

It had a blotter, a green-shaded lamp, and two neat stacks of papers. We both sat. "What is it I can do for you?"

"A week ago Friday I got a rather odd phone call. A woman suggested I visit your cemetery."

He cocked his head and looked surprised. "For what purpose?"

"She didn't say."

"And you did?"

"I did."

"To what end?"

There was a knock on the door.

"Come in," he said.

"I'm back, Director," said a nicely dressed middle-aged woman who I assumed was Mrs. Cook.

"Thank you, Addie. I'll let you know if I need anything."

She looked at me and smiled. He looked back at me.

"Well, there was one small thing."

He kept looking, expectantly.

"I noticed the grass on one of the graves was a bit disturbed."

Now he looked confused.

"What does that mean?"

I shrugged. "In the specific sense or the general sense?"

"How about both?"

"Disturbed means it looked a bit mounded, like it had been tampered with, not flat like the others."

"We do have burials, Mr. Manning. The area naturally would be mounded until the dirt settled."

"Not from seventy years ago."

He laughed. "No, probably not. So, in the general sense, why are you bringing this to my attention?"

"Because the woman who called me has a missing nephew." I told him about Rentel and the police, at least as much as was in the papers.

"What's this woman's name?"

"Susan Janice."

He shook his head. "While that's an interesting story, I don't know why you're here or what all this has to do with our cemetery."

"Well, I'm thinking someone who was connected to the Rentel case pointed Mrs. Janice to your cemetery, and I found that grave."

"And you think one has something to do with the other?"

"I've known stranger things."

He laughed. "So have I, but they've been in books. I think it more likely that your imagination is vivid. You should have been an author." He smiled politely.

I smiled. "Perhaps."

"I also heard you had a meeting with Mr. Quark that didn't go very well."

"No, we probably won't be seeing each other socially."

He laughed. "Quark does have that effect on people."

I couldn't help saying, "A PR director?"

He sighed. "Well, some things are out of my hands."

I knew why it was out of his hands and knew he wouldn't continue that conversation.

"Anything more I can do for you, Mr. Manning?"

"No. I appreciate your time." We both stood and shook hands.

"If you come up with anything more… substantial, do give a call."

"Thanks."

He called Mrs. Cook and told her I was leaving. She told me my escort would be there momentarily.

Howie walked me out. On the way I asked if he knew anything about the cemetery. He said one of the night custodians had taken him there a week after he started. He said it was kind of an initiation for new employees. He thought it was spooky. Swore he heard whispers.

"Something going on at the cemetery?" he asked.

"Not that I know of. Just trying to tie up some loose ends."

"I get it. You can't talk to a stranger, especially one who works here. But I get around. If you need help, call me. You got something to write on?"

I gave him one of my cards, and he wrote his number on it.

"That's a direct number to the dormitory," he said.

"Dormitory?"

"Yeah, I live here."

"Really. Do many live here?"

"Just two of us right now. It's not the Ritz, but they don't charge, and I'm saving for a place of my own."

I gave him another card and said to call me if he had any concerns.

"Concerns about what?" he asked.

I smiled. "About anything strange, Howie."

He winked at me. "Got it."

People watch a lot of TV. They want to be involved in something mysterious and exciting. But people die in real life just as much as they did on TV. I didn't plan on calling Howie.

On the way home I thought about what I had told Bridgewater and what I hadn't told him, mainly that Mrs. Janice was also missing. I hadn't said I thought an extra body was in one of his graves... even *thinking* that sounded crazy. But if that wasn't it, what was the phone call to Susan about?

On the way home my phone rang. It was Paul. He and Ralph had different talents and were my best operatives.

"Hey, Spencer. Just checking in."

"No sign of Malone?"

"None. Talked to a few neighbors. Last anyone remembers was at least a week ago, but they couldn't remember exactly which day."

"Who's on it with you?"

"Rebecca. Want us to continue?"

"Run shifts until Friday morning and then call it off." I knew he would have left my card with the neighbors, and hopefully they'd call if he showed up.

"Got it. No news is bad news. See ya."

The list of missing people was growing, but Barker and Malone were only missing from me, and that by choice. And as far as I was concerned, Yancy wasn't missing. But I hoped his car being towed would start some people in the Fourth wondering.

*   *   *

I WALKED IN THE DOOR with hot dogs and fries a little before one. Yancy was watching the noon news.

"I was about to raid the ice box," he said.

"Hope you're okay with mustard and relish."

"No onions?"

I gave him a look and he laughed. I grabbed two bottles of beer out of the fridge and hesitated as I set them down.

"Don't worry, Spencer. That was a bad night. I'll keep it to one."

I nodded... and hoped. But I realized if he wanted to drink he had plenty of opportunity when I wasn't there. I told him about my talk with Bridgewater as we ate. He asked a few pertinent questions. My answers didn't get us anywhere.

"What about my car?" he asked.

I took the last bite of my first dog. "Next on my agenda."

"What are you going to do?"

"Move it to where my friends in the Third can have it towed ASAP."

He looked up at the ceiling. "My baby and the Lincoln Park Pirates." He shook his head.

Lincoln Park Towing was the scourge of the tow business in Chicago, and unfortunately for Jerry they had the city contract.

"I'll put in a good word, but at the moment that's the least of your worries." I bit into the second dog. "I'd kinda like to know where your gun is." As we ate in silence a thought occurred to me. When I finished, I called Carol.

"Hey, kiddo, I need an op at my house ASAP. I'd prefer Chester."

"Something going on I should be concerned about?"

"Nope. Being proactive. Tell him to be prepared to stay overnight. Might be for a while, so bring whatever he needs."

"Got it."

"What's that about?" Jerry asked.

"Occurred to me that you may need an alibi for whatever happens with your gun. When I'm not here you'll have company. It'll be one of my operatives, hopefully Chester, a retired cop."

"Good idea. Too bad you're not on the force."

I laughed. "Sometimes it feels like I am."

Chester rang my bell forty minutes later. He had retired from the force fifteen years ago. He and Yancy would get along fine. I explained the situation and told them I wouldn't be back until around ten. It was Gin night at Stosh's.

Chapter 22

I PARKED MY CAR ON A SIDE STREET ONE BLOCK WEST OF Cicero, a little north of Montrose, and took a bus down to the bar. I drove Yancy's car back up north and parked on Cicero in close proximity to a tavern in a spot with an expired meter.

It was ten to five when I got to the station and two before as I walked into Stosh's office.

"I hope this is a social call. I'm done for the day," he said drily.

"In the two minutes you have left you can order a tow on Yancy's car which is now in your precinct." I gave him the address. He picked up the phone and hung up at a minute after five.

"You're paying for overtime."

"Take it out of my winnings. We eating in or going out?"

"Eating in. I've got something to do that'll take fifteen minutes. Warm up the grill when you get there." That shoulder as he walked out seemed pretty cold, but there was obviously something else on his mind. It might be a long night.

***

THERE WERE DEFROSTED STEAKS in the fridge along with a bowl of mashed potatoes. I slid the potatoes in the oven and was putting the steaks on when I heard a car pull into the drive. When I was working on a case, our meals became opportunities to pick Stosh's brain. Sometimes he thought of something I hadn't, and sometimes I ended up frustrated because his methods were constrained by the system. Mine weren't, to a certain extent. But I knew I couldn't do anyone any good from a jail cell. We took the food and bottles of Schlitz to the card table in the living room.

He took a bite of steak and smiled. "Perfect. So tell me."

"I'm worried about the gun… it's gonna pop up somewhere."

"Yeah, Yancy needs to be able to provide an alibi. I suggest—"

"Already covered. I have one of my men staying with Yancy… as of today."

"Which one?"

"Chester."

He nodded as he chewed. "Good. An ex-cop makes a good alibi."

"Yancy is edgy."

"Of course. He's a cop. He needs to be doing something, especially when it's his butt on the line."

"I gave him Susan's journal just to keep him busy."

"Good. Maybe he'll find something."

"Maybe, but it's mostly therapy, make him think he's helping. I've been through it several times."

"Ya never know."

"And I discovered that Quark, the PR guy at Walker, is related to Lansing's wife."

He took a bite of steak and said, "So?"

"So, a connection between the attorney general and the phone call about the cemetery."

He kept eating. "I'm not going to let your conspiracy theories ruin my steak. You sure you don't want to throw in the chief of police and the mayor?"

"Come on. I'm just collecting information… same as you. At some point the pieces fit and you've got a picture."

"Just don't be making accusations you can't back up with more than what's in your head."

I stabbed a piece of steak and scooped into what was left of the mashed potatoes.

"That it?" he asked.

I had saved the best for last. "One more thing. Yancy told me this morning. When he and Barker were sent to Rentel's the second time, they were told to look for a watch, Amos Grant's watch. They found it and arrested Rentel on suspicion of murder charges."

"I already told you that. Certainly enough to justify the arrest."

"Yes, but."

"But what?"

"They weren't only told to look for the watch. They were told *where* to look for it."

He stopped chewing. "Crap. By who?"

"Whom. He didn't say."

"Doesn't have to. Almost surely the chief of detectives."

"McElroy," I said.

"Yeah."

I waited while he took another bite... and then another and then asked, "And who tells McElroy?"

He didn't answer right away. "Take my advice for once and stay out of this."

"How well has that worked in the past? Besides, I started this... whatever the hell it is."

"You can do a lot by taking care of Yancy. Let me look into a few things."

"Yancy's taken care of. What things?"

"Things." He sighed. "By the way, only prints on the gun box are Yancy's. The guy wore gloves."

"Figured." We both silently finished eating. When he set down his fork, I said, "Looks like Rentel was set up."

"Looks that way. Long rap sheet. The public would find him guilty long before the trial. Easy case for the state."

"But easier if they had a confession."

"Much."

"So they lean on him. How far do you think they'd go?"

He leaned forward. "Spencer, I'm not saying anyone leaned on anyone."

"Hypothetically, let's say a guy resists, maybe because he didn't do it. How far would they push?"

He just stared across the room.

"And does everyone have a limit?" I continued. "If a guy knows how to inflict pain, would everyone cave in?"

He looked back at me. "Depends on the person. I'd give you up if a dentist even *told* me he was going to drill without novocaine."

"I'm hurt."

He blinked and looked away.

"And if someone refused to talk, could he end up in a grave in a cemetery out in the middle of nowhere?"

He took in a lot of air and let it out slowly. "A dead guy can't confess, Spencer."

"No. I'm not saying they wanted him dead. It just might happen that way. And if it didn't happen that way, where's Rentel? And where's Susan?"

"Let Oak Park work on Susan."

"Sure, lots of manpower devoted to her." I drank the last of my beer. "Stosh, Yancy says there's a goon squad. Rentel was framed and then disappeared. Two and two add up to four."

"Not always. Lots of other explanations."

"Like what?"

He didn't answer.

"Would you see if you can find him in the system?"

"I'll make some calls. I'm gonna change." He pushed away from the table and walked out.

While I was cleaning up the dishes, Stosh came in wearing sweats and said, "Not in the mood for cards. Let's call it an evening." He walked out.

When I was done, I knocked on his closed bedroom door.

"Yeah."

"Let me know if your looking into things gets anywhere."

He didn't answer.

"Goodnight."

"See ya, kid."

I hadn't seen Stosh so withdrawn since Francine died. It was hard to watch. I knew there was, something going on at the station, but there always was and he usually didn't bring it home with him. Or maybe he didn't want to accept the possibility that two and two might equal four.

Chapter 23

SINCE MY EVENING HAD ENDED EARLY, I CALLED ROSIE AND asked if she could stand some company. If I insisted, she said. Stosh would give me up in the dentist chair, and Rosie would rather watch paint dry. A guy might get a complex. It was a warm evening and the sky was clear, so I suggested going to Montrose Harbor and sitting on the rocks at the end of the point. There were no parking spaces in front of her old, stone apartment building, so I double-parked and called her. Two minutes later she appeared in jeans, carrying a light jacket, wearing no makeup, with her light-brown hair pulled back in a ponytail. She looked plain and simple and beautiful. We got to the beach just in time to see a faint line of red appear on the horizon as the moon rose. Without the light of the moon it was hard to differentiate water from sky.

I told Rosie about my visit with Bridgewater and my conversation with Stosh. I saved Yancy's account of the planted watch for last. She was more concerned about that than Stosh had been.

"If you were me," I asked, "where would you go with that?"

"I'd tell a trusted police official."

"I did that. He didn't seem too concerned."

She squeezed my hand a bit tighter. "He asked you to give him some time to look into things."

"Without telling me what those things were."

She laughed. "You made that choice. There's that blue line, and you're on the other side of it."

"As close to it as you can get. You're forgetting what I've done for the department."

She turned toward me and took my hands in both of hers. "For which the department is always grateful. But you made a choice not to wear the uniform. There are consequences of that you have to live with."

I let go of her hands and put my arm around her. The moon was half above the horizon and spilling a shimmering red pool of fire on the water. "I know. But some of those consequences are good."

She laughed. "Like bending the laws when it serves your purpose."

I wasn't going to deny that. "But bending gets results. Which makes me think cops bend the rules too."

"Some."

"Any that you know of?"

"It depends what it is. Holding off filing a report happens all the time."

"How about planting evidence?"

"Not that I know of," she said without having to think.

"How about physical violence to a suspect?"

She didn't answer right away. "I can't imagine, Spencer."

"What if it *is* happening?"

"It would be wrong."

"Do you think there is anything Stosh can do?"

She sighed. "That's a beautiful moon." It was almost full and had risen blood-red and was turning orange.

"You're evading the question."

"He's quietly asking all of us if we've ever heard of or know anything about a *goon squad*." She paused. "There are stories. But I've never given them much thought."

"Are you giving them more thought now?"

"Let's say I'm keeping an open mind."

We watched the running lights of a few sailboats as the moon climbed higher.

"I've got an early appointment," she said.

As we made our way back to the car, I said, "The missing gun gives this all a bit more credibility."

"It does."

"What do you think about that?"

"Nothing good."

I had to agree. Whoever stole the gun wasn't planning on using it for a paperweight. "Let's say there *is* a goon squad. Who's it coming from, and who knows about it?"

"Spencer, it takes months of investigation to get answers to things like that. And even then you might never know."

"I have a feeling Susan and Yancy don't have months."

"What about Rentel?"

I opened the door for her and said, "I think his time ran out."

***

IT WAS AFTER ELEVEN WHEN I GOT HOME. Chester was watching Johnny Carson. Yancy was asleep in Dad's chair.

"Hey, Spencer. Anything good come from the day?"

I sat on the couch. "Nothing earth shattering. Why didn't Yancy go to bed?"

"Waiting for you. He's got something."

"What?"

"Wouldn't tell me. But he spent a few hours with that journal. I think he found something."

I was surprised. "Can't imagine what. I went over it three times."

Chester got up and shook Yancy by the shoulder. He slowly came alive, and as he saw me he shook his head and sat up.

"Spencer. I got something."

I waited for him to wake up.

He stretched and said, "I know who made the call to Susan. At least I think I do."

I was even more surprised. "You do? Who?"

"Well, I'd like to sleep on it and check my thinking in the morning."

I glanced at Chester, and he rolled his eyes. "Okay. Get some sleep. I'll be waiting." When his door closed, I asked Chester how the day had gone. He shut off the TV.

"Nothing worth reporting. Casual conversation, mostly about the job. He wanted to hear my old stories."

I thought for a few seconds. "My mother used to tell me she had a surprise for me, but I couldn't have it until whenever. That used to drive me nuts. But what I wouldn't give for that now."

"Roger that," Chester said. "Guess we'll find out what he's got in the morning."

"Guess so. Sleep well."

Chester headed for his room, and I shut off the lights. Morning would be here soon enough.

Chapter 24

I WOKE UP EARLY, A LITTLE BEFORE SIX. I HADN'T SLEPT WELL. I was anxious to hear what Jerry had to say. I decided to get out of bed and make coffee rather than turn over and hope to fall asleep. But Chester had beaten me to the coffee pot. He was sitting at the table with the paper.

"Morning, Chester. You're up early."

"Morning. My normal time." He turned a page and shook his head. "You know, without the morning paper I wouldn't know what day it is."

I got a cup out of the cabinet. "Should I be worried about you?"

"It's retirement. I lose track. One day blends into the next. And weekends? Forget it. They don't mean anything anymore."

I filled my cup and sat next to him. "Sounds good to me," I said.

He grunted. "Sure, if you're thirty. When I was on the job, I prayed for this. Wait till you're seventy… and be careful what you wish for."

I didn't tell him that when I parked the Mustang next to my cabin in Door County the days disappeared before I unlocked the door. But maybe he was right… maybe the view from seventy would be different. I hoped not.

As I sipped coffee, I said, "Jerry didn't give you any hints about the caller?"

"Nope. Patience is a virtue." He folded the main section and started in on sports.

"How has he seemed?"

"Bored, but nervous. Can't sit still."

"Don't blame him. That gun would make me nervous too. You think he'd leave if you weren't here?"

"In a second."

"Wouldn't blame him for that either. I'd go nuts sitting on the sideline if my butt was on the line."

He laughed. "You'd go nuts no matter whose butt was on the line."

I agreed. "If he's not up at seven I'm waking him." I didn't have to. At a quarter to he walked in, looking tired and needing a shave. Two more pieces of toast popped up as he sat.

"Morning, Jerry," I said. Chester nodded. I added the toast to the pile and got a jar of peanut butter.

"Morning, guys. What day is it?"

We both laughed as Chester pushed the front page of the Trib across the table.

I didn't even give him time to finish pouring his coffee. "So, whaddya got?"

He took his first drink and squinted at the cup before he set it down.

"Vicki Gable. She's a clerk in Records." He took another drink.

I figured I shouldn't have to ask a cop how he knew. I didn't.

"She's been there almost twenty years and plays the Beach Boys non-stop all damned day long. Has a little cassette player. Drove everybody nuts. I mean, I got nothing against the Beach Boys, but all damn day long."

"Drove?" I asked.

He nodded. "They got her her own room with only one desk."

"Why treat her so special?"

"Because she *is* special. She does an amazing job. I think she has a photographic memory. Ask her a question about a case, and she knows just where to look, sometimes doesn't even have to look. If she handles a file it gets handled right, nothing missing, everything squared away. She's a stickler for details. But boy that music drove everybody nuts."

Chester and I made eye contact. "So the call was made from her phone," I said. "But it wouldn't have to be her. Maybe she left for the little girl's room."

Jerry shook his head. "People would sometimes need something from the files in her room, and there were times she wasn't there. But they'd turn off the music."

"She didn't mind that?"

"Oh, yes, she did. But she never said anything... just turned it back on."

Another glance from Chester. We were thinking the same thing.

"So, it would be a perfect cover for someone to go in there when she wasn't there and make the call without turning off the music."

He nodded. "That's what I needed to think about. There's three other people in Records, two women and a man. None of them are that smart. And none of them would care."

"And why would she?" I asked as I added peanut butter to a piece of rye.

He reached for the toast plate. "Because she has a passion for doing things the right way. She'd even make us sign reports so she could read the signature."

"Imagine that," Chester said with a smirk.

"She drove everybody nuts, not just with the music."

We all ate in silence for a few minutes.

"I know it's a little nuts," Jerry said, "but it's more than we had before."

"It is that," I said.

"I could call her," he said.

"Only if you have a death wish," Chester said. He hadn't stepped into the conversation so far, but I knew he was paying attention, and I valued his opinion. Thirty-five years as a cop bought a lot of credibility.

Jerry looked at him with a bit of resentment. I didn't believe I had to explain the situation to a cop, but evidently I did.

"Look, Jerry," I said, "your gun wasn't stolen to shoot at tin cans. Somewhere along the way here it's going to be used in a crime, and you're going to be in the cross hairs. You were told to disappear. If they need a fall guy, who better than the guy who has skipped town? Guilty by inference. They get a warrant, and the case is as good as solved. And if you are never found, either because you have done a great job of disappearing or because they gave you some help, all the better. You're guilty, and the case is solved without the expense and trouble of a trial."

He started to look worried. He should have been worried before.

"What about Barker? He was told to disappear too."

"It's a great plan. They have a choice. But if it were me, I'd pin it on the easiest patsy. Maybe the one who left his gun where it could be stolen."

He held his cup but didn't drink. "They didn't know they'd get my gun."

"Nope. Added bonus. Icing on the cake."

"You're making some assumptions, Spencer," Chester said. I knew that, but I didn't respond. When I didn't, he continued. "Like that there is a *they*. And if there is a they, who is it?"

"Somebody broke into his apartment and stole his gun."

Chester nodded. "Yup. Not saying that didn't happen. Just saying that might not be tied to the cemetery call. Maybe several things going on here."

I hated when logic got in the way of my conjecture. But this conjecture was on pretty firm ground. "I'll give you that, and maybe so. But my plan is the same no matter. And my point to you, Jerry, is that, as far as anyone but a handful of people are concerned, you have disappeared, and you need to stay that way. Your car was found abandoned, and you are off the grid. A phone call puts you back on. At the moment, that gives us an advantage."

He let go of his cup. "Yeah, but I'd feel better if I was doing something."

"Would you feel better dead?"

He just looked at me.

"Remember who told you to disappear."

His face changed as he remembered and thought about why.

"And who told *him*?" I asked. "He didn't make that decision all by himself. The guys who are supposed to protect you are telling you to disappear."

Jerry looked like he had just lost his best friend. This was even worse.

"Well, cheer up. Chester will teach you how to play Casino. And there's a Cubs game on this afternoon."

That didn't cheer him up. "I'm a Sox fan."

"I'll pretend you didn't tell me that," I said with a smile.

"What's the plan?" Chester asked.

"Need another chat with the lieutenant and figure out a way to see Vicki Gable. She married?"

"Nope," Yancy said. "Husband left a few years back. Probably not a Beach Boys fan."

"Give me a description."

"Middle aged, average looks, brown eyes and hair, five foot five-ish, maybe a hundred and forty. Dresses kinda frumpy."

"She go out for lunch?"

He shrugged. "Probably. Everybody does sometimes."

"Is there a favorite spot?"

"Diner called Broken Promise. On Madison a block west of the station."

"Know what she drives?"

"Nope."

Chester stood up. "We'll clean up." He picked up dishes. "By the way, the fridge is pretty empty."

"I'll stop for food on the way back. Anything special either of you want?"

They both shrugged.

"Okay, I'll stop at the butcher and get something unhealthy."

"Roger that," Chester said.

I didn't know exactly how Jerry felt, but pretty close. Sometimes when I shook a tree I had a rough idea of what would fall out, but other times not a clue. I just had to wait to see what would happen. But it had never been my butt that was in the cross hairs. Knowing that something was coming and not knowing when had to be stressful. The kind of thing that could tip an unstable person over the edge. And, based on his visit to the bar, Yancy was already near the edge. But there had to be some solace in knowing that when it did come you had a wall around you. So he had two big things in his favor... me and Chester.

Chapter 25

STOSH LOOKED UP, SAW IT WAS ME, LOOKED UP TO THE CEILING, and crossed himself. "Maybe I should get you an office... clear out the janitor's closet and get you a stool."

"That's what I love about you... you always make a guy feel at home. Key to the executive head?"

He just gave me an icy stare. When I closed the door, he stared harder and finally said, "I made some calls about where Rentel is being held. People who should know, don't. One of them said it was like he had disappeared."

"Maybe not only *like*. But I *have* made some progress. Yancy knows who made the call to Susan."

"Yeah? How would he know that?"

I explained. By the time I was done, the ice had melted.

"Still leaves some room for someone else," he said.

"Agreed, but not much."

He shook his head. "I hope he doesn't go crazy on you."

"That's what Chester's there for."

"Yeah, that was a good call. He was one of the best detectives we ever had. And most respected. There wasn't one person at any level who had anything against him, and I can't think of anyone else I can say that about. He could have gone much higher. Don't know why he didn't."

"Really? I know someone who would've stayed a sergeant if he didn't need the money."

He sighed.

"I have a question," I said. When he didn't respond, I said, "Something stinks… bad. Do I get some help, or am I in this alone?"

"You already have some help. I—"

"I know. You're looking around." I knew he had asked about the goon squad, but if I said anything he would have known who told me. And I didn't consider that much help.

"I can't tell you everything I do. There's the—"

"I know that too. I'm not on the force."

"I have procedures, a code of laws. Those mean everything."

"Sometimes they need to be bent, even broken."

"And sometimes I do bend them. Breaking them is another story."

"So you'd never break one."

"Never say never. Everything depends on the situation. Breaking would be a level of serious I haven't seen in my thirty-two years."

"Let's assume it was Gable who made the call. Now we know who started all this… where the leak came from. But where is Barker? And how about Malone? And does this go higher than McElroy?"

"All good questions."

"Think the guy who gave you the names would have anything else?" I asked.

"Maybe, but not on the phone. If he knows the world outside the walls knows about this, he may loosen up. But don't count on anything. He likes his job as much as the rest of us."

"Well, I guess that's something. Thanks."

"We've got a chain of command and jurisdiction and twelve other things I've got to pay attention to or my ass gets chewed out."

"And you wonder why I went private."

I just got a stare. There was a knock on his door. "Come."

Rosie stuck her head in. "Oh, sorry to interrupt. Didn't know you were interviewing candidates this morning," she said with a smile.

Not smiling back, he looked like he was thinking.

"What?" I asked.

"Close the door and have a seat, Detective."

"Spencer, I've been thinking about something else. What you just told me makes me think I should do it sooner than later."

I glanced from him to Rosie. She looked like she already knew but was waiting for him.

"We've been asked by DEA to help with the drug problem."

"You already do drugs."

"More. They want undercover cops to help infiltrate the gangs."

"They already have that."

"Our people know a hell of a lot more about the local situation. They want to ramp it up. Chief Swalee has been talking with them for almost a year."

"So how does that fit into this?"

"If I could get permission to use our undercover agents for this…"

That was a big step. And that was the big difference between him and me. If it were me, I'd just do it. He'd have to go through channels, and this would go all the way to the top. And the people he'd have to convince along the way would want to hear why. But cops didn't like dirty cops.

"Saying you could," I said, "who are your people?"

He glanced at Rosie, and she glanced back. My heart dropped.

"Tell him?" she asked.

"Tell him."

She took a deep breath. "Remember my trip to California?"

"How could I forget?"

"DEA training."

None of us said anything.

"You still want me to do something?" Stosh asked.

Tough question. I usually had few qualms about putting my life on the line. But I remembered the Riverview case. Rosie's life had been on the line, and I often thought about it. It was her job, and she chose to do it. She had chosen to do this, too, but not this new twist.

"Got something else?" I asked.

"Be careful what you ask for, kid."

I was sure this would come back to weigh on me later. "How

long will this take to put together?"

He shook his head. "*If* I can put it together, maybe a week, and that's being hopeful. Gotta run it by several command layers and deal with the brass who are going to look at me like I'm nuts and want more to go on than some Beach Boys fan made a phone call about a cemetery that somehow implicates police personnel."

I sighed. "Now, when you put it that way… it does sound a bit crazy. You think the brass will listen?"

"They'll listen. It's what they'll say that concerns me. I'm walking on pretty thin ice here, and thin ice has a tendency to break."

"At least it's not *your* department."

I got a serious look. "Anyone wearing a badge with CPD on it is my department."

"Understood."

"If your theory has any truth to it, it's serious and we'll get involved. But I sure could use more than what you've got."

"There's Yancy's gun and the fact that he's disappeared."

He groaned. "Perhaps not something Yancy wants made official. And there's the little asterisk by that word disappeared… like not really."

I wasn't sure how to answer him, and I was pretty sure I didn't want Rosie involved.

His intercom buzzed.

"Yeah."

"Your ten thirty is here, Lieutenant."

"Thanks, Kate. Give me a minute." He turned back to me. "Look, kid, I'm doing what I can with what little I got to go on. I'll let you know what works out, and you let me know if you get anything else."

"Okay. One more thing. I need a home address and auto info on Vicki Gable."

"See Kate."

Rosie and I walked out. When we were halfway down the hall, I asked who her partner was.

"Vazquez."

"Well, that makes me feel a *little* better."

We stopped before going into the detective room.

"You don't want me involved in this do you?" she asked.

"I don't want you doing DEA undercover work."

"But you're willing to put yourself into situations that we would not."

"Different."

She slowly shook her head. "Not different at all. Double standard."

"But you're—"

"A police detective. A good one who is well-trained and goes by the book and doesn't take unnecessary chances."

I looked at her and took a deep breath. "I'm sure of all of that. But just because you're a cop makes this more dangerous. Cops know each other. It's pretty likely that someone in the Fourth would know you're undercover."

She folded her arms over her chest. "How about this? If I can show you that that's not a possibility, would you feel better about it?"

"Maybe. But I can't imagine how that would be the case."

She smiled. "If you don't recognize me it's likely no one in the Fourth will either."

I laughed. "Did they teach you magic tricks out there?"

"Kinda. Deal?"

"Throw dinner in and you've got a deal."

She put out her hand, and I shook it.

"Steak with all the trimmings," she said.

"My thoughts exactly!"

***

SHE WENT INTO HER OFFICE, and I walked back to see Kate. Fifteen minutes later I had the information on Vicki Gable. She drove an '82 Buick Regal and lived on Neva near Harlem and North Avenue. I stopped at the deli and made it home in time for lunch.

Chapter 26

I WANTED TO HAVE A LOOK AT VICKI GABLE. AT TEN TO FIVE, there were several open spots, but I knew they would go quickly. I parked in front of an empty lot taken over by weeds across the street from 1734 Neva, a brick ranch that looked, except for different colored shutters, like most of the rest on the block. Most had single-car, detached garages. The afternoon was warm enough that I could leave the window down. The sun was a perfect, bright circle behind a thin layer of gray clouds, and a dog was barking in someone's backyard. While I waited, I thought about Rosie.

She was right about being a good detective, and she was right about the double standard. And she wouldn't have been chosen for the training if she wasn't good at her job. And she was perfectly capable of taking care of herself. And… and… But undercover situations never went according to plan, and I was worried. I also wondered if I had put more effort into our relationship, if we had firm plans, if she would have accepted the training. A part of me wanted those plans. As I listened to the barking, I knew I had to stop second-guessing. With everything in my life, I took the attitude that I had to do what I had to do and what would be would be. I had to trust that Rosie could make her own decisions wisely. I was thinking about what Rosie's undercover strategy would be when I realized the dog had stopped barking.

At ten to six, a Buick regal pulled into the driveway and stopped before getting to the house. A lady matching Yancy's description of

Vicki got out and opened the trunk. As Yancy had said, she was pretty much average everything, with short brown hair, but not anywhere near the sixties hippie I had envisioned, with a plain, green dress down well past her knees. She took out a box, walked to a neighbor, rang the bell, and handed the box to the lady who answered, an older woman who was surely someone's grandmother. Vicki then pulled her car into the garage and let herself in at the side door.

On the way home I thought about how I was going to approach Miss Gable. I stopped at a record store and bought a Beach Boys cassette.

***

I PULLED UP TO THE GARAGE and saw Chester and Jerry sitting on the deck, each with a bottle of beer. I locked the car and stepped up to the deck.

"Nice to see you two relaxing," I said. "Appears everything is peaceful."

"Hah," said Jerry. "Except for the fact that I'm going nuts here."

"Which *here* do you mean?" I asked. "You can't possibly mean the one where you're in nobody's crosshairs and you have this big lovable teddy bear to keep you company."

"Hah," he said again. "You mean to babysit me."

I was getting tired of the *hahs*, and the point where I would get tired of Jerry was on the horizon. I was tempted to hand him his suitcase and wish him well. But I needed him to spring the trap. He was the bait... bait that I was taking very good care of.

"Interpret it as you like," I said as I headed for the back door. "Why not think of it as your own personal relocation program?" I got a beer, noticed the steaks on the counter, and headed back outside. Chester was lighting the grill. It was warm enough to eat on the deck.

As we ate, I told them about Vicki and the plan I had come up with on the way home. They pointed out the holes but couldn't come up with anything better. After dinner we played Gin, but Jerry couldn't keep his mind on the game and quit. Chester and I switched to Casino.

Chapter 27

FOR SOME IT WAS THE END OF THE WORK WEEK, AND THERE was a weekend to look forward to. But I didn't have a work week.

Carol was talking to Watson when I came in the back door of the office. He wasn't talking back. I was willing to bet he wasn't even awake. But that was okay. The night he had saved Billy up at Aunt Rose's had earned him a sleepy retirement.

"Morning, Carol."

"Morning, Spencer. Any progress?"

I gave her a quick review and told her I'd be gone before lunch. Before I sat at my desk, I took a business card and pushed a dead moth into the trash can.

At ten, Carol came into my office and told me she'd be upstairs for a bit with Watson, trimming his nails. She said she'd lock the front door.

"Pedicure?"

"Just a trim this time. If you make an appointment, I'll see if I can fit you in."

I frowned at her. When I bought the building, I had a stairway built from the office to the apartment above for Carol and Billy so she wouldn't have to go outside. It came in handy, especially in the winter.

Fifteen minutes later I heard a noise that I assumed was Carol. It wasn't. It was two men who had come in the alley door. Carol had locked the front. We kept the alley door locked, too, but someone had forgotten to do that after he came in.

One was well over six foot tall. The other was closer to five eight. The tall one had shoulders that looked like he could have pulled a semi, and his neck was almost as wide as his jaw. His hands were almost as big as dinner plates. The other one was a lot skinnier. He had a pointy nose, and his black hair was slicked back. Neither one showed any hint of friendliness.

"Something I can do for you?" I asked.

"Yeah, there is," the one with the shoulders said with a little rasp to his voice. But neither one said what it was.

"You boys got names?"

Shoulders said, "Seems to me you're in no position to ask."

The smaller one just watched.

"And what position would I be in?"

"One where you listen while we talk."

I turned in my chair and reached slowly for the drawer that held a gun.

"I said listen, not be reachin' for nothin'. Hands on top of the desk."

I folded my hands on top of the desk.

Shoulders continued. "You've been askin' questions about a cemetery. You—"

"I didn't—"

"I said listen. If you're talkin' you're not listenin'."

I wanted to tell him I could do both at the same time, but I kept that to myself.

"You don't know what you're gettin' into. One way or the other, you're gonna stop askin' questions. This is one way, the other is... well, not as polite."

I didn't respond.

"Understand?"

I hesitated.

"I said understand!"

"Ah, I wasn't sure if I was still supposed to be listening."

He laughed. His shadow didn't. "Smart-ass shamus. Give me a reason to not be polite."

When I didn't give him a reason, he repeated, "Understand?"

They stood straight and tall in their black suits and white shirts. They looked straight out of the *Blues Brothers*. There were guns under the jackets, but the guns wouldn't come out unless I gave them a reason, and I didn't plan on giving them a reason. But Carol didn't know that. I saw her without moving my eyes away from them, and I saw what she was holding.

The sound of a shotgun cocking is the best attention-getter in the world. And those two guys had exactly the right reaction. The looks on their faces made my day, perhaps even my year.

"Okay, boys. Take out the guns and set them on the floor, two fingers, one at a time. You first." I pointed to the one with the shoulders. They both complied. "Kick 'em over here." They did. "Now, let's see some ID. Just reach in easy and toss your wallets on the desk."

They hesitated. The big one had a look on his face like a deer in the headlights—utter confusion. He was used to having things go his way and didn't know what to do when they didn't. The best weapon I had was not my gun but the arrogance of someone who thought he was invincible. That and greed were the downfall of many. I had to assume these two had planned this visit. They knew it was just me and my secretary in the office. And they had totally discounted the woman sitting at the front desk.

I smiled. "Seems to me that Remington double-barrel *now* puts me in position to ask."

They tossed their wallets to the desktop as I reached into the drawer and pulled out the Taurus 9mm I kept at the office.

"Okay, Carol. I got it."

"Do you want me to call the police?" she asked.

"Not yet. We're going to continue our conversation first." I kept the Taurus in my hand.

She gave me a questioning look and headed back to her desk.

I looked at their driver's licenses and at them. Same pictures. Addresses in Chicago. The big guy was Thomas Darny, the little one Nicholas Jetter. I set those aside and looked through the rest. Credit cards and one other ID. I set it all down and, still holding the gun, looked at them for a reaction to what I'd seen. There was none.

"So…" I said. "FBI?"

The big one decided to talk. "Listen, Manning, mind if we sit?"

He had suddenly become friendly. "Chairs are for guests. Explain."

"Pretty simple," Darny said. "We're on a case. You're gettin' in the way, askin' questions, screwin' up what we've been workin' on for months."

"What case?"

He shook his head. "Can't say, other than the mental facility is involved."

"Who you working for?"

He shook his head some more. "That's all I can say. You've been out there. What prompted your visits?"

Prompted my visits? "Looking into some missing people."

"And who would that be?"

"I get no information from you, and I'm supposed to share everything?"

Jetter gave Darny a worried glance. Darny shrugged and said, "Suit yourself."

I did suit myself. I used the intercom and asked Carol to come in. I handed her the wallets.

"Make copies of everything in the wallets, please."

"Hey!" said Darny. "That's government property. You can't do that."

"No?" I pushed the phone toward him. "Feel free to call your supervisor."

He looked confused and said. "There's nothing illegal here."

"I disagree. But it'd be tough to make a case for threats and in-timidation… a waste of my time. But I'm not fond of threats."

"Just friendly advice, Manning," Darny said.

"Good to hear. And to keep it friendly, I'll keep a copy of your info."

Carol came back in with the wallets, and I told her to hand them back. They both looked through them.

"You going to back off?" Darny asked.

"Get out."

He gave me his best tough guy look and started to bend down to pick up his gun.

"Nope," I said. "I'll keep the guns."

"You can't—"

"This gun says I can. Get out."

They left by the rear door.

Carol came back into my office after locking the door, shaking her head. She put the copies in front of me.

"How many times have I told you to lock the back door when you come in?"

"Several."

"Well, now you know why." She sat.

I smiled. "Hey, not an issue when I've got an office manager with a shotgun. That course was just in time." She had just received her permit and taken a gun course that included shotgun training.

She smiled back. "Not something I want to do again any time soon."

"But it'll make a helluva story for Billy to tell his friends."

"Billy's not going to find out."

"Well, keep it in your arsenal if you ever need a *hero Mom* story."

She laughed. "Some hero. The course didn't teach me how to stop shaking."

I smiled. "Deep breaths. You were great."

She relaxed in the chair. "Those guys really with the FBI?"

I laughed. "No. It's all a load of horsecrap."

"So then..."

"I know where the load is... it seems to be following me around. What I need to find is the horse. And I can do that better if the horse doesn't know I'm coming."

"Couldn't Stosh help with the IDs?"

"Maybe, but I can do better than that. Please make another copy I can take with me."

I made a phone call and then headed out for lunch.

Chapter 28

I GOT TO THE BROKEN PROMISE AT TWENTY TO TWELVE AND sat in a booth near the back. A haze of cigarette smoke hung from the ceiling, slowly swirling in the moving air from the fans. There were two waitresses, one behind the counter at the register and the other setting tables. I set my cassette player on the table and put my headset plug into the jack. I popped in the Beach Boys cassette and pushed play. It started somewhere in the middle of "California Girls." I stopped it, turned the volume all the way up, and pulled the plug partially out of the jack. I ordered coffee and a ham sandwich and watched the door. At ten after, Vicki Gable came in, alone, a black shoulder purse slung around her neck. The crowd had arrived in the last half hour, and the conversation level had risen.

As she looked for a booth, I pressed play and the song blared.

As I fumbled with the plug, a waitress yelled, "Hey! Turn that down. What do you think this is… a concert hall?"

I got the plug in and apologized. I listened to the song through the headphones and ate my sandwich. Vicki Gable approached my booth and thanked me for the music.

"You like the Beach Boys?" I asked.

"They're all I listen to," she said with a friendly smile.

"They're the best. You wanna join me?"

"If it's not an imposition."

"No, not at all. Please." I motioned to the bench, took out the headphones, and turned off the player.

She sat.

I held out my hand across the table. "Spencer."

She took it. "Vicki." She looked like she didn't know what to say next. She was saved by the waitress. But after ordering soup and tea she was back to the awkward situation, two people having nothing but a moment of music. It was awkward for me, too, for several reasons, and I decided to level with her sooner than later.

"Vicki, there's something I want to tell you. I'm a private investigator, and I'm looking for someone."

She looked very confused, and I sensed that she was on the verge of leaving. But I hoped that the crowd in the diner, which probably included several cops, would give her a level of safety that would keep her there.

"Susan Janice," I said. There was a slight sign of recognition as she remembered why that name mattered to her. "And I need your help." The waitress brought her tea and soup and refilled my coffee.

She blinked quickly for a bit and then said, "Why would you need *my* help?"

"Because you made a phone call about Martin Rentel… told her about a cemetery."

Her eyes changed immediately as she looked around at the other tables. They held a look that might, in another situation, be mistaken for insanity. I couldn't tell if it was fear or anger, maybe both. I fully expected her to get up and leave, but she didn't. Instead, with a shaking hand, she took a spoonful of soup. I let her think and looked around at the nearby tables. No one was paying any attention to us.

When she looked back at me, her eyes had lost the fear, but she was very nervous.

"Do you have ID?" she asked.

I took out my wallet and handed her my license.

She studied it for ten seconds and then handed it back. "Any relation to Chief Manning?"

"My father."

She nodded slowly. "He was a fine man."

She sipped her tea and then asked, "Does anyone else know

about this?"

"No." I could tell by her eyes that she had made a decision.

"There's another diner called the Full Cup on North Avenue a few blocks east of Harlem. Can you meet me there at eight?"

"I can."

She stood and opened her purse.

"I've got it," I said.

She nodded, started to say something, and then just turned and left.

I motioned to the waitress for the check.

She dropped it on the table and started to clear the plates. "Didn't your friend like the soup?" she asked.

"It was fine," I said with a smile. "She remembered something she forgot to do."

"Too bad. You have a good day."

"You also. Thanks." I left a ten on top of the check and walked out, realizing on the way to the door that Vicki hadn't asked how I knew she had made the call.

Chapter 29

A YEAR AGO, I HAD A CASE WHERE I CROSSED PATHS WITH Special Agent Thward, agent in charge of the Chicago office of the FBI. He was arrogant and a pompous ass who had nothing but contempt for private investigators. But I had won him over with my charm, and he and I had ended on better ground. Or maybe that was because I had stepped aside and let him take all the credit.

I hated the thought of a trip to his office. He was a chain smoker, and it was filled with a haze. I had felt badly for his secretary, Mrs. Mitchell. She was in an outer office, but the air wasn't much better than in his.

Traffic got worse the closer I got to the Loop. His office was in a high-rise on Michigan Avenue. I had the choice of parking in a vacant lot for five bucks or a city garage for twenty. I cringed as I pulled into the garage, but my Mustang didn't belong in a vacant lot.

I got a surprise as soon as I opened the door to Thward's office. There was no cigarette smell.

"Mr. Manning!" an excited Mrs. Mitchell said.

"Mrs. Mitchell. How nice to see you again."

She got up from behind her desk and gave me a hug.

"Not that I'm complaining, but what's that for?"

"That's for the air I breathe. Agent Thward told me you made a deal with him… you'd let him take all the credit for the case last year if he'd do something about the smoke in the office."

I had forgotten about the deal. And now that I was reminded, I remembered that at the time I had no hope he would hold up his end.

I laughed. "And he went through with that?"

She raised her arms. "Living proof."

"Good for you, Mrs.—"

"Peggy. You are my hero, Mr. Manning."

I smiled. "Spencer. Is he available?"

"Yes." She knocked on his door and ushered me in.

He came around his desk and shook hands. "Spencer Manning. I didn't figure to see you again any time soon."

"Crime doesn't stop, Special Agent Thward."

"No. Job security is pretty good. What brings you here?"

I sat and told him about my visit from the Blues Brothers and handed him the envelope. He opened it and looked through the documents.

"Ring any bells?" I asked.

He shook his head and laughed as he rolled an unlit cigarette between his thumb and forefinger. "These two worked for me for a couple of years up until a year and a half ago when I let them go. I heard they had gone into some kind of private enterprise. I assumed it wasn't all above-board, but this is the first time I've run across them, and obviously it isn't."

"You had trouble with them?"

"Everyone had trouble with them. They worked on the east coast and didn't play well with others. They were given a choice… transfer and shape up or get booted."

"Lucky you. Not easy to get fired from the FBI. What happened to get them tossed?"

"I'd rather not say. Paperwork is still being sorted out." He shrugged.

"And what have you heard about them?" I asked.

"Not a lot. I figured they'd be bending the rules somewhere else."

I pointed out the obvious. "Impersonating an agent is more than bending."

He smiled and tapped the cigarette tip on the desk. "It certainly is. Can I copy these?"

"They're yours."

"I have a few men who will love taking care of this," he said.

"Well, if you don't mind, I have another idea."

He smiled again… this time bigger. "I kinda figured you would." He shook his head. "If those two idiots are involved, whatever they're doing is gonna go south somewhere along the way. What's the idea?"

I smiled. "You got someone who can drive a tractor?"

He frowned, but he listened. And by the time I had left we had worked out a rough outline of a plan.

***

WHEN I GOT BACK TO THE CAR, I called Chester to tell him I wouldn't be there for dinner. I asked how Jerry was doing. He had taken to pacing. I had time to take care of some errands and find a burger joint.

Chapter 30

I DROVE UP THE INCLINE AT RIDGELAND AVENUE, THE ANCIENT boundary of Lake Chicago, the result of the glacier-melt ten thousand years ago and, in a few more blocks, easily found an open spot in front of the Full Cup. I got there early and sat in the car for a few minutes, wondering if Vicki would show up. By the time I got out of the car at ten to eight, the wind had picked up with a cool breeze out of the northwest. A scrap piece of paper caught my eye as it lazily followed the wind. I watched it dance past a few storefronts and then up as it disappeared over the roof of a laundry. As I turned toward the diner, I realized this case was a lot like that scrap of paper, just following the wind. Maybe my life was too.

Before I got to the door, I saw a homeless person step out from behind a car and come toward me. I knew the homeless problem was getting worse in the city and moving into the nearby suburbs. His hair was long and dirty, and he wore a threadbare, stained jacket. I gave him a couple of bucks as he passed, and he nodded a thank you.

Vicki Gable was also early, but not as early as me. I already had a cup of coffee. She looked the same except she had changed to slacks.

"You found it okay?" she asked.

"Sure. Have you eaten?"

"Yes."

The waitress came by, and Vicki asked again for tea. Service would be good… there were only two other couples in the diner.

We looked at each other for a minute in a mental tug-of-war, wondering who was going to say something first. I thought it should be her. It eventually was, but not before I saw the decision made in her eyes... the decision to trust me. But the question she asked wasn't what I was expecting.

"So, if Mrs. Janice is missing, how do you know about the cemetery?"

I had wondered how much I should trust her and how much I should tell her. She had very quickly left me with no reason not to trust her. That was a smart question. I decided to tell her the whole story. By the time I was done one of the couples had left.

She listened patiently and then said, with a bit of a knowing smile, "So you're not a Beach Boys fan?"

I laughed. "More Miles Davis and Coltrane, mostly the ballads. I'm sorry for the ruse."

Her smile broadened. "That's perfectly okay. It was clever." She took a sip of tea. "And probably the only thing that would have worked."

"I have a lot of missing pieces here... I'm sorry, is it Mrs. Gable?"

"Vicki is fine, as long as I can call you Spencer."

I nodded. "Your phone call was very cryptic. You told her she would find answers at the cemetery. Answers to what question?"

Her lips parted, but she paused and looked sad and slowly shook her head. "I don't know. And now that poor woman is missing too. And all she wanted to do was find her nephew."

"Was he released?"

She leaned closer to me. "The paperwork says he was. But I'm guessing he never left the building, at least not on his own accord."

"Why do you say that?"

"Because the signatures on the paperwork were forged."

I found it hard to believe what I was hearing and was starting to wonder if Vicki was some kind of a conspiracy nut. Maybe there were other reasons she was in a room by herself.

"Let's say that's true." She raised her eyebrows but didn't say anything. "How do you know that? And if you know that why didn't someone else catch it?"

She didn't have to prove anything to me, but she looked very determined. "Because I'm very thorough, and I've been doing it for a long time. No one else would even look at the forms other than to see there was a signature." She finished her tea and looked a bit flustered. "I've been accused of being *too* thorough. There's too much paperwork to pay that kind of attention, I've been told."

I didn't doubt the paperwork. I heard it from Stosh all the time.

"Have you told anyone?" I asked.

She looked at me for a few seconds before shaking her head.

"So what's going on at the cemetery, and how do you know?" I asked.

The waitress came up and asked if we wanted refills. We said no. She put the check on the table and said they were closing in ten minutes.

"I'm afraid I don't know what's going on, Spencer."

I was hoping for more than I already knew, which was next to nothing. "You told her she'd find answers at the cemetery. Why did you say that?"

"I overheard a conversation between two men. There's a small empty room in the rear of the second floor. It's next to our old file storage room and next to my office. There's a vent through the wall. I just heard one of them mention Rentel and say maybe they could use the cemetery at Walker for that too. The other man asked what Walker was, and he said the Walker State Mental Health Facility."

"Do you have any idea what he meant by *for that too?*"

She tilted her head and said, "I'm sorry. That's all I heard. Someone came into the file room."

"Do you have any idea about what they might have meant?"

"I've thought about it. I have twenty wild guesses, none of them with any facts behind them. And now poor Mrs. Janice is missing."

"Did you recognize the voices?"

"Never heard them before."

"Would you recognize them if you heard them again?"

"Maybe, at least the one who mentioned Walker. He had a raspy voice."

"And you're sure you had never heard either one before?"

She slowly shook her head. "No, I hadn't."

"Do you think they're part of the police force?"

She shrugged and played with her cup. "They have to be, don't they? How else could they be in there? But I know everybody in the building."

I had no idea, but another odd thing added to the list didn't surprise me.

I got a look from the waitress. "I think we're wearing out our welcome. Thanks for meeting with me, Vicki."

She was still playing with her cup. "One more minute. How did you know it was me?"

I smiled. "I was wondering if you'd ask. I told you about Susan's journal. Well, when she wrote about your call, she also wrote that she heard Beach Boys music in the background."

She sighed. "I thought I was being so secretive." She pushed the cup away from her. "So, whoever gave you my name was somebody from the station... who knew I liked the Beach Boys."

It wasn't a question.

I laughed. "I hear the people who know you like the Beach Boys is just about everybody."

She looked embarrassed. "I guess I should do something about that."

"Hey, people do worse things."

"I have a question," she said with a slight smile.

"Shoot."

"Are you brave?"

I smiled back. "That depends."

"On what?"

"Whether or not someone is looking." I smiled and she laughed.

The ten I left on the table made for a very nice tip. As I held the door for Vicki, she asked if there was anything she could do to help. I told her I didn't think so and gave her my card in case she thought of anything or anything else happened. I was particularly interested in the identities of the two men. And she gave me her home number in case I needed anything from her. She said she was more than glad to help, and maybe she'd be able to. Indeed, having a person on the inside was certainly a plus.

Chapter 31

I HAD PLANNED ON DOING SOME YARD WORK BEFORE GOING to Stosh's for lunch, but Saturday dawned with a spring drizzle, the kind that was going to last all day. We all chatted about the case at breakfast without adding anything of value to the growing puzzle of disconnected pieces.

As I finished my eggs, I said, "I have a question, Jerry. I've been to the facility twice. The first time I saw Quark. The second time I saw Bridgewater. Both times someone at the station was tipped off that I was there. Any ideas who that might be?"

He shook his head.

"I'll narrow it down a little." I told them about my visit from the Blues Brothers. "After the first visit you and Barker were told to disappear. After the second I got a visit from the Blues Brothers."

He still looked blank. "Sorry, could be just about anybody." He looked forlorn.

"Do you have any idea who it might be at the facility?" Chester asked.

"It obviously needs to be someone who knew I was there both times. Quark and his secretary were outwardly hostile. Quark was quickly antagonistic about my questions about the cemetery. But the same kid had escorted me to the offices both times. And there's the old man at the front desk. And who knows who talked to whom after I left."

"Sounds like Quark and his secretary have something to hide."

I smiled. "I'd love to nail those two to the wall."

"How about Bridgewater?" Chester asked.

"Certainly possible, but my gut feeling says no. He seemed too clueless to be involved."

I took care of several chores before leaving at eleven thirty.

***

AS USUAL, STOSH HAD THE SANDWICH FIXINGS laid out and waiting. We had an hour and a half before the start of the Cubs Phils game, and we talked about the case over lunch. We both wondered if the game would be called because of rain.

"So, kid, you got anything new?" He glanced at the envelope I had left on the card table on my way in.

"Yup. Met with Vicki Gable. She has no idea what's going on at the cemetery. She just overheard a conversation between two men whose voices she didn't recognize. One mentioned the name Rentel and said maybe they could use the cemetery at the Walker State Mental Health Facility."

"Use how?"

I shrugged as I chewed a bite of roast beef on rye. "That's all she heard."

"So nothing new there. I've never met this Gable. What's she look like?"

"Not what I expected."

"What did you expect?"

"An aged hippie from Woodstock."

"And?"

"More like my third-grade teacher. Very prim and proper." I described her.

"You know, kid, not everyone at Woodstock was a hippie."

I looked at him with disbelief. "*You* were at Woodstock?"

"Hardly, but your folks were."

My disbelief changed to shock. "What!"

He laughed. "They never told you?"

"No, but you'd better!"

"Your mother wanted to go. Your father was somewhat less than enthusiastic. But she insisted. Said she'd go by herself if he didn't want to."

That I believed. Mom could be headstrong when she was set on something. "I can see her saying that, but I can't believe Dad would go along."

"He thought there would be violence, and he wanted to protect her."

I laughed. "She could have done fine all by herself."

"Hey, he was her white knight. And there *were* threats of violence. No way he'd let her go alone. But it turned out pretty peaceful." He took a bite. "Only real violence was when Peter Townshend hit Abbie Hoffman in the head with his guitar."

"What?"

"It was something like five in the morning Sunday, and The Who hadn't gone on yet. Peter had been backstage drinking tea, probably spiked, and was not in a good mood. But they finally got on. They finished "Pinball Wizard", and he was tuning his guitar. Abbie Hoffman was sitting offstage and chose that moment to get up and grab the mike and take off on one of his social injustices. He had been volunteering in one of the medical tents… most likely using LSD to stay awake. Peter didn't take well to someone interrupting their set and hit him in the head with his guitar."

I laughed. "I would have loved to have seen that."

"Well, your folks did. Surprised they never told you."

"Maybe not something a young teenage kid would understand."

"Or, as I remember, a forty-year-old police chief."

We laughed and sat for a bit in silence as I thought about my mother the hippie.

"What's in the envelope?" he asked as he set down his empty bottle.

I took the documents out of the envelope and set them in front of him. "I had a visit from these two guys yesterday morning. Suggested I stop asking questions. Told me I was interfering with a case they were working on."

He laughed as he raised his bottle of Schlitz. "You do tend to do that." He took a drink.

I told him about Carol and the shotgun. He thought that was hilarious.

"Only one problem," I said. "I showed their pictures to Thward, and he said they were let go by him a year and a half ago."

"Impersonating a fed. That's a nice chunk of jail time. He going after them?"

"At some point. I asked him to wait. Told him I had a plan."

"Which is?"

"Well…" I took another bite.

He smiled. "You don't have a plan, do you?"

"Not exactly, but I do have a rough outline, and Thward is willing to play along. If I'd have had them arrested right then, whatever they were involved with would fold up. Now they're feeling safe… and these two guys are too stupid not to make mistakes."

We were listening to the noon show on WGN radio. The host said the game was delayed.

"That's one way of looking at it," he said. "But it's always good to get bad guys off the streets."

"Vicki said one of the men had a raspy voice that she'd be able to ID. So did Darny, the big guy in my office. I wonder if they have anything to do with this goon squad rumor."

He gave me a harsh look and looked at the pictures again. "I'll have someone check out these addresses. Be nice to know where we can find them when we want to."

I nodded. "And one more thing. The two goons said I was interfering with their case. How did they know what I was doing?"

"Good question."

"Must be someone at the facility. My guess would be Quark."

He gave me a playful smile. "Don't jump to conclusions. By the way, have you thought about Thward?"

"What do you mean?"

"He either has some respect for your methods or he wanted to be able to deny that he ever knew you."

"Let's hope for the first."

"You can hope all you like. If I had to put money on the table…"

"Yeah, whatever."

"So, you've got two missing civilians and three missing cops. At least that's what someone wants it to look like. But you know where Yancy is, and you think Barker is off to places unknown with his family. That leaves Malone as the only cop unaccounted for. You had someone on his place, right?"

"Until Friday morning, and then they pulled off. No sign of him."

"And a missing gun."

"Yeah." I sighed. "Whatever is going on, they couldn't have expected to find his gun. That's going to change the plan."

"Yeah, and not in a good way."

We both knew that someone was going to end up dead by means of a bullet from Yancy's gun. Who and when were the big questions.

"You want another bottle?" he asked.

"Sure."

He came back with two bottles and said, "So you still have no idea what the cemetery has to do with all this?"

"No. But I think that grave was dug up, and maybe others. I want to have someone who knows about grass take a look at it."

"Who would that be?"

"How about the Cubs groundskeeper?"

He laughed. "Good luck with that."

"Hey, who can refuse a mystery and a free lunch?"

"Let me know how that goes."

I cleared the table and cleaned up the lunch fixings.

When I got back, he was shuffling the cards.

"I talked to my guy at the Fourth," he said. "Gave him what you know. He says there *is* a lot of pressure from the top to close cases, but that's the same for all of us. Doesn't give any credibility to your goon squad."

"Can't imagine he would. If that *is* happening, whoever is responsible isn't advertising it. And if someone finds out they're not likely to make waves."

He just looked at me. Hard to argue with my logic. And hard to admit it might be happening… after all, these were the good guys.

At a quarter after one, the radio announcer said the game had been postponed and would be made up as part of a double-header on Sunday. As Stosh was dealing the cards, the phone rang. He answered and listened and said he'd be there in twenty.

He hung up and said, "You wanna take a ride?"

"What's up?"

"Body. Found in the back of a garbage truck."

"I think I'll pass. I've got enough on my plate. And I've got a dinner date with Rosie at six."

He stared at me. "This *is* your plate. It's Malone."

"Jesus."

Chapter 32

THE DRIZZLE WAS VERY LIGHT WHEN WE GOT TO THE ALLEY behind a grocery store on Western. The truck was from a private company. Most of the green paint was faded or scraped off and "BEST DISPOSAL" in white letters was painted on the side. The alley was closed off at both ends, and there were police cars everywhere. I could see a body on the ground behind the truck, although it didn't look much like a body. It was bloated and gray and covered with garbage. Officer Kelly handed the lieutenant two wallets in an evidence bag and glanced at me. He was wearing gloves.

"Wallace and I were the first to arrive, Lieutenant. The body was on the ground."

"How'd it get there?"

"Driver pulled him out."

"Where is he?"

Kelly pointed to the yard across the alley. "Guy with all the tattoos."

We all looked in that direction. A brawny guy was sitting on the grass with his head in his hands. He wore a cut-off sweatshirt that showed off his collection of tattoos on both arms. He had a crew cut and tats on his neck.

"Get a name?"

He pulled his notebook out of his pocket. "Max Brown."

"Body was in the dumpster?" Stosh asked.

"Yes."

Stosh and I glanced at each other.

"So how does he know there's a body?" Stosh asked.

"I asked that," said Kelly, looking proud of himself. "He rolled up the dumpster and hooked it up. As it was lifting and the back was opening, the back gate jammed. He jiggled the controls, but nothing happened. Couldn't get it to go up or down. While he was trying to fix it he glanced in the dumpster and saw a hand sticking out of the garbage. And here's the weird part… he thought the hand moved. So he reached in thinking the guy was alive, leaned up over the edge, and pulled the guy out."

I knew what happened next. There was a pool of lunch on the ground next to the body.

"The wallets were on the body?" the lieutenant asked.

"Yes, back left pocket. Left front for his badge wallet. When I saw that, I…"

The lieutenant nodded. "It's okay, Kelly. Anybody see him pull the body out?"

"No. And he didn't see anybody. Wallace is talking to neighbors."

"Okay. Good job, Kelly. You got plastic or a tarp in the trunk?"

"Plastic sheet."

"Good. Get him covered up. Let's keep him dry. And see if you can keep the reporters away from the driver. I don't want any photos of this in the papers."

Kelly nodded. "Sure thing, Lieutenant."

Stosh looked at Malone and said to me, "Okay, kid, you got my attention."

I sighed. "We need to get somebody from the Fourth to ID him."

He shook his head. "Won't be easy, even for his friends. We'll have to wait for prints."

We walked away from the smell and stood by the back door of the grocery. A crowd had gathered in the parking lot as officers strung yellow tape.

"His body wasn't meant to be found," I said.

"No. It was meant to end up buried in a mountain of city garbage."

An unmarked car pulled up, and Detective James got out and

walked over to where we were standing.

"Lieutenant... Manning," he said.

"James," I said.

The lieutenant gave him the rundown. "Let's talk to the grocery people. Find out why no one noticed a body in their dumpster."

"Right, Lieutenant."

As he walked away, Stosh said, "Let's have a chat with the driver." As we walked across the alley, someone from the coroner's office showed up. Right behind him was an evidence team. Detective James intercepted all of them.

We stood in front of the driver. He didn't look up. The rain had stopped.

"Mr. Brown," said Stosh.

He rubbed his head and finally looked up. Stosh showed his badge.

"I'm Lieutenant Powolski." He didn't introduce me. Brown looked at both of us with a blank stare but didn't stand.

"You pulled the body out of your truck?"

"Yeah."

"Did you move it after you got it out?"

He shook his head. "When I saw he was..." He took some deep breaths. "When I saw he was dead, I just left him lay."

"And threw up."

For a big, brawny guy to look so embarrassed was oddly disturbing. He nodded.

"Any idea what caused your truck to jam?"

He stretched out his legs. "Hydraulics. Line broke... piston froze up... something like that."

"Has that happened before?"

"Yeah. These are old trucks."

"How often do you make this pickup?"

"Twice a week."

"Uh huh. How long you been doing this?"

"Eighteen years."

He turned to me. "You have any questions?"

"The body was in the dumpster, right?"

Brown nodded.

"Why would someone not notice a body in their dumpster?" I asked. "Especially one that smells because it's been decomposing?"

Brown shrugged and looked at me like I was an idiot. "You never smelled a dumpster?"

"Thank you, Mr. Brown," Stosh said.

As we walked back across the alley, avoiding the puddles, I said, "Those were all questions James will ask again."

"Yeah, but now I don't have to repeat the answers to you."

As we stood looking at the plastic sheet and the distorted body of a police officer under it, a ray of sun glinted off the side of the truck.

The doc from the coroner's office removed the plastic.

"Any info, Doc?" asked the lieutenant.

"Looks like strangle marks on his neck. Wide, like maybe a clothesline."

"Time of death?"

"Gonna be tough. There's food here. Produce garbage gives off heat. That would keep a body warm."

"Okay." Stosh looked at me and shook his head. "Let's get the hell outta here."

It was a quiet ride back to his house. I thought about the kind of people who put people in dumpsters. Chicago was famous for bodies showing up in any number of places, but that was a long time ago… or was it? Larry Maggio, the current crime kingpin had assured me more than once that they were businessmen these days. But I wasn't naïve enough not to realize that their business and that of the guy who ran the grocery were two different things. But in some ways they were the same... both had to do things to stay in business. The grocer had to make sure his shelves were stocked and his prices weren't out of line. Because if he didn't, he'd go out of business. Larry had to… well put people in dumpsters. Because if he didn't, he'd go out of business.

But put a cop in a dumpster? It wasn't Maggio. But a little voice had been telling me that this was about drugs, and the drug scene had changed with the long arm of the cartels taking over. And that arm didn't care who it threw in dumpsters.

As Stosh pulled into the drive I asked if he had a plan.

"Yeah, be in my office at nine Monday morning."

"For?"

He parked next to my Mustang and shut off the car. "For a meeting with the captain. If he's gonna find it hard to believe somebody, I'd rather it was you."

"Wouldn't you rather get all the credit when this gets solved?"

"I can do both. Have a nice date."

He waved over his shoulder as he walked to the back door.

Chapter 33

IT WAS FIVE MINUTES AFTER SIX WHEN I FOUND A PARKING
spot two buildings down from Rosie's apartment building. I was hur-
rying and not paying attention as I bumped into a homeless woman
coming out of the alley between buildings. I almost knocked her over.
She was slumped over, had short, mostly gray hair and was wearing a
ragged, dirty sweatshirt and wrinkled brown slacks that were too long.
She looked like she had been rummaging in a dumpster. I felt sorry
for her and dug into my pocket. As I handed her some bills, I only
glanced at her face for a second, but that made me feel even worse.
She had a scar from her nose to her lip, and her left eye was bruised.
I turned away quickly and hurried to Rosie's door and rang the bell
inside the foyer.

As I waited for the buzzer, I heard the outside door open behind
me and a scratchy voice say, "Thank you, sir, but I don't need your
money."

As I turned, ready to argue about being too proud to take a hand-
out, she started to laugh and said, "But maybe I'll keep it to remember this moment by."

My jaw dropped as I looked closer. Her beautiful, long brown
hair was gone.

"You can close your mouth now."

She took out her key and opened the door, and we took the stairs
to the third floor without saying a word. When we were in her apartment, she said, "Satisfied?"

"Shocked."

She laughed again. "What you said was somebody would probably recognize me. And I said—"

"Okay, I'll give you that. But that doesn't mean I feel any better about it."

She put her hand on my arm. "We do our jobs, Spencer. And both of us are good at it."

I thought about that for a minute. "Do you have an assignment?"

"No. But if I'm asked, I'll take it."

I put my arms around her and hugged her. When I let go I smiled. "I take it we're not going out for dinner."

"Give me some time to clean up. We still gotta eat. And you're buying."

As she walked away, I asked, "You hear about the body in the garbage truck?"

She said she hadn't as she pulled the sweatshirt over her head. "Tell me after a shower."

***

WE DECIDED ON PIZZA. On the way to Salerno's, I told her about Malone. While we drank beer and waited for the pizza we talked about the case.

"Hard to see how all this fits together," Rosie said.

"Missing pieces. And maybe it doesn't."

"What are you staring at?"

I shook my head. "Gray hair."

"You don't like it?" she asked with a smile.

"Not so much."

"Me either." She took a long drink. "How's Yancy doing?"

"Not happy."

"I wouldn't think so. Not easy waiting for a truck to hit you."

I set down my bottle. "But he has Superman to stop the truck."

She raised her glass.

"So, your training was for drugs. Can you make me feel better about it?"

"Probably not, but it was thorough."

"I assume you would go undercover as a drug addict. Drug addicts have needle marks."

She pushed up the right sleeve of her blouse. Needle marks.

"What if whoever runs a test?"

"I've got a powder to add to the sample."

"And they wouldn't search you?"

"Not my bra."

"Hopefully."

She nodded. "Hopefully."

"You'd be in a situation all by yourself."

"Well, yes, but there is a safety net."

When I just looked skeptical, she said, "I have glasses with a tracker in the frame. They know where I am at all times."

"That doesn't make me feel any better. What if—"

"Spencer. Stop. I—"

The pizza arrived, and we ate in silence.

Halfway through she reached out and took my hand. "It'll be fine, Spencer. But thanks for worrying. I worry about you too."

I nodded and stared at her.

"What?" she asked.

I shook my head. "It's the gray hair. I've never dated a woman in her sixties."

She laughed.

I suggested we go back to her place. We'd just make it for Star Trek at nine. She gave me the Vulcan salute, fingers properly displayed, and smiled. I returned it, and we headed out.

***

I GOT HOME A LITTLE BEFORE TEN THIRTY. Chester was reading, and Yancy was asleep on the couch. I nodded at him.

"Tough day at the office?" I asked.

"He musta walked ten miles pacing back and forth."

"You doing okay?"

He smiled. "Living the dream."

"Mind if I turn on the TV? There's some news you need to see."

"I've already seen it. It was on the six."

"Jerry see it?"

"Nope. He was on the deck cooking burgers."

I turned the set on.

"At six the body wasn't identified," he said.

"Not for the public. It's Malone."

"Oh, Christ. Maybe we shouldn't tell him."

"Maybe not."

At the end of the news, he asked, "You up for a game of chess?"

I glanced at the table in the corner where the chess board was set up. The pieces were still where they were when my last game with Dad was interrupted. Perhaps my refusal to accept reality. But maybe it was time to let that go.

"Sure," I said.

"You in the middle of a game with somebody?"

"I was." I thought for a bit. "But the game's over."

"Were you white or black?"

"White."

He walked over to the board and studied it for a minute.

"Whose turn?"

"Mine."

He nodded. "You should have castled a couple moves ago."

I laughed. "I certainly should have. But I had a plan."

He smiled. "How'd that work out?"

"Not very well. Set up the board."

We played to a stalemate and woke up Jerry at a quarter to twelve so he could go to bed.

Chapter 34

MONDAY MORNING WAS SUNNY AND WARM WITH A LIGHT breeze coming in off the lake. Jerry had heard about the body in the garbage truck Sunday morning. The news was calling it name unknown. I got to the station at ten to nine and poked my head into Stosh's office.

"Come on in and sit. We got a couple minutes."

"Anything from the coroner?" I asked.

"Nope. This'll get priority, but they're short-staffed."

"So why the meeting?"

"He needs to be in the loop, and I can't authorize without his signoff." He gave me his serious look. "Here's the rules. Just give him the facts, without any smart-ass comments. Got it?"

I nodded.

"Okay, let's go."

I waved to Kate as we passed her office. Her smile always made my day.

Captain Perez was on the phone, so we waited in the outer office and made small talk with Mary. In less than a minute he told us to come in.

"Lieutenant... Spencer. Have a seat, gentlemen."

We got as comfortable as you can get in the captain's office. He had a cigarette burning in a crystal ashtray. One of the windows was half open, and traffic provided background noise.

"I understand you both were at the scene Saturday," he said.

The lieutenant took a deep breath. "Yes, sir."

"Anything from the medical examiner?"

"Nothing yet, sir. We're working with the Fourth on Malone's whereabouts."

Perez nodded and smiled. "Let's just talk off the record, Lieutenant. You can skip the *sirs*."

Stosh nodded.

Perez clasped his hands on top of his desk. "From your call, I understand there is a possibility that this may have something to do with something Spencer is working on?"

"Yes…" He paused, trying hard not to say sir. "I'll let Spencer tell you about it."

It took fifteen minutes to go through everything. He didn't interrupt. I told him about the cryptic call from Susan Janice, my visit to the cemetery, and my meetings with Quark and Bridgewater. Then I told him about Susan and her tie to Martin Rentel and the anonymous call she got and the two detectives in the Fourth who were told to disappear. I told him about Barker and Yancy and how I had figured out that it was Vicki Gable who had made the call to Susan, and I told him about the goon squad and the planted watch in Rentel's apartment and Yancy's stolen gun.

He had been watching smoke curl up to the ceiling. When I mentioned the goon squad, he looked at me. I kept talking, and he got up and walked to the window where there was a lovely view of the parking lot. I told him about the two ex-FBI agents who paid me a visit and suggested I mind my own business and the raspy voice Vicki had heard in the fourth precinct building. By the time I was done, the cigarette had burned down to the filter.

I didn't tell him about Stosh's contact at the Fourth, my visit to Thward, or my hiding Yancy. I especially didn't tell him about something that kept bothering me… that Quark was related to the DA's wife. That was a fact, but one that would have made me sound a bit over the edge.

He came back to his desk and sat and glanced at both of us. "That's a lot to take in," he said.

I waited for the rest.

"And you think all this has something to do with Sergeant Malone?"

"It's certainly possible."

"How?"

"Timing. I don't like coincidences."

"What would he have to do with Rentel and all the rest?"

"I don't know yet. My guess is nothing. Maybe he saw something he shouldn't have."

He pursed his lips. "So, why are you telling me about something happening in the fourth precinct?"

"Because something smells bad."

"A dead mouse behind the refrigerator smells bad. Doesn't mean a crime has been committed." He picked up what was left of the cigarette and stubbed it out. "There's a lot there that sounds pretty... well, fanciful, for lack of a better word. For instance, this goon squad... do you have any proof?"

That was the problem with my whole story. It was just a story. There were several believable characters, and I could tie everything up into a great plot, but I had no proof.

"It's not hard to put the pieces together," I said.

He smiled, a bit condescendingly. "The courts need a bit more than that, Spencer. I have some questions."

I nodded.

"How do you know the detectives were told to disappear?"

"Detective Yancy. And Barker left in a hurry."

"But Yancy didn't leave."

"No, he said he didn't know where to go. He picked up a bottle instead."

"And how did you know about Gable?"

"Yancy. Like I told you... the music."

"And the goon squad?"

I wasn't happy about where this was going. "Yancy."

He nodded. "So, all this is based on a detective you found buried in a bottle at his favorite tavern who, if he was told to disappear, didn't have the sense to do that and while drunk may have… misplaced his own gun."

The lieutenant straightened in his chair. "Sir—"

The captain held up his hand and looked at me.

"And the FBI impersonators?"

"I've alerted the FBI."

"Uh huh." He lowered his chin and looked at me over his glasses. "For the sake of conversation, tell me how you're putting the pieces together."

All the pieces weren't together, but I'd give it a try, and I'd start with something the captain couldn't argue with. "The goal is to solve crimes, especially drug crimes and murders. And there is a much stronger push these days, coming from the chief, to get that done, especially this one… an old man in a quiet neighborhood. This started with Rentel, who has a long list of arrests, including drugs. His picture was picked out of a mug book, so they had a witness." I shrugged. "A witness and a known criminal who would be good to get off the streets even if he was the wrong guy. Wouldn't take much to help things along with a little planted evidence."

Captain Perez was looking at me harshly, and Stosh was looking out the window.

"I assume you do realize what you're saying about the police department," the captain said.

I didn't answer. It was harder to put into words than to think it.

"Do you have a theory about Rentel and Mrs. Janice? What happened to them?" he asked.

"I don't know."

"And how does Malone fit in, if he does?"

I slowly shook my head. "Best guess? Like I said, he was just in the wrong place at the wrong time. He saw something he shouldn't have."

He folded his hands again on his desk. "That's a lot to buy, Spencer." He turned to Stosh. "Lieutenant, do you have a suggestion?"

"I admit there are a lot of loose strings here. But Spencer's instincts are usually not wrong. I've looked into it a bit, unofficially. There are rumors of a goon squad. Mrs. Gable did overhear something. There are two men posing as FBI agents. There are two people missing." He paused and took a deep breath. "I'd like to get someone inside the Fourth."

"What do you suggest?"

"That we go at it from the drug angle."

He thought briefly. "Lonnigan and Vasquez?"

"Fresh off training. We'll coordinate with the DEA."

He looked at both of us. "Put it together and then talk to me again. I've got to digest all this and have a chat with the chief."

As we started to get up, he asked, "Spencer, what's your purpose in this?"

I thought about that and said, "My client is Mrs. Janice. I want to find her... alive."

He nodded. We were done.

We walked back to Stosh's office and sat.

"He didn't seem to believe that I had alerted the FBI," I said.

Stosh laughed. "He knows how you do things. Sometimes what you say isn't exactly accurate."

"He didn't ask me if I knew where Yancy was," I said.

"He knows you know, but he doesn't want you to know he knows you know."

"What? I'm not going to try and figure that out."

He folded his arms across his chest and looked proud of himself.

"But he's willing to consider this?"

"He also knows your track record. And there's a couple of other things."

I looked at him with raised eyebrows.

"One, he's none too happy about Malone. Two, if you're right, the real killer is still out there. And three... if you're right... there's a rat's nest over at the Fourth. So it's worth looking at. And if it goes south, he blames it all on you. What's on your agenda?"

"I need to get over to Wrigley and have a chat with the groundskeeper."

"You still think there's an extra body out there?"

"Only one way to find out."

"Thanks for not telling the captain about that," Stosh said.

"How do I dig up a grave?"

"With a shovel."

I glared at him.

"Oh, you mean officially? Paperwork till the cows come home and then a court order... and a lawyer."

"I have one of those."

He set down his fork. "Ben is good, but he's not a miracle worker."

"Maybe a shovel would be easier."

"Yeah, and then you'd need the lawyer for something else."

I turned to go and then remembered something. "Malone's body wasn't meant to be found."

"Right. So?"

"So, how was it moved from wherever he was killed to that grocery dumpster?"

"Good question. Let me know what you find out."

"Isn't that something *you* should be doing?"

He smiled. "We already are."

I stood and he said, "You said your purpose was to find Mrs. Janice."

I knew what he was getting at and decided to level with him. "It is. And while I'm doing that, I've got a few others." I waited for the lecture about not interfering with the police.

"Spencer. Start carrying your gun."

***

ON MY WAY OUT I THOUGHT about why people kill. Good people kill out of fear, hate, greed, jealousy, power, or money. They are the easy ones to catch because they just act on emotions and don't think about all the ways they could get caught. Then there are the bad ones who just kill because someone pays them to. They're harder to catch because there isn't any tie. Just walk up to someone you don't know and put a bullet in them and walk away.

I got in the car, rolled down the windows and headed up to Addison and east to Wrigley Field. The Cubs were on the road for ten days. I hoped to find the groundskeeper.

On the way, I called Carol and had her run info on The Greenery. I asked for the owner and a list of employees and bank activity on the males. Then I called Ben and asked him to meet me for dinner. I wanted to talk to him about the things I hadn't told the captain.

Chapter 35

ONE OF MY PARENTS' NEIGHBORS HAD A BROTHER WHO WAS the head carpenter at the ballpark. I remembered his first name… Walt. Every time he had seen Dad, the neighbor said his brother would give us a personal tour of the park anytime we wanted. About ten years ago Dad took him up on it. We spent two hours touring the clubhouse, climbing up in the scoreboard, walking the field, and exploring the nooks and crannies under the stands. With a little imagination, I could hear Pat Piper reading the lineups and Ernie yelling "Let's play two!" One of those nooks under the stands was the carpenter shop. I had no idea if Walt was still there, but I figured I'd give it a shot.

I parked in the lot on Clark Street and walked to the corner of Addison and Sheffield. The iron gates at the corner of the park were open, just as they had been ten years ago, and I walked onto the concessions concourse under the stands. I didn't remember which door led to the shop, but I heard a saw and followed the sound. Walt was cutting a two-by-four. I waited for him to finish.

"Excuse me," I said.

He turned around. "Yes? Can I help you?"

"Maybe," I said with a smile. "I'm Spencer Manning. You won't remember, but your brother was a neighbor of my folks, and you gave my dad and I a tour ten years ago."

He squinted and brushed sawdust off his shirt. The squint slowly turned into a smile. "I do remember. A cop, right?"

"Yup."

"Well, what brings you back?"

I laughed nervously. "Kind of a crazy request. I'm looking for someone who knows about grass."

He looked suspicious. "Which kind?"

"The lawn kind."

He laughed. "Ah, well that would be Randy Stone. Best groundskeeper we ever had. Let's see if we can find him."

We checked his shop two doors down, but no one was there. "Let's check the field," he said.

We found Randy talking to one of his crew by third base. Walt waited for him to finish and then introduced me. He left us, and I explained what I was looking for and asked if he'd be willing to take a ride. He said it sounded interesting and said he'd be with me in about twenty minutes. My offer to buy lunch probably didn't hurt. I leaned against the car and waited. When he came out, he was carrying a flat-bladed trowel.

***

WE STOPPED FOR LUNCH AT RAY'S, a little family diner just east of the river, and I explained as much as I could about the case. At a quarter to one, I pulled into the road leading to the cemetery. It was a bright sunny day, and the path didn't seem as ominous as when Rosie and I had been there. Birds were chirping, and the air was warm and dry.

As we walked into the cemetery clearing, Randy stopped and, after looking over the grounds, said, "This is amazing. Kinda like it's been untouched for a hundred years."

"Until you look closer."

I followed him as he walked silently down the rows of graves, stopping at some to look at the dates. At the end of the second row, he asked, "Where's the grave you're wondering about?"

We cut across the rows and stopped in front of a small, gray marker with "Bill Jenkins Died 1914" etched into it. Randy pulled the trowel out of his back pocket and walked around the grave, studying the ground. Then he knelt, set the trowel on the ground, and ran his hand over the grass along the side of the grave. He took the trowel and carefully scored a line about two feet long. With his fingers he folded back the grass a few inches. It looked like sod that had been laid.

"What's the verdict?" I asked.

"The grass here has been cut recently. Did you see how easily that folded back?"

"Yup."

"The roots haven't had a chance to take hold yet. With some time, we can find the edge all the way around. Looks about the size of a coffin."

"So this was dug up."

"Yes."

"Can you tell how long ago?"

"Based on the roots and the settling, I'd guess anywhere from a week to a month." Then he pointed to the adjacent grave. "Probably closer to a week. See the soil in the grass? They probably tarped the grass next to the dig, but some soil is in the grass."

I looked more closely. "Settling?"

He pointed to the grave. "See how it's a bit mounded in the area over the grave?"

"Yes."

"If you dig a hole and then put the dirt back, you'll never get all the dirt back level without tamping it down. It takes some time for the dirt to settle and recompact. But if you tamp it level, over time it will still settle, and you'll have a depression."

I was thinking while he was talking. "So, if you want to dig something up and not have it look like it was dug up you leave it mounded just the right amount and let it settle."

"Exactly."

"How hard would that be to do?"

"It would take some experience."

"Who besides the groundskeeper at a ballpark would be able to do that?"

"Not even a groundskeeper, necessarily. But I'd say definitely someone who works with sod."

I looked around the cemetery. "You mind taking a look at another one?"

"Why not? Where?"

I pointed to the next row, and we walked to the grave marked "Paul 1911."

"You think Paul is his first name or last?" he asked.

"Good question. Perhaps no one knew. There are a few in here with just dates and numbers... and no names. I'm guessing back at the turn of the century they got people in here who were John or Jane Does."

"Sad."

He looked at the grave for a minute and then said it also had been disturbed but much longer ago than the 1914 grave, maybe a year. I asked if he'd mind walking the rows. He glanced at his watch and said he had time. He didn't find any others that had been recently disturbed.

On the way back, he asked me to stop by the park when I found out what was going on.

"Your job is every boy's dream, Spencer," he said. "I'm jealous."

"*You're* jealous? You get paid to watch every Cubs home game in the best park in baseball and *you're* jealous?"

"You have a point. But I guess it's a little different when it's a job."

"I guess. But did I mention the part about every Cubs home game?"

He laughed.

Chapter 36

I GOT TO MCGOON'S AT FIVE TWENTY. I SAT AT THE BAR AND talked with Jack until Ben arrived an hour later and Jane showed us to our table. I ordered another beer, and Ben asked for Jameson. When Jane came back with the drinks, we both ordered steaks.

Ben sipped his whiskey and said, "I'm going to start planning my grocery list around your cases. They don't hurt McGoon's either."

While we waited for the food, I filled him in on what had happened since we last talked. Over the food, we talked about baseball and the growing drug problem in the city, mostly cocaine. I asked him how much worse the problem had become since he had started with the state.

He swirled his whiskey gently. "Over most of my twelve years, pretty status quo. But a couple years ago, the gangs started getting bigger and braver with a retinue of lawyers. And the connections in Mexico and South America have stepped up things quite a bit. There's a lot of money involved."

"Cocaine?"

"Cocaine and heroin. But just before I quit, we started seeing crack cocaine more and more."

"Better mousetrap?"

"Nice analogy. Faster and higher highs. And it can be smoked."

"How does it benefit the dealers?"

"The high doesn't last long. It's its own marketing campaign."

"Mexico?"

"Eventually, but it starts out in Columbia. Muled up to Mexico and then across the border and into the big cities."

"The DEA on it?"

"They try. But for every kid they catch with a shipment there's five they miss, or ten, or twenty."

"Why do the kids do it?"

"They make more for one trip across the border than they'd otherwise make in years doing whatever else they can scrape up."

"But they might get arrested."

He sighed. "Yeah, might. And even if they are, they spend a few months in jail or get a slap on the hand and then back in business. At best, we can only disturb the flow." He shrugged. "But even that disturbance is part of the flow. Already factored in by the drug lords."

"Who run things from their mansions with an army of protection," I said.

He just looked at his glass.

"Is the state doing everything it can?"

He thought for a bit. "It's a question of what *anybody* can do. We're trying to stop a flood with a bucket. It's all about numbers, and the numbers aren't on our side. Even if one out of five gets caught, the profits on the other four are huge, even after you deduct the lawyer fees."

"But cases get prosecuted."

"Sure. But Lansing and I didn't see eye to eye on prosecution decisions. There were several cases that I thought I had nailed, and he overruled me."

"Did he say why?"

"Not specifically. Just said he thought they were weak."

"Were they weak?"

"I didn't think so."

I saw Jane coming toward us and held up two fingers. She nodded. There were only four other tables with customers... a slow night. If it had been crowded we'd have moved to the bar.

Ben continued. "But then there were others that I thought were weak, and he got confessions. And about a year ago confessions and convictions went up drastically. Less cases were prosecuted, more criminals in jail. And now all I hear is how he wants to hit drugs hard."

"It's an election year."

"It is that." He emptied his glass.

"Why do you think convictions went up?" I asked.

"I'd like to say better police work and prosecutions, but that doesn't account for a 30 percent increase. So what do you think is behind all this?"

Jane set two fresh drinks on the table. "You boys solving the world's problems?"

"Just our little corner of it, Jane," I said.

"Good luck with that."

We raised our glasses and took a drink.

"Let me give you some facts," I said. "This all started with Susan wondering about her nephew who she couldn't find. She got an anonymous phone call telling her she could find answers at Walker. I go out to Walker and talk to Quark who was less than friendly and McElroy tells Yancy to take some time off and disappear for a while. Then, after another visit to Walker and a chat with Bridgewater, I get told to stop asking questions by two fake FBI agents. How did they know I was asking questions?"

"Quark or Bridgewater."

"And Quark is related to Lansing by marriage."

Ben swirled his drink.

"Now the fourth precinct," I continued. "Barker puts his family in the wagon and disappears. I find Yancy in a bar drowning his sorrows. And we discover his gun is missing. And Malone is found in a dumpster." I paused for a drink. "And there's a grave at Walker that's been dug up recently."

"You want me to remember all of that, start tying it up."

I took a long drink. "I lie in bed trying to get to sleep and think about how the pieces fit together. Here's my best guess. There's a big picture and a small one. The big one is about politics. Lansing is up for reelection, and Stosh tells me Grimes is bucking for the chief of police job. Convictions go up as trials go down, and rumors start about a goon squad. All is well until Susan tries to find her nephew and I start asking questions at Walker where the PR director just happens to be related to the attorney general."

"What's the small picture?"

"All the little things I already mentioned, starting with McElroy and including Rentel and Malone."

"I'm gonna need another Jameson. You're telling me the AG is involved in a cop killing? And Rentel is buried in an old grave at Walker?"

"Well, it sounds a little less plausible when *you* say it."

"A *little* less?"

I drank some beer.

"So what's your plan? The one that doesn't involve me."

"Really? Nothing about this interests you?"

He took a sip. "I'd love to stick it to Lansing. He's a pain in the ass and he's stupid, but he's not *that* stupid. He wouldn't be anywhere near any of this."

"Stranger things have happened."

"Do you have a plan?"

"Still shaking the trees. Carol will get a report on the grocery store where Malone was dumped. And—"

"Stosh isn't looking into that?"

"Sure, but I'd like to get there first. I'll get the owner and employees. And I asked for bank accounts on the males."

"Why just the males?"

"Malone wasn't meant to be found. If not for a truck malfunction, he would have been buried in a landfill. Whoever moved the body needed somewhere safe to make that happen. That means a connection with a dumpster and maybe an employee who can be bought."

"Why not the owner?"

I shook my head. "Harder to buy, and a lot more to lose. And owners don't take out the garbage. They needed someone to coordinate with so the body would be covered just before garbage day."

"Males?"

"Females don't take out the garbage either."

"Okay, that's the Malone trail. How does that help with the rest?"

"Guess what Rosie was doing in California."

"DEA training." He smiled as he watched my balloon deflate.

"Well, you're no fun. How did you know?"

He laughed. "I didn't. But you're talking drugs here, and you need someone undercover. And I have heard something about the DEA training local jurisdictions. You okay with her undercover?"

"No, but she has tried to convince me all would be okay." I told him about her demonstration.

"She'd be good at it. Is there a plan?"

"No. Stosh is working on it."

He tilted his empty glass. "I've done enough drinking for one night. And I can't listen to any more of this without drinking, so I'm calling it a night."

"You don't want to hear the rest?"

"If I keep listening, I'm sure you'll have Jimmy Hoffa in that coffin with Rentel."

I finished my beer and signaled to Jane for the check. "I'll give that some thought while I'm waiting for sleep to overcome me."

"You do that." He pushed away from the table. "Thanks for the grub. I'll look forward to the next round."

He got ten feet away, turned and said, "There's somebody who hates Lansing more than me," and started to turn away.

"Who?"

"Hey, would you respect me in the morning if I was that easy?" He walked away.

"Hell yes!" I said to his back.

He waved over his shoulder with the back of his hand.

At least that would give me something besides Jimmy Hoffa to think about while I was trying to get to sleep.

***

I DECIDED TO STOP AT THE OFFICE and pick up my gun. The report on The Greenery was on my desk. It was for the most part just what I would expect from any other business. It was owned by William Jenks, and he had owned it for sixteen years. There were seven employees, four male and three female. All of them had been at the grocery for less than five years and made close to minimum wage. One of the males, John Nichols, had only been there nine months. Two of them had no bank accounts. Four of the other five had checking accounts with balances less than a thousand dollars and steady deposits and withdrawals. John Nichols had a balance of $5,623.00 with a deposit of $5,000.00 a week ago. I made a copy of the report and slid it into an envelope.

I hadn't talked to Rosie since Saturday, so I called. There was no answer. I holstered my gun and carried it and the envelope to the car.

I wasn't ready to go home yet, so I drove to the lake and sat on the rocks until close to midnight. I tried to put all the pieces together, without much success.

As it turned out, neither Jimmy Hoffa nor Ben's mystery person were what got me to sleep. Putting together a plan *did…* and I was going to need some help.

Chapter 37

TUESDAY MORNING, CHESTER WAS ALREADY ON THE DECK with coffee when I poured a cup at six. I pulled a jacket off its peg by the door and joined him.

"Morning, Spencer."

"Chester. How's our guest doing?" I set the cup down on a wicker table and watched the steam rising.

"About the same. Pretty nervous and tired of watching TV." He took a sip. "Speaking of which, you hear the news?"

"What news would that be?"

"Frazier Thomas had a massive stroke yesterday."

"Oh, no." Frazier was the host of Family Classics, Garfield Goose, and had taken over from Ned Locke, "Ringmaster Ned," on Bozo's Circus, the most successful kids' TV show ever. It was now called the Bozo Show. "You have any details?"

"No. Happened at the studio. Doesn't sound good."

"What a shame."

We listened to the birds and sipped coffee for a few minutes until Jerry joined us.

"You making any progress?" he asked.

"Hard to tell. There's so many loose threads. But I do have a plan."

Chester set his cup down. "I'm thinking all those threads aren't related. You may have several different paths. What's your plan?"

"They may *not* be related, or one may have led to another. I gotta think it all started with drugs, and it started before Rentel showed up. So if we make that assumption, let's think backwards."

"So?" Jerry asked.

"Somebody in the Fourth is stealing drugs."

"Whew," he said as he stretched. "That's a big bite you're taking there."

"Just a theory."

Chester took a drink as a squirrel ran across the end of the deck. "Let's see if the pieces fit."

"Okay," I said. "We're assuming somebody is stealing drugs. How would they go about that?"

"I don't know about today," Chester said, "but in my day whatever came from a bust was logged in by the detectives leading the team to whoever was in charge of evidence."

"Hasn't changed," Jerry said.

I drank the last of my coffee. "So if someone was going to steal some, it would be between the bust and the evidence locker."

"Or at the bust or at the evidence locker," Jerry said.

"How easy would that be to do?" I asked.

"Not terribly hard," Jerry said. "Especially if both detectives were in on it. Depending on how it's packaged, you'd just have to slip a packet into your pocket." He thought for a minute. "And if you were planning on it, maybe you'd have a special pocket inside your jacket. Wouldn't be hard to make off with a kilo, especially if it was packed in halves."

"How big would that be?" I asked.

"A kilo?" He shrugged. "'Bout the size of a large paperback."

"So maybe a crime of opportunity," I said. "Nothing is planned… just take advantage of a situation if it arises."

"Sure."

"So a cop takes drugs off the street and then puts them back on and supplements his income."

Chester shook his head. "Not how *I'd* do it."

We waited as he thought and then said, "It'd make a good retirement plan. Stash it away and start selling it years, even decades, later."

"Then he wouldn't have to worry about where to hide the money or money above his income in his accounts," I said.

"He'd just have to hide it somewhere," Jerry added. "Maybe for a long time."

I smiled. "And I know of the perfect place—somewhere no one would ever look."

They both smiled at the same time.

"And Vicki said one of the men she overheard said they could use the cemetery for that *too*," I said.

"But we don't know what *too* means," Chester said.

"I can guess," I said and picked up my empty cup. "Let's eat."

***

I TOLD THEM ABOUT THE GROCERY store employee over scrambled eggs and bacon at the dining room table.

"Exactly what I'm talking about," said Chester. "We catch criminals because they're dumber than rocks."

We switched the conversation to Frazier. We had all watched him on one of the shows and talked about favorite memories. Then Jerry switched the subject.

"Spencer, I'm going crazy here. We haven't heard anything about my gun." He shook his head. "I just don't think I'm in danger. If I was out there, I could help."

I looked at Chester, and he nodded.

I finished my orange juice and said, "Jerry, there's something you don't know."

He looked at me with raised eyebrows.

"Remember the body in the garbage truck?"

"Yeah? So?"

"It was Malone."

His look quickly turned to shock and then sadness. "Jesus. I can't believe… he was ten months from retirement."

I let him sit with that for a few seconds and then said, "Jerry, whatever's going on here, these people are willing to kill to cover it up… and kill a cop. I can't keep you here, but this is the safest place in the world for you right now. Nobody knows you're here, and you have Chester. But if you want to leave, there's the front door."

His gaze came back to me, and he whispered, "I get it." He turned and looked out the window like it was freedom drifting away and then turned back to me. "So what are you going to do about the drugs?"

"The less you know the better."

"And how does the rest fit in?" asked Chester. "Malone and Rentel and Susan."

"Don't know, but I'm betting it does. If you find a bunch of pigs, they're probably all eating from the same trough."

Chester laughed. "Where the hell did that come from?"

"I spent a couple summers on an uncle's farm in southern Illinois as a kid. I loved watching the pigs."

"Well, maybe that explains some things," he said with a smile.

I got up from the table with my plate. "I'm gonna get dressed. Make up a food list along with anything else you need, and I'll shop on my way home."

"Know when that will be?" Chester asked.

"Late morning or early afternoon. But I won't be home for dinner."

Jerry handed me the list on my way out, and I headed for the station.

***

STOSH WASN'T IN HIS OFFICE. Kate told me he'd be in a meeting most of the morning. So I added a note to the report and left it with her. The note said, "Official wheels turn slowly."

Chapter 38

ROSIE WASN'T IN THE SQUAD ROOM, SO I CHATTED WITH THE desk sergeant on the way out for a minute and then headed for groceries. The list was longer than I had expected, what with several items that included ice cream and chips of various sorts that I wouldn't normally have bought. But I figured Jerry deserved a few indulgences. There were also things like spices and herbs and a few things I needed help to find. I figured those weren't from Jerry.

We all had lunch on the deck in the midday sun. Chester made Chicken Parmesan. There was a gentle breeze, and the deck thermometer read seventy-five, a perfect spring day.

"By the way," Chester said. "Your neighbor across the street stopped by. Said she noticed somebody strange in the house and figured you had company."

"Damn. That would be Ann. I should have told her. She's our neighborhood watch commander."

"Good that somebody's paying attention."

"Did she see Jerry?"

He shook his head and washed a bite of chicken down with beer. "Nope. When the bell rang he was in the kitchen, and he stayed there."

"Good. I'll tell her you're an uncle."

He nodded. "She brought homemade chocolate chip cookies."

"I always look forward to her cookies. But I usually don't have to share them."

"Don't worry about it," said Chester. "I already had a couple. By tomorrow you won't have any to share."

I didn't have plans until dinner, so I spent a few hours cleaning up the garden and doing a few chores. By five thirty I was parked across from the Full Cup.

***

I CALLED VICKI'S HOME NUMBER after I had parked. There was no answer. I tried every fifteen minutes after that and finally got her at six thirty. I asked if she still wanted to help. She did. So I invited her to dinner. She said she'd be there by seven. At five to, I saw her walking on the other side of North Avenue.

"I was wondering if I'd hear from you," she said as she slid into the booth.

The diner was about half full and noisier than the last time.

"I appreciate your coming," I said. "I need some information and am hoping you can help."

The waitress arrived with tea that I had presumed to order for her. We both ordered omelettes.

"What is it you're looking for?"

I explained my drug theory to her. She didn't seem surprised.

"If that's happening, do you have any idea who it might be?" I asked.

She sighed and took a sip of tea. "Ten years ago I would have said you're crazy. Now... could be about anybody. There was a change in the atmosphere when Captain Meyer took over five years ago."

"How do you mean?"

Her brows furrowed. "Nothing I can put my finger on. Just not as tight a ship. Several new people who just seem to have a different attitude. It used to be about doing what was right. Now, I'm not so sure."

"But nobody in particular?"

"Tell me what you want first."

I liked that she didn't want to dirty someone's name without being sure.

"Let me preface this with I have no idea what is going on. But whatever it is seems to have to do with drugs. And if someone is skimming drugs there might be a pattern. I'd like you to go back through the last five years and see who was involved with the larger busts."

She laughed. "Five years is a long time."

"Well, as much as you can."

"What do you mean by larger?"

"Well, use your judgement, but anything over five kilos. I'll give you one to start with. About four years ago I was involved in the Macek case. Drug bust that went south, and he killed a detective."

She nodded. "I remember."

"Start with that. I want to know how much coke was logged."

"Okay. Easy enough."

"When do you think you can get it?"

"Tomorrow at lunch."

"Great. Thanks, Vicki. One more thing. I think the two men you overheard are named Darny and Jetter. Could you see if they're on the payroll?"

"Sure. No problem."

"And if they are, how long."

She nodded.

"But make sure nobody knows you're looking. I don't want you involved in this."

She laughed. "One advantage of having my own office is nobody sees what I'm doing. I'll see what else I can find too. How do you want me to get it to you?"

"I think the less we meet the better, so give me a call tomorrow after work."

She smiled as the waitress set our food on the table. "Okay."

"When all this is over, I'll buy you the best steak in town."

She picked up her fork and said, "I can't wait to see where you think that is."

"It'll be a surprise."

While we ate, we shared stories about how we ended up doing what we do. The omelettes were good, but I preferred steak to be my source of protein.

As I held the door for her I asked if she wanted a ride home. The warm evenings had turned chilly.

Smiling graciously, she said, "No, thanks. After a day sitting at a desk, I enjoy the brisk walk."

I had to admire her for that. It had been longer than I wanted since I had taken an early morning run.

I started the Mustang and called Rosie as I sat at the curb. Still no answer, and I wondered if I should start to worry. But perhaps she was working nights with the new role. And perhaps she had forgotten to tell me that. And perhaps not. I decided to worry just a bit.

Chapter 39

THE FORECAST FOR WEDNESDAY HAD BEEN FOR SUNNY AND temps near seventy. At seven, the first part was accurate... not a cloud in the sky. But a gray day would better have matched my mood. Except for riling a couple of characters out of the Blues Brothers, I wasn't getting anywhere. But I was counting on those characters to still play a role. Chester scrambled eggs, and the three of us ate and talked about the case without adding anything new. But I hoped Vicki's digging and a visit to Cook County Jail would change that. As I started to clear the table, Chester asked if I'd be home for dinner.

With a bit of sarcasm, I said, "No, dear. Dinner tonight with Stosh."

He shook his head. "It's so hard planning meals when I have no idea when you'll be home."

Jerry looked at me and said, "The next line is 'you knew about my job when you married me,' but if you say it, I'm leaving."

We all laughed.

I cleaned up the mess, and by the time I was done it was after eight thirty, and I called the station. I needed another favor, and I had no hesitation in asking. But Kate answered Stosh's private line. I explained that I wanted an interview with Anthony Macek, currently residing on death row in County. A few years back I had needed to talk to a prisoner in the same situation at Stateville in Joliet, one of Illinois' maximum-security prisons. Approval for that had taken three days. I hoped that it would be easier for Stosh to get me into County, what with it being in his jurisdiction. Kate said the lieutenant was in with the captain for at least an hour, but she'd see what she could do. I figured she could do just fine, seeing as he would have handed it off to her anyway. She called back twenty minutes later and said I had an appointment for eleven.

***

WHEN I WAS IN HIGH SCHOOL, Dad had given me and a few of my friends a tour of Cook County Jail. It certainly made an impression. My sociology teacher had told the class that deterrence didn't work. She was of the opinion that showing kids where they might end up had no effect. After the tour, I told her she was wrong. There was no way I was going to do anything that would give me even one night in that jail. She told me it all depended on what street you grew up on. I also thought that if someone was lucky enough to get out of there they'd straighten their life out and not do anything to go back. But one of the jailers told me the recidivism rate was high due partly to three meals a day and a roof over your head. The tour made me realize how lucky I was.

But as bad as County was, Stateville was worse. I would always remember the face of a prisoner being led down the hall coming toward me. He was dressed in gray and both his feet and hands were shackled. There was a chain attached to his hand shackles that went around his waist, and a guard following behind him held a chain attached to the waist chain. Another guard carried a shotgun. The prisoner had no expression on his face. He may as well have been a robot.

***

THE INTERVIEW ROOM FOR THE COUNTY PRISONERS on death row was the first room at the bottom of the stairs in the basement. It was tiny, only big enough for each of us to sit on either side of a bullet-proof glass window. The room was situated such that I didn't have to enter the cell block and the prisoner didn't have to leave. A separate entrance with double iron gates and a holding area led into the cell block. I had been searched before I came down and had to empty my pockets into a tray that was placed in a locker. They had also taken my picture and attached it to an authorization slip. The only thing I carried down was the slip.

I waited ten minutes before two guards appeared with Macek who had both his wrists and ankles shackled. One of the guards entered the room and walked up to the window. I held up my slip, and he made sure the picture matched my face. "You've got five minutes," he said. "I'll knock when you've got a minute left." When he left the room, Macek walked in and sat.

Macek had been told who wanted to see him. But we had never met, and my name had not been brought into the case, so there was a possibility he would have declined to see me. But I figured if you live in a four-foot by seven-foot cell with concrete walls and only get out two hours a day and that cell is twenty feet from the electric chair, you'd be glad for any reason to get out. The chair wasn't currently being used, but it was still there.

He was thin and lanky, and his hair was jet black and pulled into a ponytail. He had an inch-long scar on his left cheek. The chain made a clanking noise as he rested his hands on the shelf in front of the window. He said nothing.

I looked into his emotionless blue eyes and said, "My name is Spencer Manning. I'm a private investigator. I have a question about your case."

He just stared at me.

"I need to know how much cocaine you had when you were arrested."

That brought a slight flicker in his eyes that struck me as amusement. I had thought about how I would have felt if the roles were reversed, and I had no idea. If there was some hope that something had happened that might change the fact that he was going to die, his lawyer would have been sitting across from him. Whatever I wanted wasn't going to change his life one bit.

He dragged the chain on the counter as he moved his arms. The amusement left his eyes, and he stared at me hard. My time was running out, but he was thinking, and I figured the only way he was going to answer was if he got through whatever he was thinking.

After what seemed like several minutes, he said, "You could get the amount from the cops, so why are you here asking me?" The way he said it made me know it was a question he wasn't asking me. He shifted in the chair. "So, perhaps you have reason to believe the amount the cops ended up with wasn't the amount I had on me."

I let him think.

"But why would you care?" he asked.

That question *was* for me.

I certainly didn't have time to tell him the whole story. "Because right is right, and wrong is wrong."

The guard knocked on the door. I had little time left and just as little hope that I'd get an answer.

The raise of his chin was barely noticeable. Five seconds later he said, "Twenty-two kilos."

I nodded. "Thanks."

As the door on his side opened, he said, "Be nice to know if right gets made right."

"If this goes down, the grapevine here will be buzzing."

There was a bit of interest in his eyes. Maybe what I was doing *would* change his life.

***

THE SUN WAS SHINING, but sitting across from Macek had made my mood worse, and it wasn't good to start with. I needed a change of scenery, and I was hungry. I had the whole afternoon free before dinner with Stosh. I fired up the Mustang, rolled down the windows, and decided a drive would do me good. Maybe to a cemetery. Maybe to the cemetery where this all started. I needed another excuse to walk into Bridgewater's office. But first, lunch at Ray's. The last time I was there the waitress had told us they were adding a fabulous

Chicken Kiev. I had no idea how you could make Chicken Kiev fabulous, but I suddenly had a taste for it.

On the way, I had the radio on and heard that Frazier Thomas had died. A Chicago icon was gone.

Chapter 40

THE KIEV WAS GOOD, BUT IT WASN'T DIFFERENT FROM ANY other Kiev I had ever had. As far as I was concerned, Chicken Kiev was one of those dishes you could ruin, but there was nothing special about it from one place to another. But they were proud of it. Ray even came over to see how I liked it. Of course, I raved about it. He said it was his mother's recipe. I couldn't tell the difference from the ones I got from the butcher.

It was a warm spring day with a promise of summer in the air. I left my jacket in the car and walked down the path. As I stepped into the clearing of the cemetery, I smelled the smoke of burning leaves, probably from a leftover fall burn pile. I wandered the grounds for a bit and ended up in front of the 1911 grave. I listened for Howie's whispers, but all I heard was the chirping of birds hidden in the trees. After a few minutes I felt like I was being watched. I turned around quickly but no one was there. I scanned the tree line and saw nothing. I walked between the rows and thought maybe I'd have to come back at night to hear the whispers. As I was walking, I still had the feeling I was being watched.

I headed back down the path that led to my car. After I made the turn and was out of sight of the cemetery, I doubled back through the woods, picking my steps carefully so I didn't make any noise. Five minutes later I was in the trees on the edge of the clearing, fifty feet south of the path. I had a clear view of the cemetery... and the old man standing in front of one of the graves, holding a rifle. A black lab sat by his side. I watched him wander from grave to grave for a couple of minutes, followed by the dog, and then he sat in the grass in front of one. The dog sat next to him. He stared at the grave, lost in time. That's what people did in a cemetery… that's what I did.

I walked out of the woods and came up on him from behind. I didn't want to scare him, so I circled to the side and said hello when I was almost in his sight line. He still was a bit startled and started to raise the rifle.

I raised my hands and said, "No problem, friend. I'm just visiting."

"Sorry," he said as he lowered the gun.

I kept walking and said, "Sorry to bother you. I haven't seen anyone here before."

He stood and said, "I haven't either." He eyed me warily. "Do you work here?"

"No. Just visit now and then." I took another few steps and put out my hand. "Spencer Manning."

He looked me over and then shook my hand. "Avery Wren."

"What brings you here, Avery?"

He looked down at the ground. When he looked back up, he asked, "What brings *you*?"

I realized he had no reason to trust me and that I probably wouldn't get any answers. "Just curiosity. A friend told me about this place. I've come a couple of times and find it oddly relaxing."

He didn't respond, but he didn't leave either.

"How often do you come here?" I asked.

His face looked blank, like he hadn't heard me. Then, looking out over the graves, he said, "Every day. After lunch."

From the side, I watched him looking at something I couldn't see. The silence was broken every now and then by a bird call. "There must be some sad stories," I said.

His eyes narrowed, and he looked sad. After a bit, he said, "My brother Jimmy is buried here."

I looked at the grave in front of him. It had a number and a date on the stone. "That grave in front of you?"

He just looked lost. "Maybe."

I was torn between wanting to know more and not wanting to invade his memories. Wanting to know won.

"How do you know if there is no name?"

He looked around the grounds. "Logic. None of the ones with names are him."

That made sense, but it didn't answer my question. "But how do you know he's here?"

A robin landed on the stone in the next row and sat looking at us. He watched it as he talked.

"We grew up in the farmhouse the other side of those woods." He looked off to the north. "I still live there. My brother was, well... different. Not all there, I guess. He wasn't dangerous, just odd. And he stuttered. The kids made fun of him, and one day... well, he just stopped talking."

He looked sad. "One day we were doing chores in the barn, and I turned around and he was gone. That happened before... he'd have something else on his mind. But he'd always show up. That time he didn't. I told ma when I was done with the hay, and she said he'd be back. By dinner time he wasn't. By sundown he wasn't. She called the police, and they started looking."

He looked back at me. "That was fifty years ago."

"I'm so sorry. How did you find out he was here?"

His jaw set. "I just know." He clapped and the bird flew away. "The police checked at the hospital. They said he wasn't there. But I always figured he was. We knew it was a place for crazies, and we heard the stories... people not knowing who they were and never getting out. They did experiments." He pointed to the grave. "They ended up here in this cemetery. There are five graves with numbers. My brother is one of them."

So the answer was, he really didn't know, except in his gut. And maybe that's the best place to know when you get right down to it.

"What kind of experiments?" I asked.

He shrugged. "You know. Brain things... to find out how they work."

I didn't know, but Avery wasn't going to be able to tell me.

He looked around the grounds again and then back at me.

"You believe in ghosts?" he asked.

I laughed nervously. "Don't know for sure."

He nodded slowly. "I hear them sometimes. If the wind is right, I can hear them through the trees."

"You hear ghosts?"

"Yeah. They talk in code… beeps."

"Beeps?"

"Yeah, beeps."

"Like a horn?"

He shook his head. "Nope. Just little beeps."

It crossed my mind that maybe Jimmy wasn't the only odd one in the family. "Do you come here at night?"

"Nope. I figure they need their privacy."

"When was the last time you heard them?"

"Don't know exactly. Week ago, maybe two."

"Why the rifle?" I asked.

He shrugged. "Just habit, I guess. This used to be pretty wild country. Lots of coyotes. They're afraid of you by themselves, but if they come at you in a pack…" He lifted the rifle.

I thanked him for telling me about Jimmy and put out my hand. But he didn't respond. He seemed to have forgotten I was there. The dog watched me as I walked away.

As I walked back to the car through the woods, I wondered about everything he had told me. Probably just the wanderings of an old man's mind. But even if that's all it was, it gave me a reason for another appointment with Bridgewater… a missing boy and ghosts that beeped.

Chapter 41

I ROLLED DOWN THE WINDOWS AND SAT IN THE CAR LISTENING to the birds and trying to make some sense out of all the odd-shaped pieces. I decided I needed another chat with Bridgewater and called Carol. It was a little before three. She said she'd let me know. She could have said what she was probably thinking... that the odds of my getting another appointment at Walker were slim. But she didn't say that, not because I was the one who signed the checks but because she had seen things that I did that didn't make much sense turn out pretty well. But in case she met with resistance, I told her to mention a missing boy named Jimmy Wren. I sat some more, this time wondering why Rosie wasn't answering her phone. I turned on the radio and listened to the Cubs game. They were in extra innings with the Reds.

Carol called as I was heading back to town down Lake Street. I had an appointment, but it wasn't with Bridgewater. Friday at ten, with Quark.

"And one more thing," she said. "You just had a call from a Maggie Park. Left her home number."

"Doesn't ring a bell. What did she want?"

"She didn't say. But she did say she was a friend of Ben's."

"Ah. What's the number?"

She gave it to me and wished me luck. As I reached to turn the radio back on, the phone rang again. I figured she had forgotten something.

"Yes, my dear," I answered.

"You're not my type," came the answer. It took me a few seconds to put the voice with a name. Larry, my friendly cell phone supplier at Motorola.

"Your phone works," I said.

"Yes, it does, but not for long. I've got a new one for you."

"Why would I need a new one?"

"Because this one fits in your pocket."

I laughed. "Which pocket would that be?"

"Your jacket pocket."

"That would be an improvement, but I'll believe it when I see it."

"How's tomorrow at eleven? And you can buy lunch."

"I've got an appointment at ten out west. Can you do a late lunch? I should be back by twelve thirty."

"Sure. See you at the office."

Larry and I had gone to high school together and had stayed in touch, getting together a couple of times a year.

***

THE CLOSER I GOT TO THE CITY the worse the traffic got. As I was crawling at twenty miles per hour, just west of O'Hare Airport, my phone rang and I turned down the radio. A hesitant male voice was on the other end.

"Spencer Manning?"

"Yes."

He paused and I waited.

"Are you alone?"

That was an odd question, and I considered hanging up. But I didn't.

"Yes."

"My name is Barker. You left a card with my neighbor."

"Yes, I did. Where have you been?"

"I'd rather not say. My family is still there. I'd like to meet."

I pulled past a semi and sped up to make it through a light. "What about?"

He hesitated again. "My future. I heard about Malone."

"Okay. Where and when?"

"Do you know Palwaukee Airport in Wheeling?"

"Yes."

"There's a viewing area on the south side off the entrance to Palatine Road."

"I'm familiar with it."

"You available at nine tonight?"

"I can be."

"Okay. I've got a Ford station wagon."

"I've got a blue Mustang."

"See you then. Thanks."

"Yup."

By the time we hung up I was east of the airport on Irving in rush hour traffic. There was no good route to get to Stosh's that wouldn't be just as crowded, so I stayed on Irving. I'd get there when I got there. But the drive would be a bit better after the call from Barker. Whatever he had to say would certainly be interesting.

I turned the radio back up. The game was over. While I was on the phone, Leon Durham had hit a game-winning homer, and WGN had left the Cubs game for the end of the Bob Collins Show.

***

IT WAS TWENTY AFTER SIX when I pulled onto Stosh's drive. He was sitting on the porch. I had just shut the car off when the phone rang again. How did I ever live without a phone in my car? It was Vicki calling with dates and names.

"There are six dates, Spencer."

She gave them to me along with the detectives. The dates went back four years. Two of the dates were the same team, and one of those was Barker and Yancy. The rest were all different. I was expecting more similarity. I thanked her for checking.

As I was about to say goodbye, she said, "Spencer, I know you didn't ask for this, but there's something that may be useful."

"Yes?"

"On all but one of them, McElroy was the one who logged in the evidence."

I thought about that for a bit. "He was a detective then?"

"Yes. In charge of the evidence room."

"Interesting. When was that?"

"About three years ago. And I found your two men. They've been on the payroll for fourteen months."

"As what?"

"Special investigators."

"Seems odd."

"Yes, it does. Anything else I can do?"

"You can forget we ever talked. Call me if you run across anything else, but be careful."

"Sure. Hope you figure this out."

"Me too. Thanks."

I hung up and hurried out of the car before the phone rang again.

Chapter 42

"HEY, KID," STOSH SAID AS I WALKED ACROSS THE LAWN. "HOW did you ever get by without a phone in your car?"

I laughed and sat next to him. "I was just wondering the same thing. It does come in handy. What's for dinner?"

"Got a taste for pizza. How about Little Italy?"

"Sounds good. I've got an appointment at nine, so that should work."

He waved to a neighbor. "Working nights?"

"Do you remember my telling you that Detectives Barker and Yancy were told to take time off and disappear?"

He just raised his eyebrows.

"Well, Barker has unofficially reappeared."

"Maybe I didn't want to hear that."

"Then pretend you didn't."

He rolled his eyes. "Let's eat. You're driving."

On the way, he asked, "How did you hear from him?"

"Who?"

"The person I don't want to hear about."

"I left a card with his neighbor. He evidently went back home for something."

"Where's he been?"

"He didn't say. His family is still there, and he's scared. Heard about Malone and the garbage truck."

"Yeah, that's gotta get your attention."

***

FIFTEEN MINUTES LATER WE HAD ORDERED and were working on a couple of beers. I filled him in on my afternoon visit to the cemetery and Avery and then updated him on Ben's relationship with the attorney general.

He set his glass down and said, "Lansing does get results, but he also has a reputation of being hard to work with."

"So I've heard."

We sat in silence for a few minutes watching the crowd before I said, "Had another interesting call."

He raised his eyebrows as he drank.

"I had Vicki check records to see who was involved with large drug busts."

He set his glass down and shook his head. "It's one thing you doing the things you do. It's another involving someone else."

"I know. She volunteered. She told me she's concerned about things that are going on and wants to help if there's anything she can do. And since she works by herself, checking records is easy."

He gave me a doubtful look. "So?"

I explained my theory to him.

"And?"

"No pattern with detectives, but for a couple years McElroy was in charge of the evidence room."

The pizza arrived. The waiter set the pizza on a stand and cut two slices and placed them on our plates. "Another beer, gentlemen?"

"Please," I said.

We each took a bite.

"And one of the cases Vicki found was Macek. When I talked to Macek, he told me—"

"Hold up," Stosh almost yelled. "You talked to Macek? How the hell did that happen?"

Kate hadn't told him. "You... sort of authorized a visit."

"Did I! When was this?"

"This morning. You weren't in your office, and I needed—"

He just stared at me and gradually relaxed as he realized that Kate must have made the call. He was willing to flog me but not her. "Whatever Spencer needs, huh?"

I had no reply that would have helped.

He just shook his head and continued eating. As he chewed, he said, "All that with McElroy doesn't mean anything."

"You mean Chief Detective McElroy who told people to disappear and probably told Barker and Yancy where to find the watch?"

"Conjecture. Hearsay. Defense lawyers love that."

"McElroy's name keeps coming up."

He picked up another slice as the waiter dropped off the beer. "So tie it to something solid. Until you do be careful where you step. I know you don't always think so, but the laws apply to you too." He took a bite and with a mouthful asked, "So, what about Macek?"

"He told me he had twenty-two kilos when he was arrested. Vicki told me only twenty were logged in."

He sighed and took a drink. "Curious, but you need more than that."

"And the two FBI fakes have been paid by the Fourth as special investigators for the last fourteen months. That seems pretty strange."

He shrugged. "Each department has the leeway for special assignments. But they're usually short-term."

I took a drink and asked, "What kind of experiments do you think they could be doing?"

"Pardon?"

"At Walker."

He rolled his eyes. "You're taking the word of some nut who hears ghosts beeping?"

"You never know. He might get things confused, but it might be based in reality."

"Maybe." He thought for a bit. "They do ink blot tests at places like that. Stuff like that."

"Maybe."

"Leave it alone, Spencer."

I took another drink, and he rolled his eyes again. He knew I wouldn't leave anything alone that looked odd.

"And then there's Rosie," I said.

"What about Rosie?"

"She's not answering her phone."

He just chewed and looked at me.

"I'm worried about her. Should I be?"

He sighed, took a drink, and set down the bottle. "She has a job, Spencer. And that job sometimes isn't your standard eight to five."

"Four days since I first called. What's going on?"

"She spent a month training for a special assignment with DEA. They don't work on a schedule."

"So, she's undercover?"

"Come on, Spencer. We keep our people safe by not telling the world what they're doing."

"I'm not the world. She had glasses with a tracker in them."

He nodded. "We know where she is all the time."

I sighed and picked up my glass. "And if she gets in trouble?"

"Lots of training and lots of experience. Twelve years of doing this job."

"Not necessarily *this* job, whatever *this* is." I took a drink. "Not even a hint?"

"Not even a hint."

"She could've called and let me know she'd be out of touch at least."

"Happened fast." He drank the last of his beer. "She'll be glad to know you're concerned."

I stared at him. "How about if we were married?"

His look of dismay cut into me.

"Really? That's where you're going with this? It's not like you haven't had more time than you deserve to ask the lady. Sometimes I wonder why she continues to give you the time of day."

"I can't believe—"

He held up his hand. "I don't want to hear it. And the answer is officially *no*. But what husbands and wives tell each other behind closed doors is out of my hands. But all that is a moot point."

"Are you done?" I asked.

"Almost. You're on the outside looking in, and that was the path you chose when you decided to drop out of the academy and walk away from the force."

"Really? That's where *you're* going with this? Perhaps you don't remember all the things I've been able to do from outside the force. Cases—"

"All greatly appreciated, Spencer. But that doesn't get you an honorary blue uniform."

I just stared at him.

He finished the pizza. I had lost my appetite. We waited in silence for the check.

When we got to the car, Stosh turned to me and said, "The truth is not meant for the faint of heart."

I faced him and forced myself to unclench my fists. "What the hell does that mean?"

I unlocked the door, and he said, "You're complaining about not being in the loop, but choices you have made put you there."

I just glared at him as I walked around to the other side of the car.

Chapter 43

IT WAS GOOD THAT I WAS TWENTY MINUTES EARLY TO THE airport. I needed some time to cool off. I pulled off the road into a gravel parking area next to small, six-tier aluminum bleachers put there so people could sit and watch the planes. I sat on the top row and took in the field in front of me over a chain link fence. In the last glimmer of dusk, I could make out three runways and a control tower and hangars in the distance. As I was watching, the lights came on along the runway in front of me. A minute later I heard the plane coming from my back, and in a few seconds it was over my head. If it had been daytime I could've made out the pilot.

The noise of the plane's engine covered the car pulling up next to mine, and as I watched the plane land I heard a door close. It was a brown station wagon. A man who was a little taller and a lot bulkier than me walked toward the bleachers.

"Detective Barker?" I said.

"Spencer Manning?"

"Well, now that we've got that settled," I said. I stood and we shook hands. As he sat next to me the lights on the runway went out. I wondered how we would break the ice. He had to be very worried about something if he was trusting a stranger. I had to gain his trust.

"So why did my neighbor have your card?" he asked.

"Fair enough." I got as comfortable as I could on a metal bench. "I was hired to find out about Martin Rentel. With a little digging I learned that you and Yancy were the arresting detectives the second time he was brought in, and Sergeant Malone was on the desk. And coincidentally the three of you were unavailable. I paid a visit to your homes and found that you had left in a hurry. I watched Yancy's apartment and ended up finding him in a bar. An interesting conversation with him followed."

The lights came on again, but on the runway to our left. In a minute we heard the plane. Before that I could hear Barker thinking.

"My turn for a question," I said. "What made you call a stranger?"

He waited for the plane to land before he answered. "Not quite a stranger. I've heard stories about Chief Manning. He has quite a legacy. I had heard he had a son who was a PI. And I'm at the point where I have to trust somebody. And somebody outside the department seems like a wise choice."

"Because somebody inside the department is *not* a wise choice?"

He nodded. "Yeah. The only one I can trust is Yancy, and I have no idea where he is. He doesn't answer his phone. And I wouldn't bet against his phone being tapped."

"This all sounds like a spy story," I said. "Tapped phones, detectives told to disappear."

"Who told you that?" he asked.

"Yancy... and more."

He was quiet for several minutes. I gave him time.

"You talked to him. Do you know where he is?" he asked.

"Yes."

"Someplace safe?"

"Yes."

"Good. What else do you know?"

"I know about the goon squad and the planted evidence and that McElroy told you to disappear." Those were all things he also knew. I wasn't telling him about the rest... at least not yet.

He took in a deep breath and sighed.

"What made you call?" I asked.

"Malone. He was one of the best men I knew. That he ended up..."

"And if he could, maybe you could too?"

He took a minute before he said, "I was concerned for my family."

"Who would do that?" I asked.

He shook his head. "No one that I know. Or rather no one that I thought I knew."

"What do you know about the goon squad?"

"Nothing firsthand. Stories, more like joking than anything else. But enough stories to make them credible. We would make arrests and when we got nowhere with interrogations we were taken off the case."

"Did you ever follow up on those cases?"

"A couple times in the beginning. I got nowhere. Files were missing. It was like they didn't happen."

"When was the beginning?"

"A couple years ago."

A car went by on the road behind us, and he looked over his shoulder. I could sense him tensing up.

"Where is your family?" I asked.

He hesitated and then said, "I'd rather not say."

That tipped my trust level for him to the plus side. I wouldn't have told a stranger that either.

"Can I ask you a question?" he asked.

"Sure."

"Who hired you?"

He looked over his shoulder again at passing cars.

"Martin Rentel's aunt. She's evidently been kinda looking out for him and was worried when the police wouldn't give her any information. She wrote the word *disappeared* in her journal."

"Disappeared?"

"Yes. I've checked through police sources, and there is no record of where he's being held."

"That's certainly odd."

That needed no answer.

"What are you looking to do?" I asked.

"Get my family somewhere safe and then find out what the hell is going on." He took a deep breath. "Where's Yancy?"

"He's been at my house for the last week."

"Really? You just take in a stranger?" More cars went by, and it took four or five before he stopped looking.

"Seemed like the thing to do. By the way, you have your gun with you?"

"It's in the car. Why?"

"I sent a man to Yancy's apartment to get some things, and his gun was gone."

"Gone?"

"Stolen. Somebody broke in."

"Oh, Jesus. That somebody is setting him up."

"Trying to."

"Looks like more than trying."

I stretched out my legs and leaned back. "Yes, but Yancy isn't the only person staying at hotel Manning."

"No?"

I laughed. "One of my operatives is an ex-Chicago cop. He's been with Yancy since we discovered his gun was missing."

"Good." He stood up and stretched. "I've had a lot of time to think about all of this. What has Yancy told you?"

"Well, he couldn't tell me any more about Rentel after he was arrested. But he did tell me about the planted evidence."

Barker was quiet.

"He told me you were told by McElroy what to look for and where to look for it."

He sighed. "Yup."

"Not exactly by the book," I said.

"But it happens. Especially lately."

"What does that mean?"

He looked around again. "The AG, Lansing, has been very clear about the conviction rate. When he started, he had a meeting with the brass and made it very clear he wanted convictions... at almost any cost."

"Who told you that?"

"McElroy."

"You think he was using Lansing's words or adding his own spin?"

He shrugged. "Hard to tell, but that was the message."

"What does *almost any cost* mean?"

He looked out over the field. "Yancy and I talked about it. We decided the inference was hurt 'em, but don't kill 'em."

"There's a fine line there."

"Yes there is."

"And maybe it gets crossed."

"Maybe."

"Were you and Yancy told to get rough?"

"No. We were told to follow normal procedures, and if we didn't get a confession to report that to McElroy."

"Then what?"

"Then, I don't know. But that's when the goon squad rumors started."

I thought for a minute. "You said you followed up on cases, and files were missing."

"Yeah."

"Do you remember any of those names?"

"Sure. Why?"

"I want to follow up on them too."

"How are you going to do that?"

I smiled. "I have a friend in low places."

He gave me five names and then asked what my plan was.

"Follow up on those names for starters." I paused. "You heard of the Walker Mental Health Facility?"

"Yes."

I gave him some of that background. "Can you tell me anything about it?" I asked. "Any personal experience?"

He sat back down. "No. I just know it exists."

"Okay."

"What can I do?" he asked.

"Well, I think the best thing you can do is keep your family safe. If I need you, I'll call."

"Two things. How are you going to call if you don't know where we are, and I don't feel too safe where we are."

"I've been thinking about that. I have a suggestion. You ever been to Door County?"

I told him about Aunt Rose's inn, and we made arrangements for them to relocate. I gave him my phone numbers and told him to call Yancy when he got settled. We shook hands, and he headed for his car.

The lights came on and another plane landed. It taxied to the hangars, and the runway lights went out. A few minutes later the tower lights went out too. That was the last scheduled flight coming into Palwaukee, and the controller was done for the day. I had read that several years ago the airport had installed a radio system that allowed a pilot to turn on the lights in an emergency if the airport was closed. I got back in the car.

I checked my watch. A few minutes after ten. Vicki was probably still up. She answered on the second ring and assured me it wasn't too late. I told her about my conversation with Barker and asked her to see if there were files on the five names.

Then I decided it wasn't too late to call Maggie and dialed her number. A tired sounding voice answered, and I wondered about calling.

When I identified myself she perked up a bit. She told me she wasn't a fan of Lansing but made it clear that she was only talking to me because I was Ben's friend, and he had told her about my distrust of government officials. We talked for about ten minutes. She told me she was the chief deputy attorney general. That meant she did all the work while Lansing got the praise. It was clear she didn't like him, and, while she didn't come right out and say it, she intimated that she would be happy to see him in jail. She wouldn't be specific because there was no solid proof. He was very careful. But there was one thing she was looking into that she was sure would lead somewhere. She had inadvertently discovered three names on the state payroll that were suspicious. I asked why. She said because checks were being issued, but with some digging she had discovered the people didn't exist. And there was a thread that led to Lansing.

I told her if she needed any help to let me know. And she told me if there was anything she could do for me that wouldn't involve jail time she was more than willing. After giving her a very general briefing on what was going on, I thanked her and told her I'd be in touch if anything came up.

I started the Mustang and did a U-turn on the gravel. Barker had been a distraction from Stosh. But as I drove I could hear his words, and by the time I got home I wondered if maybe he was right. But that didn't make me any less angry.

Chapter 44

THE SKY WAS OVERCAST FRIDAY MORNING, AND THERE WAS A light drizzle when I left for my appointment at Walker. As I crossed the river the phone rang. I looked at it and hoped Larry's new phone would be the improvement he promised. I answered and heard Stosh's voice. He didn't bother with the formalities.

"Spencer, Rentel's body showed up."

"Where?"

"Along the Fox River."

"I just crossed it. Where?"

"There's a little park off of Route 25 about two miles south of Lake."

"Who found him?"

"A teenager going fishing. He called Elgin police. They're onsite."

"How do they know it's Rentel?"

"ID in his wallet."

Whoever did it wanted the body found and didn't want any time wasted trying to identify it. "Any more?"

"Pretty badly beaten. One bullet in the chest."

"Jesus. I wonder whose gun the bullet came from. Any weapon?"

"Not yet."

I turned around and recrossed the river. "How did you find out?"

"Elgin saw the arrest record and called the Fourth. My little bird called me."

"Okay. Thanks. I'll be there in a coupla minutes."

"Let me know what you find."

"Sure." I hung up. Neither one of us had wasted time on formalities.

***

TWO ELGIN SQUAD CARS were in the parking lot at the park. One had its lights going. I parked and called Carol and asked her to cancel my appointment at Walker. I told her I'd call if I wasn't going to make my appointment with Larry. It was still drizzling, but barely.

One of the policemen came up to the car and told me I needed to leave. I showed him my license and told him I knew about the body and that it was someone I had been looking for. He stared at my license and then at me and told me to wait in the car. He walked down a path toward the river to where the other officer was standing, presumably over the body. I watched him talk and point in my direction. After a short discussion, he walked back up the path. I rolled down my window as he approached the car.

"You can stay, but pull over to the side so we can get a response team in here."

"Mind if I take a look?"

His stance changed from polite to tough guy.

"Yes." He turned and started walking away.

"Hey," I said. "You find the gun?"

He turned and said no without any politeness.

"You will," I said to his back.

He turned and stared at me for five seconds and then walked away. I rolled up the window and sat in the car and waited for someone with more authority to show up. In five minutes someone did. Almost at the same time, another squad, a paramedic, and an unmarked supervisor car pulled into the parking lot. I watched as they all went to work and patiently waited for the guy in the suit to ask the obvious questions.

They all walked the hundred feet to the river and had a conference. The paramedics came back and got a stretcher and a body bag. The suit followed them a minute later and came over to my car. I rolled my window down and waited.

He was stocky, but despite that his brown suit fit well. He was chewing on an unlit cigar and was walking with his hands in his pockets.

"Manning?"

"Yup."

He looked through my car and asked for my license. I handed it to him and resisted the urge to ask to see his.

He handed it back to me and said, "Lieutenant Santone. You were looking for this guy?"

"I was."

He looked at me some more. "How long?" The cigar waggled as he held onto it with his teeth.

"Coupla weeks."

"Um hmm." He looked some more. "And when somebody finds him after two weeks of you not finding jack you just happen to be in the neighborhood."

"Looks that way."

"Man of few words, eh?"

I figured answering yes would have made me seem like a smart ass, and I didn't want to get off on the wrong foot. Besides, he'd figure that out if we spent much more time together.

"Mind explaining that coincidence, Manning?"

"No." He didn't want to play anymore, so I continued. "Part of the case took me to Walker. I had an appointment there at ten this morning. So I was on my way when I got the call about Rentel."

"Who from?"

I was still angry at Stosh, but I wasn't going to throw him under the bus. "After I tell you I'm not saying, you do have a couple of options, but I don't think it's important enough to go to that trouble."

He just looked at me sternly some more. He had better things to do but needed to let me know he was in charge.

"Look, Lieutenant, you've got a murder, and I know something about it. Perhaps we could act like we're both on the same side here."

He nodded slowly but not with much confidence. He took the cigar out of his mouth with his left hand and rolled it slowly between his thumb and forefinger. "Okay, let's try that. We find a body with a bullet in his chest. It's someone you've been looking for, and you just happen to be in the neighborhood."

"Right."

"Who you working for?"

"His aunt."

"Got her number handy?"

"Sure. But it won't do you any good."

"And why is that?"

"She hired me on a Friday, gave me some directions, and told me she'd call on Monday."

He raised his eyebrows. "And?"

"Friday was the last I heard from her."

"Maybe she changed her mind," he said.

"Maybe the Cubs will win the World Series."

I got a hard stare. "What're you... a Sox fan?"

"Nope. A realist. I got a call from her son who said she was missing. She is."

He studied the cigar. "Your track record seems a bit tainted. You report it?"

"Yup. Oak Park has come up empty."

He thought for a minute. "What directions did she give you?"

"To visit the cemetery at Walker Mental Health Facility."

"And do what?" He swatted at something buzzing at his ear.

"Look around."

"Look around." When I didn't respond he continued. "That's it? Look around?"

"Yup."

"Seems a bit odd."

"Not only seems."

"What did you find when you looked around?"

"Everything you'd expect to find in a cemetery." I wasn't going to give him all my cards, at least not at the moment.

"I would imagine." He took a deep breath, let it out in a huff, and looked at my card. "I can reach you at this number?"

"Yup."

He nodded. "Expect a call." He turned and walked ten feet before he turned back. "You asked Officer Daniels if he had found the gun."

"I did."

He tilted his head. "Like you expected him to find a gun."

I shrugged. "He was shot, wasn't he?"

"Yes, he was. But if you shot someone would you leave the gun behind for the police to find?"

"Nope."

"Then why did you ask?"

"Just curious."

He hesitated before saying, "Yes, you are. I'll call you when I need you."

As he was walking back down the path to the river, Officer Daniels yelled, "Lieutenant, we've got a gun."

I was reaching for the ignition when Santone stopped and slowly turned back to me. "You stay put." Santone joined the other two officers in the weeds about ten feet uphill from where the body was. I was tired of being a bystander, so I got out and headed toward the river. The drizzle had picked up a bit but not enough to melt me. At the edge of the parking lot I passed the paramedics carrying the stretcher with Rentel in a black body bag as another unmarked black car with several antennas pulled into the lot.

***

SANTONE SAW ME COMING but didn't say anything. I stayed about twenty feet away, close enough to see the area but far enough that he wouldn't tell me to leave. The area where Daniels was crouching was trampled. Weeds were flattened and stalks were broken.

Santone stood with the other officer outside the trampled area. "What kind of gun, Daniels?"

I considered telling Santone that the gun was a Glock, but there were times when the little man who sat on my shoulder was able to stop my tongue before it invited my foot into my mouth. It was odd enough that I happened to be in the area when someone found Rentel. And a bit odder that I knew they'd find a gun. If I were able to tell them it was a Glock they'd want to spend hours asking me how I knew. I would do the same. I had other things to do with my hours.

"It's a nine millimeter Glock, Lieutenant. Right size for the hole in his chest."

They left the gun on the ground while Daniels went for an evidence bag, and Santone walked back to where I was standing.

"So evidently there *is* someone who shoots someone and leaves the gun behind." He was talking to me but looking out over the river.

"Evidently."

"And you knew about it."

The guy on my shoulder was still telling me to keep my mouth shut.

"Doesn't make sense," he said with a bit of showy concern. He pulled the cigar out of his mouth and spit a piece of leaf on the ground. "No, it sure doesn't. Make any sense to you, Manning?"

"Well, looks like there was a struggle. Maybe Rentel has ahold of the gun and pulls it as it goes off and the guy drops it."

"Why doesn't he pick it up?"

"Maybe he hears someone coming and needs to get away. He looks for it but it's down in the weeds. He leaves in a hurry."

Santone looked at me and nodded as he stuck the cigar back in his mouth.

"Let's say all that's the way it happened. There's one little problem."

"Which is?"

"You didn't see the body. This guy Rentel was beaten up pretty badly. Hardly in any shape to struggle much." When I didn't respond, he continued. "Another odd thing. Have to wait for the coroner. Gunshot was new, but some of the bruises were old. But still… he didn't look like a guy who was going to put up much of a fight." He paused. "Got an explanation for that, Mister PI?"

I did, and maybe he'd be willing to buy me a beer someday to hear it. But for the moment I was keeping it to myself. But the guy on my shoulder had done all he could for one day. "Nope. Too busy thinking about how to clean up my track record."

He laughed. "You do that. You also count on another chat when we get into this. So be available."

"No problem." As I turned to leave, I said, "You ever smoke that thing?"

"Nope. Gave it up for Lent."

I gave him a two-finger salute and headed back to the parking lot.

Chapter 45

I WAS LATE GETTING BACK TO THE OFFICE BUT ONLY BY TEN minutes. Larry was sitting on the corner of Carol's desk showing her the new phones. Watson glanced at me and then went back to sleep.

"Okay, those are the kid's toy phones. Where are the ones that work?"

"Funny. You wanna keep the one you got just say the word."

I picked up one of the phones and looked at it and then at Larry.

"It's a prototype," he said. "And it *will* fit in your pocket. And this is nothing. The idea people are way ahead of the production teams. You wouldn't believe what they're talking about. The day is coming when your phone will take pictures."

Carol told me to call the office. I went out in the parking lot, leaned against the car and called. It worked. I slid it into my pants pocket and went back in.

Larry was smiling. "Fits in your pocket."

"But it's uncomfortable."

"Really? From you who bitched about how big the last one was? You're gonna complain about the one that fits in your pocket?"

I shrugged. "I'm just sayin'. Not real comfortable." I thought I'd leave it in the car unless I was in a situation where I might not be able to get back to the car. "Same deal?" I asked.

"Sure. The coverage keeps getting better with more towers going up all the time. Keep letting us know where there are dead spots."

"Okay. Thanks. Buy you lunch?"

He looked at his watch. "If we can make it quick."

"Let's go next door and get subs. Come with us, Carol?"

"I have something I want to finish. Bring me back a number three."

"Sure."

"And here's a couple messages. Lieutenant Powolski called twice." She handed me two notes. The other was from a fellow who called every few months trying to get me to sell the Mustang. I tossed both. I'd call Stosh at home later.

"Plans for the afternoon?" Carol asked.

"I have one appointment."

"Nothing on the calendar."

"No, surprise visit."

"Okay. Good luck with that. You want me to reschedule Walker?"

"Yes, please. See if you can get something for Monday. Thanks. And please type up an affidavit. Use the standard form Ben gave us. I want it to be by Chester and say that Jerry Yancy has been in his custody twenty-four hours a day at my address since Tuesday, May 1. Can you do it before I leave?"

"No problem."

"Thanks. Five copies please. Put the original in the safe."

Larry and I got subs and brought them back to the office and ate with Carol. I saved a bite for Watson. It was the only way he paid attention to me.

***

I HAD FOUND EARLY ON THAT SEEING PEOPLE was more successful if I dropped in without an appointment. That way nothing sudden could come up that would result in a phone call canceling the appointment. The chances of that working in a police station were not quite as good, but I was going to drop in on McElroy and take a shot.

The desk sergeant told me McElroy was in and asked what I wanted. I told him I had information about the Rentel case. He asked my name, and I told him Spencer. He pointed to the wooden chairs along the wall and picked up the phone. Ten seconds later he told me someone would be right out. A minute later a woman in her fifties came over to the chair.

"Are you Mr. Spencer?"

"Yes."

She smiled and said, "Come with me."

We wound our way through halls and desk areas until she finally motioned me through an open office door and into a room about the size and décor of Stosh's... early functional. McElroy, a man I guessed to be in his forties with combed back brown hair and a nose that had been broken at least once, stood and motioned me to another spartan wood chair. He was sturdy and had about two inches on me. He didn't offer a hand.

"Mr. Spencer?"

I smiled and said, "Well, Spencer Manning to be more accurate." I handed him my card and sat.

He did a barely noticeable double-take, enough to make me pretty sure he knew the name, and looked at the card.

He showed a smile and said, "Most people give both their names when asked."

I kept my smile. "Well, I'm not most people."

As he sat he said, "I'll keep that in mind. I'm Chief Detective McElroy. You have information about the Rentel case?"

"I was hired to find out what happened to him by his aunt, Susan Janice. She seemed to think he had disappeared. Your precinct wouldn't give her any information."

"Ah, well then this is your lucky day. His body turned up this morning."

"Is that right?"

"It is."

"Body must mean he's dead. What were the circumstances?"

"I can tell you what you'll hear on the news tonight. Found by a kid somewhere out by the Fox River. A bullet in the chest."

I nodded and let that sit for a bit. "And before that he was in your custody."

"He was."

"For the murder of Amos Grant."

"Yes."

I shifted in the chair, trying to get comfortable. "His aunt thinks there was no way he would have done that."

"We had evidence that says otherwise."

I was wondering where the line was as to how much information McElroy would give me. I found it with my next question. "What evidence would that be?"

"I'm sure what with your history you know I can't answer that."

We stared at each other briefly. "So you're saying someone wanted him dead and put a bullet in him and dumped the body along the Fox."

"Looks that way."

I gave him my best confused look and said, "Then help me out with this. Grant wasn't a crime figure or a gang banger or someone who was in any way connected to anything outside the law. Right?"

He just looked at me, without the smile.

I continued. "He was some average old man who lived a normal life who was in the wrong place at the wrong time."

He still didn't respond.

"So what reason would there be for someone to want Rentel dead?"

The smile came back. "I'll give you this much, Manning. Rentel wasn't exactly an upstanding citizen. He had a sheet as long as his arm. This probably had nothing to do with Grant and something to do with his other... activities."

I smiled too. "Now why didn't I think of that?"

He shrugged. The lady who escorted me knocked on his open door and told him he had a meeting in five minutes.

"Hate to cut this short, Manning, but you said you had some information."

I had to think fast and come up with some. "Yes. The aunt has been missing for two weeks."

"And where does this aunt live?"

"Oak Park."

"Not to be callous, but that is Oak Park's problem. Now—"

"One more question. If you had Rentel in custody with solid evidence, how does he end up dead next to the river?"

He stared at me a bit longer than the last time. "He escaped during transport."

I looked surprised. "When was that?"

"You're done. Good luck with the aunt."

I stood and thanked him for his time. It took a lot of self-control not to say the other things that were on the tip of my tongue. Like asking what he knew about Walker. Like asking if he'd ever planted evidence. Like calling him on the *escaped during transport*. Like my missing drug theory.

***

I SAT IN THE PARKING LOT and called Carol on my new toy. I had an appointment at Walker at three on Monday. It was getting on toward four, and I had a taste for a cheeseburger. By the time I fought rush hour traffic and pulled into my driveway, it would be dinner time. So I called home and asked Chester if they wanted me to pick something up. They did. I briefly told him about Rentel.

***

CHESTER WAS SITTING ON THE DECK with a martini when I pulled up to the garage.

"How's things on the home front?" I asked.

He smiled. "One of us is enjoying retirement. The other is bouncing off the walls."

"I bet." The first ball had dropped. Now we just had to wait for the second. And I wasn't sure what to do when it did. I sat next to Chester and asked how he thought we should handle it when the police said they were looking for Yancy.

He took a sip. "Been thinking about that."

"And what do you think?"

"I think my babysitting fee doesn't include that much brain work."

"Big help you are."

"Retirement has its advantages." He took another sip. "But the little thinking I did do left me without a good answer."

I sighed. "Yeah, me too. The obvious answer is turn him in and have his name cleared."

"Yes, but…"

"But we don't catch a rat that way," I said. "If they think their trap is set we can set our own."

"Two problems," he said.

I stretched out my legs.

"One, kinda dancing around the law."

I smiled. "I've been accused of that very thing. Two?"

He hesitated while taking a longer sip of his martini. "Would Jerry be part of the trap?"

I also hesitated, but I didn't have a martini to cover my hesitation. "No, he wouldn't be *part* of the trap… he would *be* the trap."

"Then point two is, Jerry should probably have a say in this."

Of course he should. But Jerry was about to come off the tracks. "Agreed. I'll put the food in the oven, and we can talk."

I figured we had the advantage over whoever was framing Jerry. We knew what the trap was… we just didn't know when they would spring it. And we could choose to step into it or immediately defuse it with Jerry's alibi, Chester. But for the moment, all we had to do was keep Jerry from climbing the walls.

After venting his frustration, Jerry agreed to setting a trap. He wanted to get whoever was setting him up. I gave them each a copy of the affidavit and asked them to sign it. It made Jerry feel better, but he was still nervous and a bit irrational. But I did have a thought that calmed him down a bit. I told him about Barker and asked if he wanted to talk with him. He did. So after dinner I called Aunt Rose and, after catching up with her, Yancy and Barker talked for a half hour.

While they were talking, I went out to the car and called Vicki. All five files were gone.

Chapter 46

STOSH WAS SITTING ON THE PORCH WHEN I PULLED INTO THE drive. The noon sun was making its way into his shade. I left the windows down and got out.

As I stepped up onto the porch, he said, "You didn't call."

"Figured I was seeing you today, and you didn't say it was urgent." I sat in the wicker chair next to him. He didn't say anything.

"So what was it?" I asked.

A kid with a mutt on a leash walked by and waved to Stosh. He waved back.

"What happened out at the river?"

"A Lieutenant Santone of the Elgin police suggested that I knew more about the body by the river than I was saying."

"And why would he think something silly like that?"

"There was the fact that I'd shown up before he did."

He nodded.

"And I may have asked the officer if he'd found the gun."

"Brilliant."

"Yeah, probably should have kept that to myself."

"And had they?"

The sun crept up onto my knees. "Not at that point, but they did before I left."

"You see the body?"

"No. But the lieutenant told me he was beaten pretty badly and confirmed the bullet in the chest."

"Um hmm. Anybody wonder why the gun was left behind?"

"Santone brought that up. Said it seemed strange."

"Years of police work," Stosh said with sarcasm. "And you said?"

"Well, somebody had gone to the trouble of making it look like there had been a struggle. I suggested maybe the gun had been dropped in the weeds."

"Why not just pick it up?"

"Somebody came along, and whoever dropped it needed to get out of there."

He nodded. "Santone buy that?"

"Didn't seem to. How does a guy beat up that bad put up a struggle? And then he pointed out that the bullet hole was new, but some bruises appeared to be old."

He shifted his chair so it was out of the sun. "That it?"

"Says we'll be talking again."

"Yes, you will."

"Lunch?"

"Sure." He lifted himself from the chair and pushed it back against the wall. I did the same.

***

I SET UP THE CARD TABLE in the living room while Stosh got out the sandwich fixings. We carried sandwiches and macaroni salad and Schlitz to the table and finished half our sandwiches in uncomfortable silence. I wanted to find out about Rosie, but I wasn't going to be the one to bring it up. He took a long drink and broke the silence.

"Nothing new on the aunt?"

"Haven't heard anything."

"What happened with Barker?"

"He confirms what Yancy said about the evidence and that they were taken off the case and told to disappear by McElroy, but he doesn't know any more than that. But listen to this. He gave me five names of cases he and Yancy were taken off of. I gave the names to Vicki. The files are gone."

He sighed heavily and shook his head. "Lots of pieces that need to be pulled together."

"I'm working on it."

"Is Barker safe somewhere?"

"Yup." I told him about Aunt Rose's.

With a full mouth, he said, "The Spencer Manning room and board service. Door County comes in handy."

It had for several needing a place to disappear, including Stosh. "You seem to—"

He stopped when the phone in my pocket rang.

"What the hell's that?" he asked, looking startled.

I laughed. "My new toy." I pulled it out and answered, watching Stosh's startled look turn to confused. It was Chester. Howie Egan had called home and wanted to talk to me. I had put Howie's number in my contact list. I thanked him and told him not to expect me for dinner.

Stosh put out his hand, and I handed him the phone. "You gotta be kidding." He looked at it from every angle, like he didn't trust it. "What a world. I wish Francine could see this," he said with a faraway look. I ate the last of my sandwich and took a long drink before he took a deep breath and looked up at me. He wiped his mouth and set the napkin on the table.

"So, kid, what about Yancy?"

I couldn't give him the honest answer to that question. Ignoring the warrant that was surely coming in order to use Yancy as a trap wasn't something I could share with a by-the-book Chicago police lieutenant. "Haven't decided yet." That was partly true... I hadn't decided how the trap was going to work.

"You better decide soon."

"I've got until someone figures out whose gun they've got. That might take a bit with the extra layer of Elgin."

"Your time runs out when a warrant is issued."

"Technically."

He sighed. "Yes, technically you could end up in jail. Harboring a fugitive is pretty high on the serious scale."

"I'm well aware of that. But someone would have to know what I know before the cops show up at my door."

He shook his head. "These aren't fools you're dealing with. We catch most criminals because they're stupid. These people aren't."

I laughed. "I beg to differ. If I'm right about even a bit of this, it's *all* pretty stupid. Outright breaking the law and thinking they can get away with it because they wear a badge?"

"Yeah, it stinks. But where's the evidence? All you got is hearsay and some pretty wild theories."

I pushed back my chair and stretched out. "But theories that make sense."

"From the angle you're looking at them. Maybe they make different sense from a different angle, or none at all. Maybe all this is part of a different picture… a bigger plan where everyone is working together to catch criminals."

I laughed. "It's easier to believe in politicians and people in high places lining their own pockets." I shook my head. "An attorney general coming up for reelection who wants convictions at any cost, a sheriff who wants to make a name for himself, a chief of detectives who is in the right spot at the right time to make a few bucks… yeah, everybody's working together to catch criminals. And then there's the two morons impersonating FBI agents. And you're going to tell me these are all coincidences?"

"Nope. What I'm telling you is you got no hard evidence. Lots of things that look odd, but how do they fit?"

I sighed and pushed away from the table. "I'm looking."

"Well, when you find some let me know."

I wasn't going to ask about Rosie. I didn't want to give Stosh the satisfaction, and he had made it pretty clear that he wasn't going to tell me anything. But I sure wanted to know. As I started to stand, I hesitated.

"Don't ask," he said with a look that said he meant it.

I gathered plates and headed for the kitchen. "I gotta make a call."

I rinsed the plates and called Howie.

"Hey, Spencer. You said to call you if anything odd happened."

"Yeah. What happened?"

"Don't really know, but you said to call."

"Sure. Go ahead."

"I was out for a walk last night about ten. I do that every night if it's not raining, just to check the grounds. There's a wing in the back of the facility that's not used anymore. Last night there were lights on in two of the rooms."

"And there haven't been before?"

"Not since I've been here. And I asked Hank about it... he's the old guy in the dorm. He's been here forever. He says that wing hasn't been used in ten years."

Stosh came into the kitchen and got another beer. He held one up to me, and I nodded. He headed back to the living room.

"Coulda been just someone looking for something. Maybe that wing is used for storage," I said.

"Maybe. But I went up and tried to look in the window. The shades were down, and I couldn't see anything but light around the edges. But as I was walking away I heard the start of a scream."

"Start?"

"Yeah. It was muffled pretty fast, like someone put a towel or something over someone's mouth."

"Could it have been a screech from someone dragging some-thing across the floor, like a bed or a table?"

"I suppose. But it sure sounded like a scream. I stood there for a few minutes but didn't hear anything else. The lights went out and I left."

I wondered how much Howie's imagination was running away with him. I had planted the seed that something was going on, and things tend to be more suspenseful at night.

"I'll look again tonight," said Howie.

"Tell you what," I said. "How about I buy you dinner, and I'll take a walk with you."

"That'd be great! But I don't have a car."

"I'll pick you up. But I don't want to be seen. How about you meet me at the cemetery at six?"

"Sounds good. See you then."

I stood for a minute, thinking about what Howie had said, looking forward to an adventurous evening.

Stosh was shuffling the cards when I returned to the table. He looked like he was thinking about something.

After a few shuffles, he said, "You know, you need to be thinking about Barker too."

"What about him?"

"I can't decide if you're Lancelot or Don Quixote, saving damsels on your white horse or tilting at windmills... maybe both. It's not just Barker who's at risk, it's his whole family."

I picked up the bottle of Schlitz and clenched my jaw. "I'm well aware of that. They're all safe at Aunt Rose's." I took a drink.

He nodded slowly. "So you'd like to think. You've been very lucky so far, but one of these days luck is going to catch up with you. You—"

"Hey! You refuse to tell me about Rosie, and now you're telling me how to run my affairs. I'm good at what I do."

"Good has a lot to do with it, but so does luck."

"Just get off my back." I slammed the bottle down on the table.

He squared up the cards in front of him. "I see. Well, if that's how it's going to be, you know all that inside information you've gotten from me?"

"Yeah."

"Well, no more. It stops right now."

I can't say I was surprised. We were both angry, and he was venting. I had been frustrated by him before, but never this angry, never angry at all. I didn't know how to deal with it besides letting time cool it off. Neither one of us liked to talk about problems, especially Stosh. When Francine died I didn't remember him ever saying anything about how hard it was.

"Got it. I'd better be going."

He just nodded and put the cards back in the box.

Chapter 47

HOWIE AND I GOT BACK TO THE CEMETERY A LITTLE BEFORE ten. I grabbed my jacket, put on my Cubs ball cap, and we walked up the path. There was no moon, and standing among the graves in the dark was a bit eerie. The only sound was the chirp of crickets… and me slapping at mosquitoes.

Over dinner, Howie had given me as much history of Walker as he knew. Most of it came from stories Hank had told him. Hank had been there forever, according to Howie. When I asked him how long forever was he shrugged and said thirty years. Evidently the place had been a lot busier thirty years ago. The dormitory had beds for ten men, and they were almost always full. Over a hundred patients filled most of the rooms, including the wing where Howie had seen the lights the night before. Now there were only seven. Six of the eight admin offices were unoccupied. Now, it was just Bridgewater and Quark. There used to be six doctors. Now there was just one. There used to be a large cleaning staff. Now there was an outside company. There was a kitchen with part-time help and two orderlies who delivered food and provided other services for the patients. The Walker State Mental Health Facility was a mere shadow of its former self. I asked Howie if he knew what had happened. He didn't. They had just hired a new man to take care of the grounds. His name was Thomas. Howie was relieved that he didn't have to drive the tractor anymore.

I had told Howie about the man I had met in the cemetery and asked if he had ever seen him. He had, but they hadn't spoken.

Howie had just waved to him when he was mowing the lawn. And when he came back down the next aisle the man was gone.

I had also told Howie what the man said about experiments and asked if he knew anything about that. Hank had told him there was a time when the doctors used electric shock treatments and something about cold water baths. But as far as Howie knew, nothing like that went on now.

As we walked into the cemetery, I asked him when he had last dug a grave.

He scrunched up his lips. "Hmmm. That would have been just after I started, almost a year ago."

That didn't fit with my theory. "Are you sure? It wasn't more recent?"

"Yup. About a year ago." As we walked farther into the cemetery, he said, "But a couple weeks ago I got an order to uncover an old one."

"Uncover?"

"Yeah, just dig down to it."

"Did you think that was strange?"

"Nope."

Seemed strange to me. "Who told you to do that?"

"That woulda been Hank. But the work orders come from Bridgewater."

"Do you remember which grave it was?"

"Sure. Over that way." He pointed west.

We stopped in front of the 1914 marker. "There it is."

"Did they say why?" I asked.

"Yup. I asked. Said there was something personal needed to go in the coffin that they forgot. I thought that was real nice of them to make sure whoever it was had their wish. Especially with all the extra trouble."

"What kind of coffin was it?"

He shook his head. "Just a plain old pine box. Sure hope I get better than that when my time comes."

My theory was back on the table. Something was being stashed in that coffin. "Did you see them open the coffin?"

"Nope. I came back later that day and filled it back up and set the grass."

"Which day *was* that?"

"It was a Friday. A week ago."

I thought about that. I had my second appointment at Walker on Wednesday, and on Friday they were digging up a grave.

"Where do you put the dirt?" I asked.

"I put a tarp on the ground next to the plot and put the dirt on that."

That explained why there was so little dirt in the grass. And then I had a thought.

"Howie, does your tractor have a backup alarm?"

"Sure, they all do. It beeps."

Of course it does, I thought.

"Should we head over to the facility?" Howie asked.

"Give me a couple of minutes." I wanted to spend some time with the graves, in the quiet darkness.

"Sure."

As my eyes adjusted to the dark, I could see the outlines of the headstones. I walked past the graves of people who had lived troublesome lives, the kind who leave ghosts behind. I figured if there was such a thing as ghosts this would be where they were. A mosquito buzzed my ear, and I smacked it, leaving me with a sore ear. I showed her. If there *were* ghosts here, they had an advantage—no blood.

I didn't know what I was looking for, and I didn't find it. The crickets were still singing, and as I reached the middle of the cemetery the leaves started to whisper in the wind. Ghostlike shapes danced at the tops of the trees where they met the sky. I turned in a circle looking through the trees for lights and saw none. Avery's house was to the north, and the facility was to the south. But the trees blocked the light from both. I walked back to Howie who was standing where I left him. He didn't seem to be bothered by the mosquitoes.

"Aren't they biting you?" I asked.

"What?"

"What?! Mosquitoes. I'm getting attacked."

He thought that was funny. "Nah. Never have been. Used to drive my brother crazy. Ma said it was because he was sweeter than me. Some people just attract 'em."

***

"LET'S GO," I SAID.

"Follow me," he said.

I sighed. "No problem there. I can't see a thing through those trees." I was wondering if this adventure was worth it.

As he headed down the aisle between rows of graves, he turned and asked, "You have a gun?"

"Not on me."

He stopped and turned. "Don't you think you should? I mean, you wouldn't be here if there wasn't something going on, right? Something you might need a gun for?"

"Maybe at some point. But I doubt that's tonight."

"Oookay," he said, obviously not agreeing with me. While we walked, he said, "Sam Spade always carried a gun."

Probably not always, but I didn't argue with him. I followed him toward the woods, thinking about the growing list of people who thought I should carry a gun.

"Where are you going?" I asked.

"There's a path here. It'll take us back to the facility."

After just two steps in I could barely make out Howie who had opened up a ten-foot gap between us. If the route we were taking was a path, it was well on its way to being reclaimed by the forest. Crunching dead leaves, I pushed branches out of the way and slapped at mosquitoes and could barely see Howie ten feet in front of me, much less a path. When I was paying more attention to the mosquitoes than the branches, one whipped me in the face. I grabbed it and broke it off.

"I heard something on our left," I said.

"Well, could be a deer... or a coyote."

"A coyote?" I said nervously.

"Probably a deer," he said. "Probably wouldn't hear a coyote… unless they were in a pack."

"Great. That makes me feel better."

"Like I said, probably a deer. Even if it *is* a coyote, it won't bother two of us."

Unless it's out with friends, I thought. I took a couple of quick steps to catch up to Howie.

Five minutes later we came into a field of grass and weeds, and I could make out the outlines of the facility buildings. They looked much different from the rear. There was a little light over the roof from what I assumed were lights in front of the building, and there was a red light on top of a tall tower. Howie gave me a tour.

He pointed to the left at three single-story structures, each a few hundred feet long and joined at a hub in the center, like the arms of an octopus. "Those are the main buildings on the left. The second one from the left is where the offices are where you were. The others are patient rooms, but most are empty." I didn't see any lights, at least none in the rooms. The field was sparkling with fire-flies. I wondered if they ate mosquitoes.

He pointed past the wing on the left. "On both sides of the wings are a cafeteria, an exercise room, a TV room, and more offices. Not used much anymore."

I looked up at a sky as black as crude oil, dotted with many more stars than I could see in the city. It reminded me of the trips we took when I was a kid. On clear nights, Dad would pile the family and the telescope into the station wagon and ride out to a forest preserve far enough from the city to see a sky just like this. I thought it was magical. And, though they must have been there, I didn't remember the mosquitoes.

Saturn was just above the horizon in the east, and I knew Jupiter would be up within a half hour, following Saturn across the sky. Sprinkled across the sky were a thousand twinkling pinpoints of light. Dad would tell us stories about the constellations and the men who tried to make sense of it all, including the ones who were burned at the stake for suggesting there might be life on other planets around those twinkling stars. We understand a lot more today than they did then, but we still understand very little. When Howie called my name I looked down at the building and thought of the men who had been burned at the stake.

We started to walk across the field. In the distance from and to the right of the last wing were two more buildings. One, larger than the other, looked like the barn Rosie and I had seen on our first visit. Howie confirmed that it was indeed a barn. Evidently this land had been a farm in the eighteen hundreds, and the barn and the other building were remnants of that. The barn was used for storage of records and was where the maintenance equipment was kept. The other building had been converted into the dorm.

As we made our way across the field, another wing came into view. Each wing had a door at the end. Howie said that was where he had seen the light. I followed him to a stand of trees about fifty feet from the building. Something ran ahead of us into the trees.

Howie pointed toward the building and said, "Third window from the center hub is where I heard the scream. One window to a room."

The whole building was dark. "I don't see any lights. How many staff are on duty?"

"Two orderlies. They have an office in the front. There's a doctor on call."

"Anybody at the front desk?"

"Nope. The door is locked at eight. The orderlies, me, Hank, and the new man are the only ones here until the cleaning crew comes in at ten. But they're only here three nights a week."

"Where's the new man?"

Howie shrugged. "He's hard to keep track of... kind of disappears. Don't know where he goes. Then I'll find him asleep in his room, and I never saw him come in."

I laughed. "That sounds mysterious. Where did he come from?"

"Don't know. He asks a lot of questions, but he doesn't answer any."

I looked out of the trees and only saw outlines in the dark. I changed the subject. "You said the shades were down?" I said.

"Yes. I could see light around the edges, and the shades were lit up. But I couldn't see anything when I got up close and tried to look into the room."

"Is there a basement?"

"Yes. There's a basement under all the wings... and tunnels."

"What's down there?"

"Storage rooms and mechanicals like heating and air conditioning and electric panels."

"I'm gonna walk up to the window."

"Okay. I'll hoot like an owl if I see anything."

Howie couldn't see me rolling my eyes. "Okay, you do that."

I started at the third window. The shade was down. But I noticed something Howie hadn't mentioned. There were bars on the windows. I stood there for a few minutes and heard nothing. I went back to the first window and walked along the building. There were ten windows, and the second and fourth were the only ones where the shade was up. I looked into those rooms and could barely make out sparse furniture, a bed with sheets and metal rails, and a dresser. Then I rounded the end of the wing and caught a slight whiff of skunk. I looked around the field and didn't see it. But then it was so dark I would have barely made out a person. I turned and walked down the other side. As I started down the wall a light went on in one of the middle rooms and spilled onto the grass. I swatted another mosquito on my neck and swore under my breath. My whole neck itched.

I hugged the building, and as I neared the room the light went out. When I got to the edge of the window, I stopped and listened. Quiet. I took off my cap, leaned across the edge, and peered in. There was dim light coming from somewhere in the hall, and I could see enough to see that there was no one in the room. Then I was poked in the back by what felt like the barrel of a gun.

"Don't move," a low voice said from behind me.

I wasn't planning on it.

"Hands up, and turn around slow."

As I turned I saw the gun was a rifle, an old one. He had backed off a couple of feet.

"Be careful with that, now," I said.

"I'm not the one that needs to be careful, mister. You're trespassing. I could've shot you already, and no one would be the wiser."

I had no doubt about that. We were only a minute from a road, but it seemed it was the middle of nowhere. People out here were probably used to gunshots, and Avery would think it was ghosts.

In the dark I could just make out a shape. He was about my height but bulkier and smelled of cigarettes and motor oil. He had on a ragged jacket and a straw hat and looked to be about sixty. Had to be Hank. He must have been the man who told Rosie and I to leave, but it was too dark to tell for sure.

I gestured at the rifle. "Tell you what, Hank. How about you point that at something besides me, and we can talk?"

"I ain't..."

The barrel lowered a bit, and he looked confused. He took a step closer to me, and I could see him squint. "I know you?"

"No. No reason you should."

He had forgotten about the rifle. It was pointing off to my left side.

"But you know me."

"Howie told me about you. He was showing me around back here."

He was still squinting. "I still don't see no Howie."

"He's on the other side."

"Well, let's just go see."

He motioned with his head and pointed with the rifle. I walked past him and back along the building. We rounded the end of the wing, and I continued across the field toward the trees.

"I still don't see no Howie," he said.

"He's in the trees." As we got nearer I heard an owl hoot.

We entered the woods, and I stopped. This was where I had left him, but there was no Howie.

"I'm done listenin' to your fast talkin' mister," Hank said.

I took a deep breath and called Howie's name.

"I'm up here," came the reply.

"Up where?" I asked.

"In the tree."

Hank answered. "What are you doin' up a damn tree, boy? Get your ass down here."

I couldn't have put it any better.

When he dropped to the ground, I repeated Hank's question.

Howie was standing close enough that I could see his smile. He looked proud of himself.

"I figured owls don't live on the ground, so if I had to hoot I'd better be up in the tree."

"What are you blabberin' about, boy?" Hank asked.

"This here's Mr. Manning. He's a detective. Something going on here he's looking into."

The rifle was still pointing at me. "That right mister?"

"That's right."

"You got some ID?"

I started to reach for my wallet.

"Nice and slow now. You wouldn't have a gun under that jacket would you?"

"He doesn't carry a gun," Howie said. He sounded kind of excited.

"Okay, get the ID."

He looked at it closely. Not much he could see in the dark. He looked back at me and lowered the rifle. "What say we go back to the dorm and have a little chat?"

"Lead the way," I said. Didn't see any point in it, but I wasn't the one with the rifle.

***

THE OUTSIDE OF THE DORM was in pretty bad shape. There were a few boarded up windows, pieces of asbestos tile siding were missing, and it had been a while since anyone had thought about painting trim. The inside wasn't any better. We sat in a large, open area just inside the door that was lit by a lamp with no shade. The couch cushions were torn in a few spots, and the room could have used a cleaning crew. I tried not to touch anything.

Hank offered a drink, and I thought it polite to accept but dreaded what it would be. I was right to dread. I didn't see the bottle, but it wouldn't even have made it as bar whiskey. We talked for almost an hour, mostly Hank talking in a monotone and me listening. Along the way, trying not to scratch the mosquito bites, I gave him enough of my story to cover my presence but not enough to give any real information. He didn't seem too interested.

With a few questions, I got Hank talking about the facility. He had indeed been there forever, as he also put it, and knew a lot of the history. He had seen many admin types come and go, and the new batch was just another page in the book. They were all worthless. Didn't take much to run the place in his opinion, especially these days with so few patients. He was surprised he still had a job.

"I noticed there are bars on the windows," I said. "Do you know why?"

Hank shrugged. "Used to have some pretty violent characters in there, I guess. Wouldn't want them gettin' out."

I nodded.

"Where's the new guy?" I asked.

He shrugged. "Who knows. He comes and goes."

I took as few sips of the whiskey as possible, and at one point he asked if something was wrong with it. I told him something at dinner wasn't agreeing with me.

After almost an hour, I asked him if he had ever noticed anything odd at the cemetery. He took a drink and then pursed his lips.

"Well, no. Not at the cemetery," he said with a slight slur.

"But something odd?" I asked.

"Not that you'd be interested in."

"Might be."

"Year ago or so. Nothing to do with whatever you're doing."

"Like to hear about it anyway."

I looked at Howie. He wasn't drinking either, but in his case it was because he was falling asleep.

"Yeah, about a year. One of the doctors disappeared."

There was that word again. "Disappeared? How does a doctor disappear?"

He shrugged. "Beats me. But he just didn't show up for work one morning. Cops came and everything. We all got interviewed. Never heard what came of it, but never saw him again."

"That *is* odd," I said. "What's his name?"

He shook his head for about five seconds and narrowed his eyes. "Don't remember."

I looked at my watch and then at Howie. He was snoring. "Well, I appreciate the information, Hank. I'd best be going. Looks like Howie's done for the night. Can you get me back to the cemetery?"

He shook his head. "That's one place I stay away from. I figure the poor souls there have been bothered enough while they were alive." He got up and walked into the dark hallway at the back of the room.

Chapter 48

I WOKE UP HOWIE, AND HE LED ME BACK THROUGH THE WOODS with me waving my arms to try and fend off the mosquitoes. As we walked, I realized the word *disappeared* was gnawing at me. By the time we got to the edge of the woods, it was more than a gnaw.

I wanted to get out of mosquito hell more than anything, but I turned to Howie and asked, "Do you know where they keep the records?"

"Sure. Room at the end of the hall from the offices."

"Can you get me in there?"

He shrugged. "Sure. I got keys to everything."

"Now?"

"I suppose. Nobody else in there but a couple of orderlies, and they're asleep by now. Why do you want to get in there?"

"I want to see the personnel records. See if I can find that missing doctor."

He looked confused. "What missing doctor?"

I guess he had slept through that part. "I'll tell you while we walk."

***

WE GOT INTO THE BUILDING and made our way down the dark admin wing. At the end of the hall, he opened a door that led into a room filled with filing cabinets. He closed the door and turned on the light. There were no windows.

"Do you need to stand guard outside?" I asked.

"Nah. Like I said, the only two here are asleep. And even if they're not, they're not coming back here."

"And Hank? He was obviously watching outside."

Howie laughed. "Once he has a drink and heads down that hall he's done for the night. A bomb wouldn't wake him."

"How about the new guy?"

"Probably asleep. But he doesn't have keys to the buildings."

I found the cabinet that was labeled "Personnel" and leafed through the folders that held lists of employees by year. They showed names, position, hire date, and termination date. I considered taking the folders but figured that it was so easy getting in I could do it again if I needed to.

I went back five years and compared lists. There were six doctors in 1981 and the same six in 1982. But in 1983 there were only four. Lee and Cassidy were not on the list. I looked back at 1982. Both had termination dates, Lee in June and Cassidy in October.

Howie was standing in a corner, leaning against the wall, eyes closed. But he wasn't snoring. I replaced the folder and pulled out another that had individual records. I looked through Quark's and Bridgewater's and didn't find anything unusual. I thought of looking through patients' files to see if I could find one for Avery's brother. But, despite Howie's assurance, I didn't want to get surprised in this room, and if his brother had been a patient here it was likely he hadn't given his name.

I decided that even though there was nothing that seemed important other than Lee and Cassidy, the rest of the information would be good to have. So I pulled out the folders I had gone through and wished I had that camera phone Larry had talked about. But at least I had a phone. I called the office and left a message on the machine about the six doctors and the information on Bridgewater and Quark. If I needed anything else I'd come back.

I replaced the folders and poked Howie in the shoulder. He didn't move. A loud yell of his name woke him up.

"What are you doing here?" he asked.

"Come on, Howie. Wake up. Spencer… you let me in."

He shook his head, looking dazed. Slowly it came back to him.

"Oh, yeah."

"Let's go."

The skunk smell was a bit stronger, and the mosquitoes were still attacking. I was never so glad to get back in the car. I had it with mosquitoes… and Howie.

Chapter 49

I SLEPT IN SUNDAY MORNING. I DIDN'T MAKE IT INTO THE kitchen until after nine, lured by the smell of bacon. Chester and Jerry were still at the table with the paper.

"Late night?" Chester asked.

"Late and useless."

"Eggs and bacon in the oven."

"Thanks." I filled a plate, poured coffee, and joined them.

Jerry folded the sports section and said, "Mine was useless too. I've lost track of how many in a row that is."

I took a forkful of scrambled eggs and a sip of coffee. That gave me time to not react to Jerry's frustration. And I knew if I were in the same situation, there was no way I'd be doing nothing.

"I do appreciate your patience, Jerry. Something should break soon. Have you heard they found Rentel's body?"

"On the news last night and in the paper," Chester said from behind the paper, which he lowered. "They said he had been shot, but they didn't say anything about the gun."

I hadn't heard anything on the radio. I finished a mouthful and sighed. "It's like a chess game, except you can't see the board."

"Isn't there anything we can do?" Jerry asked.

"Keep doing what I've been doing," I said. "Shake the trees enough and something'll fall out."

"Which tree is that?" Jerry asked.

"I've got another appointment at Walker Monday. Those people aren't fans of mine."

"And how is that helping?"

"It's only helping if my theory is right. This is all about McElroy. I've gotta get his attention."

Chester folded the paper and set it on the table. "How are you going to do that?"

"My visit to his office was a waste. I figure the people at Walker will be dialing his number if they get fed up with me." I tapped my fingers on the table and thought about another idea that had been gnawing at me.

"What does the lieutenant have to say about all of this?" Chester asked.

I finished the last of the eggs and bacon and told them about my last visit with Stosh. I was still angry about him cutting me off from information.

Chester drank some coffee. "You know, he could be covering your ass, something you have a habit of putting in jeopardy now and then."

"And how do you figure that?" I asked.

"Deniability. If you knew the cops were looking for Jerry before it became public knowledge, you'd be in a corner. Admit you'd been hiding Jerry or be charged with obstructing justice."

"I'm not hiding him," I said vehemently.

He shrugged. "Call it what you like… they'd have a case. Stosh is just buying you time."

Then there was Rosie. I wasn't done being angry yet.

"What was useless about last night?" Chester asked.

I started to tell them when Jerry said, "I'm going for a walk."

"Pardon?" I said, suddenly worried.

Chester laughed. "He paces up and down the bedroom hall. He's wearing a path in the carpet."

Jerry started to get up, and I asked him to wait. He sat back down and looked at me expectantly.

I wasn't sure where I was going, but I needed to get it started. And Jerry's gun was sure to hit the news soon.

"Jerry, I know you're not happy about waiting here doing nothing. Neither am I." He was looking at me hopefully, like a kid waiting to get a present. "I need to flush out McElroy. If you'd be willing to—"

He about jumped out of the chair. "Hell yes! Willing? I'd be willing to get in the ring with Spinks… with no gloves. And I'd win. I'm ready to explode here."

I smiled and shook my head slowly. "You don't know what I'm going to ask."

He sat up straight, put his hands flat on the table and said, "Doesn't matter. I gotta do something."

We were all quiet for ten seconds. Chester had a little sparkle in his eye. I had a feeling he knew where I was headed.

"What is it?" Jerry asked.

"I want you to call McElroy and tell him you know where he has the drugs stashed, and you want a cut."

Jerry laughed, loud and raucously. "Is that all? I thought you were gonna have me kill somebody."

I waited till he calmed down. "That's all, but that's a lot. He'll come after you."

He raised his arms and looked around. "In my secret haven? He has no idea where I am."

"But he will as soon as a warrant is issued for your arrest and I have to give you up."

He lost his excitement. "So how does this help?"

"It does two things," Chester said. "It gets McElroy worried about you. And it gets him to move the drugs."

"And what good does that do?" Jerry asked.

I leaned over the table. "We catch him in the act."

He thought about it for a minute, trying to follow the plan, and then nodded. "I'll do it. When?"

"Monday morning. As soon as you think he's in his office."

"That would be after roll call. Seven thirty."

I nodded. "Get him on the line and just tell him that. Hang up quick so they can't run a trace."

"Got it." He got up, brought his dishes over to the sink, and went for his walk.

"How do you figure to catch him?" Chester asked.

"Be there when he does it."

"Not what I meant. More like how will you know when he's gonna move?"

I grinned, and he rolled his eyes.

"Got that covered," I said. He didn't ask how. Chester operated like Ralph. All he needed to know was what he needed to know. But even though that was covered, some things weren't. I'd need to make another trip to the cemetery.

I told Chester about my night at Walker.

"So you figure McElroy was feeling some heat because of your visits and needed to move his stash of drugs to a more secure spot?"

"Yup. Don't know how often he skimmed drugs, but it would be a chore to dig up a grave every time. So he kept them somewhere else, maybe somewhere at Walker, and added them to the coffin when he had a large haul."

"Maybe once a year," Chester said.

I nodded. "Maybe. But I think this time was prompted by my asking questions. They got nervous."

Chester finished his coffee and set the mug next to his plate. "And if you're right about all this, somebody at Walker is involved."

"Exactly. Just gotta figure out who."

He smiled. "You have a plan for that?"

"I do," I said with a bigger smile.

"So they're hiding drugs in the coffins... not bodies?"

"Well, not Rentel's body. But Rentel couldn't have been the only one they beat up." I told him about the missing files.

"This could be a huge can of worms." Chester ended the conversation by throwing a wrench into the works. "Of course, you're assuming your theory about the drugs in the grave is correct."

I sighed. "There is that."

He stood and picked up his plate. "Good luck with that."

I didn't reply. If I was right, I had everything. If I was wrong, I had nothing. But, at the moment, it was all I had.

Chapter 50

CAROL WAS PICKING UP AFTER WATSON WHEN I PULLED INTO the spot in the alley. She looked up and leered at me.

"Where is he?" I asked as I got out of the car.

"He only does three things. Eat, sleep, and this. Now that he's done with *this*, he'll be back to the second." I started to say something about his saving Billy at Aunt Rose's but thought better of it. Carol had never been upset about taking care of Watson before. There must have been something else wrong about Monday morning.

There was nothing I could say that wouldn't have ended in trouble, so I held the door for her after she deposited *this* in the trash can. As I stood there, I thought about my not doing anything to take care of Watson, besides paying the bills. But I was hardly ever around. I didn't get to play with him either. Next time I was there I'd take him for another walk.

As we walked in, she said, "A Lieutenant Santone wants you in his office."

"When?"

"An hour ago."

"Well, that's not going to happen."

She shot me a look. Still not happy about the *this* evidently. "He wasn't happy. Another Spencer Manning fan."

"I don't want to talk to him now. I've got that three o'clock appointment at Walker. Would you call and tell him I can be there around one?"

She nodded.

I sat at my desk and pulled the shoulder holster with the Taurus out of a locked drawer. I didn't want Howie thinking less of me.

Carol buzzed the intercom and told me Santone would meet me at noon at Danny's Pizza, a block north of the station. I had a feeling I was buying.

***

I DROVE PAST THE POLICE STATION and a block farther north pulled into the parking lot at Danny's. I took my phone from the tray on the center console and slid it under the seat. I wasn't that comfortable with it in my pocket. I looked at it like I looked at my gun. Both were there in case I got into trouble, and I was pretty sure I'd be okay with Santone.

I was early. So was Santone. He was sitting all alone at a long wooden table in the middle of the room. I thought he was wearing the same suit. There was an unwrapped cigar in the top pocket. About ten other people were scattered around the room.

Santone waved to the bench across from him and said, "I already ordered… half pepperoni half sausage. Hope you're a meat eater." He took a drink of what looked like Coke.

"My mother's rules make me eat the occasional vegetable, but only occasionally."

"Yeah, must have been a mother thing." He didn't bother with any more pleasantries. "While we're waiting, let's fill in some blanks."

A waitress came and asked what I wanted to drink. Coke worked.

"Be glad to help if I can," I said.

He looked surprised. "After our last conversation that's not the attitude I expected."

I shrugged. My attitude tended to change when I wanted something.

"Any blanks in particular?" I asked. I knew exactly which blanks and had been rehearsing my answers.

The waitress set the Coke in front of me. "Pizza will be right up."

"Thanks," I said.

"Let's start with how you got there so fast," he said.

"Like I told you, I had an appointment at Walker."

"And that had something to do with Rentel?"

"Yup."

"And that was?"

I repeated what I had told him at the scene.

"Same story you told last time."

"The truth never changes."

"Hmmm."

The pizza arrived. The waitress placed it on a silver serving stand and cut two slices and put them on our plates. I thanked her. She warned that it was really hot.

"Then there's the gun," he said.

I waited. And we both let the pizza sit and cool a bit.

"You knew it was there."

"No, I thought it might be."

"And how would that be?"

"It's what I do. I get hunches about things, and I'm usually right."

We each took a bite. Not as good as Gino's but pretty good.

"Um hmmm. And what's your hunch about who the gun belongs to?"

I finished chewing and took a drink. "No hunches about that." That was the truth. Knowing isn't a hunch.

He wiped his mouth. "Well, everything about this is odd. Odd that you were there, odd that you knew there was a gun, and who the gun belongs to is even odder."

I didn't mention his grammar. When I didn't respond he continued.

"Odd enough that I'd think an expert like you'd have a hunch."

"Didn't say I was perfect." We ate some more. "You gonna tell me who it belongs to?"

"Nope."

"Maybe I could help."

He looked at me with a squint. "Maybe, but I've been told to keep it quiet."

"Really?" I could see why, and I could see his wheels spinning trying to figure if I knew or not. "Sounds intriguing. If you know, I'd think it would be all over the news. What's so hush hush?"

He smiled. "Well now, answering that wouldn't be so quiet, would it?"

I smiled back. We ate some more.

"We seem to be back where we were Friday," he said.

The waitress was walking toward us. I held up two fingers, and she turned.

I finished the last of my Coke and said, "Except for one thing. What do you know about the doctor who disappeared from Walker about a year ago?" I didn't want to tell him I didn't know which doctor. The less he thought he was giving me, the better. I wanted him to fill in the name.

He squinted at me again. "More important, what do *you* know about it?"

"Not much. But this case started with a missing person... Rentel. Then his aunt goes missing. Then I find out about this doctor who didn't show up for work one day. And the thread tying them all together is Walker."

He picked up the last piece of pizza, took a bite, and slowly chewed.

"So let me see if I got this straight," he said. "You keep what you know under your hat and I'm supposed to spill about an old case."

"So you do know about it?"

He sighed and gave in. "I was a sergeant at the time. It made a bigger splash than it should have cuz he was related to one of our council members."

"How much did you learn?"

He stared at me as the waitress brought the Cokes. "Nothing, not a damned thing."

"As in... nothing?"

"Oddest case I've ever had. He didn't report to work on Wednesday. He didn't come home Tuesday. No paper trails after that."

"How do you know he didn't come home?"

"He lived in a quiet neighborhood where everybody notices everything. No one saw him come home, and the lights in his house didn't come on."

"What about his car?"

"Didn't own one. Took buses and cabs. There was a bus that stopped in front of Walker. Talked to the driver of his regular bus. He didn't get on. The driver thought he was working late. Sometimes did. We checked with later buses. No one remembered him."

"So he just disappeared."

"Yup."

I thought about Sergeant Malone. If not for a malfunction in a garbage truck he would have mysteriously disappeared too.

"Maybe he never left Walker," I said.

He paused with his hand on his glass. I knew he was deciding what to share. He finally did.

"We talked to everybody. No one had seen anything unusual. And before you ask, no one saw him leave. They just assumed he had, like every other day."

"What about the man at the front desk?"

"Yeah, right. That was odd too. He doesn't talk. It was like talking to a brick wall. I was told he hadn't *ever* talked. I'd ask a question, and he'd just stare at me. He wouldn't write either."

"I've met him."

He nodded. "So you know." He took a drink. "So if he didn't leave, where is he?"

I had a theory. This all started with a phone call telling my client that she would find answers at a cemetery, a great place to bury a body. After all, that's what cemeteries were for. Maybe that dug up grave a year ago was for the doctor. I wasn't sharing my theory with Santone, but he wasn't really expecting an answer.

As I gestured across the room to the waitress for the check, Santone said, "So now that I've spilled about Dr. Lee, talk to me about the gun."

It took a while, but Santone had finally filled in the missing name.

"You tell me who you think it belongs to," I said.

He laughed. "Talking to you is like playing hide and seek, but I gotta keep my eyes closed. I'm the one doing all the talking." The waitress handed me the check. "I told you I gotta keep that quiet."

I shrugged and smiled. "When you want to share that we'll talk."

"You mean like I tell you about Lee and you respond with a smile?"

I was still smiling. "Like that."

"I could make your afternoon miserable."

I nodded. "I bet you could. But by dinner time you wouldn't know any more than you do now."

He took out the cigar and rolled it in his right hand, staring at me, trying to figure out if pushing me around would get him anywhere. "I'm taking that off the burner, but I'm keeping it on the stove."

"One more question," I said.

He folded his arms on his chest and leaned back.

"What would it take to dig up a grave?"

"What? Disinter a body? Paperwork and a court order that would be impossible to get after doing all the paperwork. You—"

"No. Not disinter, just dig. I don't want to remove a body… just look in the coffin."

"What the hell are you talking about?"

"Well, that's another thing I—"

"Yeah, yeah, yeah. You must be a riot at parties."

I took out a twenty and dropped it on the check.

He stood and said, "We'll have to do this again sometime."

I finished my Coke. "Anytime, Lieutenant. Good pizza."

"Always good when somebody else buys. Thanks."

I sat in the Mustang and watched him walk down the block to the police station. Not a bad guy, just another civil servant trying to do his job. A part of me felt bad about not telling him the whole story, but that part was pretty small. If I ever figured it out I'd buy him another pizza.

I watched him walk away and wondered why he wasn't willing to add two and two and get four. If you have people who disappear and a place where burying bodies is what they do, then...

He turned at the corner, and I got in the Mustang.

Chapter 51

THE DAY WAS WARM, AND THE SUN WAS PLAYING WITH FLUFFY white clouds. I had a couple of hours before my appointment at three, so I headed for the cemetery. As I drove, my thoughts turned to Rosie. Not knowing anything was very frustrating.

From Route 20 down to the cemetery road I didn't see another car. The gravel was dry, and I left a cloud of dust behind me as I drove down the path. I parked in front of the chain and walked to the cemetery accompanied by the sound of birds.

I stood next to the marker and looked south at the forest, trying to see the path Howie had used to get to the facility. I didn't see anything that looked like an opening. But as I walked toward the trees I expected to find it. I didn't. So I started east of where I figured it was and walked the line of the trees. On my third walk along the edge I found what I thought might be the right place. Looking past a large oak I could see some trampled vegetation. I walked past the oak and slowly made my way through the trees.

I wasn't sure I was in the right spot, but the trees and shrubs were less dense where I was than on either side, and there was some evidence of someone having walked there. A couple of minutes later I found the branch I had broken dangling by a thin strip of bark. I took it one step at a time and made it to the other side. As I stepped out into the clearing and looked at the facility in the daylight, I jumped as a squirrel ran up the tree on my right. The building certainly didn't seem as ominous in the daytime.

A few steps away from the woods I turned around and looked at where I had come out. It didn't look anything like the start of a path. I had no idea how Howie had found it in the dark. But if my plan was to work, I'd have to do just that. But the other side was the critical part. And the only way to give myself a chance at finding it was to walk it a few more times and maybe make the path a little more obvious. So I walked back through the woods and did it again... and then two more times before I had to go.

Before I left the cemetery, I stood at the grave where I thought the drugs were stashed and tried to get my bearings to the start of the path. There was that one oak tree that was bigger than the rest. I lined it up through the grave markers. From where I stood it was about a third of the way along the cemetery edge. Short of putting up a sign, that was the best I was going to be able to do. But this was daytime. Everything would look different at night. Worst case scenario... I'd just head in the right direction and push through the woods.

***

I PULLED INTO THE WALKER LOT at ten to three. As I walked to the door, a tractor came around the side of the building with a raised bucket full of mulch. There was a backhoe on the rear of the tractor. A fellow I hadn't seen before was driving. He dumped the load next to a maple tree. As he backed away from the tree I heard a steady beeping.

The same old man was at the desk, and he pushed the same button. I waited by the door, and Howie was there in less than a minute. As the inner door closed behind us, he said, "I hope you got more sleep than I did."

I put my finger to my lips. "You never know where ears are." But I was thinking he certainly didn't have any trouble sleeping. We walked in silence to Quark's office where his secretary was effusively pleasant. I wondered if I was in the right place. She told me Mr. Quark would be with me in a few minutes and offered me a seat on the couch. I studied the abstract art hanging on the walls while I waited. Studying didn't help any. While I was trying to decide if one was a horse or a Chevy, Quark opened his door and invited me in.

"Hello, Spencer... I hope you don't mind me calling you Spencer. You're getting to be like one of the family." He laughed. He held his hand out to the chair in front of his desk.

"Hello, Mr. Quark."

"No, no, no. Robert... please."

Wondering why the change in attitude, I said, "Okay, Robert."

"And what can we do for you today?" he asked.

"Well, I'm still wondering about the cemetery, but something else has come up."

He gave a little forced laugh and said, "You seem to find a lot wrong with our quiet little place in the country." Then he slowly shook his head. "I can assure you, there's nothing wrong at the cemetery. I asked everyone here, and no one knew of anything other than the usual disdain of cemeteries." He nodded once, quickly. That was the end of that. "Now what else has come up?"

"I heard about a doctor here who went missing a year or so ago."

He looked surprised. "And how did you hear of that?"

"Oh, just normal conversation."

He squinted a bit and took on a guarded look. Not quite as friendly as when I had walked in.

"I can't imagine how something like that comes up in normal conversation, but it really doesn't matter. But I don't know why that would concern you. We reported it to the police, and they didn't come up with a thing. He had just disappeared." He took a deep breath, let it out with a sigh, and turned to look out the window. "People have their own ways of disappearing for all kinds of reasons. We have patients who never leave their rooms, yet they have disappeared from everyday life just like Dr. Lee. The only difference is Dr. Lee made a conscious decision, for whatever reason that was."

"Unless he had help."

His eyes came back to me. "Help with what?"

"Help disappearing."

He smiled. "Our patients' minds create a world outside of reality, completely ruled by their imagination. You seem to have a rather active imagination yourself."

I smiled too. "In this business, the line between imagination and reality is sometimes very thin."

"Well, just be sure not to cross it. We do have a lot of extra rooms these days."

Despite the smile, that sounded like a threat. I didn't reply.

"Now, if there's nothing further?" he said.

"No, that covers it for today."

"For today?" He laughed. "Well, my door is always open. Watch out for that line."

I told him I would and left with a curt goodbye.

His secretary, Mrs. Starley, rang for an escort and invited me to have a seat on the couch. I said I'd stand. It never took more than a minute or two. But this time it stretched to five. Then her phone rang. After a few uh huhs, she hung up and turned to me.

"Seems our escort won't be free for a bit, Mr. Manning. But you know your way. If you'd let yourself out?"

I told her I thought I could find my way to the end of the hall. She smiled.

The hallway was empty. Made me feel kind of special to be walking down the hallowed halls all alone. I walked slowly, thinking about Rosie, wondering if I'd ever see her again... thinking about Stosh, wondering if I'd ever talk to him again. Halfway to the end I heard a door open on my left. As I turned my head to look, I heard another open on my right. I turned back that way, and something slammed into my left shoulder, pushing me into the room on the right.

Chapter 52

I HOPED THAT I WAS DREAMING, BUT I WASN'T. I WOKE UP in a dark room and couldn't see anything. I was lying on a bed, and there were handcuffs on my wrists. I reached up and touched cold rails and the other end of the cuffs. I let my arms drop back to the bed and tried to think. The last thing I remembered was being hit on my left shoulder by a linebacker. I didn't remember the hit on the head that must have caused the throbbing headache and the pain in the back of my head. I had no idea where I was or what day or time it was. But I did know one thing… next time I'd wait for an escort.

I thought about who would miss me and come looking and decided no one would. Rosie had done her own disappearing act, Stosh and I got together on Wednesday and Saturday and after our last conversation he wouldn't wonder if I didn't show up. Chester was my best bet, but he was used to my not showing up so it would be a few days before he was concerned enough to make a call. I was on my own. But maybe it had already been a few days.

Since I couldn't see anything, I listened. After a few minutes, all I had heard was my own blood flowing. At least I was alive. I didn't seem to have too many options, so I decided to go back to sleep. Maybe this was all a dream, and the next time I woke up the world would be back to normal. Maybe not. I had no idea how much time had passed when I was awakened by the door opening.

The dim light through the door hurt my head. I closed my eyes and waited.

"Wake him up," a voice said.

Someone turned on the room light, and fireworks went off in my head. I squeezed my eyes shut and tried to turn my head into the pillow.

"He's awake," a raspy voice said.

"Okay, go get a couple cups of coffee."

There was something about both voices that was familiar, but I couldn't place them. But then I couldn't even stand to open my eyes. I heard what sounded like a chair scraping across the floor and slowly opened my eyes. A few feet from my bed, sitting backward on a wooden chair, was Chief Detective McElroy. I considered two possibilities. Either he was the shining knight who had saved me from the villain, or he *was* the villain. Given the handcuffs, figuring out which wasn't hard.

When I got my eyes open, he studied me for a minute and then said, "I've got a proposition for you, Manning."

I struggled through the haze that was keeping me from thinking and tried to understand what I thought I had heard. Given the situation, it didn't make much sense. When I was sort of sure I had it right, I said, "You have a funny way of offering it."

I couldn't believe he was smiling. "Well, sorry about that. But you keep a pit bull chained up until you know he knows you're his friend."

I wasn't sure what I had to do with a pit bull. The other voice came back in with two mugs of coffee, and another piece fell into the puzzle. At the moment, I didn't remember his name, but the tall one of the two FBI pretenders set one mug on a table next to the bed and gave the other to McElroy. I looked around the sparsely furnished room. Aside from the bed, there were two small end tables and two wooden chairs, all cheap and worn. There was a heavy shade pulled over the window. Either it was nighttime or it sealed out all the light.

"Take off the cuffs," McElroy said.

"You sure about that, boss? This guy—"

"Take off the cuffs. He's smarter than you, Darny. But he's on a bed, and you have a gun." He shook his head.

"Hard to get good help these days," I said.

He smiled again.

Darny stepped over and unlocked the cuffs, squeezing each one tighter before he popped them open. As I sat up, my head objected, but it was better after I was vertical. I rubbed my wrists, picked up the mug, and took a sip. It didn't help, but it didn't hurt.

"So, what's your proposition?" I asked.

"You study history?"

"Some of it."

"Lincoln put some of his enemies in his cabinet. Better to keep an eye on them than wonder what they were doing behind his back."

I nodded.

He continued. "I figure better yet to get them to switch sides."

I looked at him over the mug and said, "And if they don't switch sides?"

He smiled and nodded his head to the right. "Darny here likes to shoot people, after he plays with them a bit."

I glanced at Darny and saw the evil smile on his face. He'd just as soon I didn't switch sides.

I thought about my options. It was good to have options and be able to make choices. If I were to believe McElroy about Darny, I only had one that let me walk out of there. Then I thought about Rentel and Malone in the garbage truck and decided I should believe McElroy about Darny.

"You're becoming a liability, Manning. I don't know how much you think you know, but it's more than we want you to know. I thought you'd back off, but you keep coming back. You're making the people here real nervous."

"What do they have to be nervous about?"

"In due time. For the moment, let me tell you what *I* know."

I raised the mug a few inches.

He took a drink and set his mug on the green, vinyl tile floor.

"Hard not to notice your involvement with some cases over the last few years," he said.

"Yes, but—"

He held up his hand. "Sure, you're on the side of the law. But you also like to bend the rules. And there's not much space between bending and breaking. You're a smart guy who doesn't give up. You'd be an asset on either side."

I set the mug back on the table. "And what makes you think I'd want to be on the... other side?"

Another smile, bigger this time. "The age-old carrot. Money."

I shook my head, trying to clear the haze. "And what makes you think I'd bite on that carrot?"

"I've done some research. Your... situation... isn't real stable." When I didn't respond, he continued. "A lot of the cases you take don't make you much money, if any. You live in your parents' house. Probably paid for. Can't afford your own place. You drive a twenty-year-old car. You have an office in a building owned by a woman whose name escapes me. Nothing that money can't help."

Evidently I didn't look so good on paper.

He paused and took a drink. "You have connections on both sides of the law that could be helpful, and when you get ahold of something you don't let go. We can use a man like that on our team."

His speech made me feel like I needed to suit up and win one for the Gipper. I picked up the mug and wrapped my hands around it. The warmth felt good. Then I remembered he hadn't asked if I wanted cream or sugar. Either he didn't care what I liked or he had picked that up in his research. Looking down at the brown liquid, I said, "Money isn't always the answer."

He laughed. "Depends on how much it is." He held out his hand to Darny who reached in his pocket and pulled out an envelope and handed it to McElroy. He held it up. "Five grand right now and the same every few months."

I was still looking at the coffee and thinking about the money. I had evidently underestimated the drug take.

When I didn't respond, he said, "How about ten?"

I swirled the coffee and watched the ripples, wondering where this would end.

When he said twenty-five, I looked up at him. I had *really* underestimated the take.

"Ah, the magic number," he said with a smile. He tossed the envelope on the bed. "I'll take care of the difference."

I kept swirling the coffee and stared at the envelope. "Where does the money come from?"

He laughed. "That's the problem. I think you already know, or at least you think you know." When I didn't respond, he said, "Come on, Manning. You know as well as I do that there are politicians and members of high society telling the world how wonderful they are while they pay for their toys with drug money. Why shouldn't we get our share?"

I had first-hand experience that he was right about the politicians and the members of high society, at least some of them. Some rich got richer and some politicians got rich. They hadn't created the problem, but they were taking advantage of it. But two wrongs didn't make a right... or did it?

"And what do I have to do in exchange for my soul?"

He looked sympathetic. "Have no regrets, sir. Every man has his price. It just took some haggling to find yours." He picked up his mug and took a drink. "You have skills we can use. Someone who is good at digging up information and doesn't mind bending the rules could come in handy."

I hadn't picked up the envelope. "And how does all this work?"

"Nothing you need to worry about. If we need you, we'll find you."

I looked at the envelope again and figured the deal wasn't done until I picked it up and put it in my pocket. I also figured if I didn't put it in my pocket I wasn't getting out of there alive. I touched it with my fingertips.

"When do I get the rest?" I asked.

"Next coupla days."

Chapter 53

I PICKED UP THE ENVELOPE, LOWERED THE SIDE RAIL ON THE bed, swung my legs over the side, and stuffed the envelope in the front pocket of my jeans... my empty pocket. My money clip and keys were gone. I felt my back pocket. My wallet was gone too.

McElroy smiled. "Welcome to the team." He was all of a sudden my best friend. He was as slick as a politician, the kind of guy you'd want to thank for burning your house down. He nodded at Darny who looked disappointed. I was sure he would rather have added to my headache.

As I stretched my shoulders, I said, "One more question."

"Not promising any answers," McElroy said.

I looked at him and waited ten seconds before asking. "What happened to Rentel?"

He thought about that. "What specifically?"

"I have it that he was railroaded. Evidence was planted, and your boys were told where to find it. Then he was… mistreated, to say the least."

"Now where did you get all that nonsense?"

"I have ways. It's one of those skills I have."

He took a deep breath and let it out slowly. "Let's put it this way. Rentel was a thug. He had a sheet from here to Pittsburgh. And who knows how many other things he was guilty of? Putting a thug like that in jail is a service to society no matter how you have to do it." He smiled at me. "It's one of those rules you like to bend."

"That sounds more like breaking."

"Fine line."

To me, the line wasn't so fine. But I had often wondered which rules I'd be willing to break if I thought it was warranted. Maybe that wasn't that far from what McElroy was doing.

"And you're becoming the judge and jury," I said.

"They're not doing that great a job."

McElroy looked at Darny and nodded toward the door. Darny left and came back in less than a minute, holding a bottle and a cloth.

"What's this?" I asked.

McElroy stood. "Well, one more little problem with you. We have to get you back to your car."

I shrugged. "I could walk."

"Ah. Without you knowing where you are." He kicked the chair back with his left foot.

Darny smiled. "Or we could hit him over the head again."

I already knew where I was. This room looked a lot like the room I had seen through the window. Same sparse furniture and a small bathroom. And besides, without knowing it, McElroy had told me. But I figured telling him that wouldn't help me any.

"Which is it, Manning?" McElroy asked.

"My head still hurts enough from the last time."

McElroy nodded to Darny whose face lit up. He was going to enjoy this way too much.

As he stepped toward me, I asked, "What day is it?"

"Monday," McElroy said.

"What time?" My watch was gone too.

He looked at his watch. "Five after nine."

As Darny took another step I made one last try. "I thought I was part of the team."

With a sly smile, he slowly shook his head. "You never totally trust a pit bull. And just to let you know what's in store for you if you get any fancy ideas…" He glanced at Darny whose eyes narrowed as he smiled.

Darny came up behind me and suddenly grabbed my left arm, bending it up behind me farther than it was designed to go but just a hair away from breaking it. He had done this before. It hurt like hell, but I wasn't going to give them the satisfaction of screaming.

McElroy nodded again, and Darny let go of my arm. I grabbed it with my right hand.

When I had caught my breath and could talk, I said, "You treat everbody on your team like this?"

"Only the pit bulls," McElroy said.

I had had enough of the pit bull crap. I stared at him as I tried to even my breaths and fill my lungs. He thought he owned me and I would do whatever he told me. And on the inside, I smiled... because the look on his face was pure arrogance.

"And who else is on this team?" I didn't think he'd tell me, but it didn't hurt to ask.

"Too many questions. But before you leave, I do have your first assignment."

I waited, still rubbing my arm, not entirely patiently.

"We have a little problem."

"That I'm guessing you'd like me to solve."

"Right. See, we know who killed Rentel."

So did I, or at least I was pretty sure, but they weren't the same person. "Good for you."

He ignored my attitude. "Trouble is, we can't find him."

After staring at him for a bit, I said, "Let me guess. You want me to."

"Seems right up your alley."

More than you know, I thought. "And who would that be?"

"One of my detectives. Jerry Yancy."

I tried to look surprised. McElroy evidently had gotten a phone call. "Why would he kill Rentel?"

He sat back down and leaned forward. "You were partially right. Rentel was railroaded. Yancy and another of my detectives planted evidence and then brought him in."

I sat back on the bed. "Why would they do that?"

He shrugged. "To make themselves look good. It's something we're not proud of, but it does happen."

"And who's the other guy?"

"Barker."

"And what does Barker have to say?"

He sighed and tried to look perplexed. He didn't quite pull it off. "He's missing too."

I laughed. "It's gonna cost you more if I have to find both of them."

"You've been paid pretty well already. And I only want Yancy."

I nodded. "Why do you think he killed Rentel?" I was very much enjoying asking questions I already knew the answers to. But talking to a member of the *team* about police business was a bit confusing.

"His service weapon was found next to the body."

I tried again to look surprised. "That seems pretty stupid. Kill a guy and then leave your gun there?"

"Yancy isn't the brightest bulb in the box. And his career has been hanging on by a thread. That's why he set up the arrest. Someone probably showed up or any number of other things that made him panic."

"Have you considered that maybe Yancy's being set up?"

He shook his head. "It all fits."

Of course it did. McElroy was the one who built the puzzle.

I leaned back against the bed. "Pardon my confusion, but I'm a bit perplexed about which hat you're wearing."

He just raised his eyebrows and furrowed his brow.

"You just handed me a sizeable chunk of money and welcomed me to the team... one of a bit questionable purpose. Yet you talk about one of your detectives like you've got your cop hat on."

He nodded slowly. "Yeah, I can see your confusion. But one has nothing to do with the other. It's like getting apples out of two different baskets. Yancy is cop business."

"Then why not have your department take care of it?"

He thought for a few seconds. "We've been trying to. But he seems to have vanished. So, you give it a try."

"Okay. But there's a blurry line there."

He furrowed his brow again.

"You're having me work on a police case and paying me with money out of this envelope." I patted my pocket.

"Let's just call it a test. Yancy just happens to be missing. I know your reputation. But let's see what you can do. You find Yancy, there will be more money."

I figured I had pushed him far enough. I shrugged. "So where do I start?"

"You'll get his address and the bar he hangs out at. You take it from there."

I stood back up. "I'm missing a wallet, keys, money clip, and watch." I held up my bare arm.

He turned to Darny but said to me, "They'll be in your car."

Darny didn't look happy about that, but he brightened up when McElroy told him to put me out. I was wishing he had given Carol some excuse to pull the trigger. He poured liquid onto a towel and, as he stepped toward me, I took a step back. Looking down at me, he grinned bigger than the Cheshire cat. The guy was born in the wrong century. He was far better suited for the Crusades.

"I wouldn't recommend resisting, Manning," McElroy said.

Darny took two more steps and stepped behind me. McElroy held up his hand.

"There's an extra five grand if you find him fast. And be careful. Every cop has a spare weapon. He's dangerous. Nobody's gonna blame you if you have to… act in self-defense."

He was telling me to kill Yancy. And I knew why. But for five grand? He nodded at Darny.

Darny wrapped one arm around my chest and pulled me into him a lot harder than he needed to. It took some effort not to resist as he covered my face with the towel. The last thing I remembered was hoping he hadn't broken a rib.

Chapter 54

THE KEYS WERE IN THE IGNITION. I LOWERED THE WINDOWS to get some fresh air and tried to shake off the drowsy effect of the chloroform. The taste and smell still lingered. Then I checked the glove compartment. My gun was still there. I reached under the seat and pulled out my phone. On the seat next to me was a brown paper bag. In it was my wallet, watch, and money clip. At least they weren't thieves. Well, at least McElroy wasn't. I was pretty sure Darny would've helped himself if McElroy hadn't been there. It was ten minutes before midnight.

There were three other cars in the parking lot. I assumed they were the night staff. Two overhead lights dimly lit the front of the building, and one light was on inside the front door. The place was shut down for the night.

The pain in my head was now just a dull ache. But when I reached back and touched the lump the stabbing pain returned. I took some deep breaths and looked at the building. It was quiet and peaceful, but because of that little voice in my head I felt there was a foreboding in the darkness of something evil. The rooms held secrets, and Walker was much more than it appeared to be. The only sound I heard was the singing of the ever-present crickets. I was wondering why they were still chirping at midnight when they suddenly stopped and the world was silent.

Also in the bag was a slip of paper with Yancy's address on it and the name and address of the bar where he spent his off hours...

Mike's. One problem had been solved. I didn't have to wonder how to get McElroy's attention. My usual strategy had worked. If you shake the trees long enough things start falling. But finding Yancy was one thing. I didn't have to look far. How I was going to make it *look like* I had found him was another. And did I want him found? I'd think about it on the way home.

I started the car and backed onto the horseshoe of the blacktop drive. Nobody noticed that a car was leaving at midnight.

***

AS LONG AS IT WAS ALREADY past my bedtime, I decided to do a bit of exploring and try and find Avery's house. It was north of the cemetery and he walked there and heard ghosts, so it couldn't be too far. I turned left out of Walker, passed the cemetery road, and turned into a dirt road I came to on the left. It wound through trees and became weed covered.

I stopped when the ruts ran out and walked the rest of the way. A couple of hundred yards in I came out into a wide yard with an old farmhouse set toward the back. A barn was at the far end. It looked like a place the ghosts would be perfectly at home in.

Before I backed the car out of the road, I called Rosie. I had been calling several times a day. Still no answer.

Chapter 55

I WENT FOR A RUN BEFORE THE SUN WAS UP. THE COOL AIR felt good. I stretched on the deck and looked at the sky. With the lights of the city not many stars were visible. But Jupiter and Saturn shone brightly about a degree apart in the western sky, and Venus was just over the horizon in the east, looking like a plane coming into O'Hare. I hadn't answered any of my questions about Yancy on the ride home last night, so I hoped the run would leave me with a clear mind. I wouldn't have any answers until after I had talked to Yancy, but I did know the questions.

I was mixing pancake batter when Chester came into the kitchen. Bacon was frying in a skillet.

"Love waking up to that smell," he said.

"Yup. Sure glad Noah got those pigs on the ark."

He laughed. "You got home late. Any progress?"

"Was an interesting evening. I'll tell you when Yancy gets here."

"I'll go get the paper."

He went out the back and got the paper from the driveway and sat at the table. Yancy walked in a minute later and made a similar comment about the bacon.

While we ate I told them about my adventure at Walker. I left the part about my assignment till last. Neither was surprised, but both were concerned.

"So the phone call worked," Jerry said.

"Yup. Pass the syrup, please."

"When do you think he'll go for it?"

"Well, as soon as possible. He would've last night, but he was tied up."

"But you won't know for sure."

"I will. I've got that covered. But I'd bet the house on tonight. He can't afford to take a chance on you."

With only a couple of bites left, I said, "There's one more thing."

Jerry picked up another piece of bacon and casually took a bite. I stared at him for a few seconds, and seeing the look on my face he stopped chewing.

"What?" he asked.

"He hired someone to kill you."

He dropped the bacon and the casual look turned to fear. "What?"

I slowly let out a deep breath. "He hired someone to kill you."

"That's what I thought you said. Do you know who?"

"Yeah… me."

His mouth opened, but no words came out.

I glanced at Chester. He was trying hard not to smile.

Yancy looked at me with squinty eyes, maybe trying to decide if he should be worried. After a pause, he said, "I'm going to assume the executioner isn't the guy who cooks your last meal."

I smiled. "If you're asking if I have plans to kill you, the answer is no."

"Well, I didn't think so, but nice to hear you say it. How much?"

My smile got bigger. "To kill you? Five grand."

Chester lost his battle with the smile and laughed.

Jerry wasn't amused. "Five grand? My life is only worth five grand?!"

I smiled. "Well, the five grand was more of a bonus on top of the twenty-five he already bought me for."

"Oh good. That makes me feel better. When is this supposed to happen?"

"Well, it's obviously not going to happen. But after he goes for the drugs, and I'm betting that's tonight, he's not going to be worried about you anymore."

"So the gun issue is dead."

I shook my head. "It's Santone's case."

Jerry threw his hands up. "So I'm stuck here?"

"Free room and board? You call that stuck?"

He just glared at me. He got up, brought his dishes to the sink, and stomped out of the room like an eight-year-old having a tantrum. A minute later I heard him pacing in the hall.

Chester took a bite of bacon. "You do get into some situations, Spencer."

I took in a breath and blew it out slowly. "Makes life interesting."

"So what do you think is going on with that grave?"

"Still seems like a good place to hide something." I told him about Howie uncovering the coffin on Friday.

"Why then?"

"If a coffin is your hiding place, you're not going to want to dig it up every time you make a score. So you save up small amounts until you have a large amount that makes it worthwhile to dig a hole."

"And it just happened McElroy had a large amount that Friday?"

"Maybe, but more likely that I was making them nervous, and McElroy wanted to get rid of the evidence."

"But it was still at Walker."

"Yes, but in McElroy's mind in a place no one would ever think of looking. Who's gonna dig up a grave?"

He nodded. "You need anything from me for tonight?"

"Aside from keeping a leash on Jerry? Nope."

"Good luck."

"Thanks."

He finished the bacon. "Will it be over after tonight?"

"It will for McElroy, but he won't know it yet. But I want more than McElroy."

He smiled. "Well, glad you cleared that up."

If he had asked, I would have explained. But he didn't ask, at least not that. Deniability. Chester had been a cop too long to be in a position where he didn't want to tell the truth.

"What time are you going out there?"

I thought for a few seconds. "He won't go till after dark." The days were getting longer, and sunset was around eight. "It won't be really dark till nine. I'll be there before that, but I expect it won't go down before ten."

He slid his knife and fork onto the plate and said, "One more question. You having dinner with the lieutenant tomorrow?"

I frowned. "Now that's a harder question."

He stood. "Thanks for breakfast. I'll clean up."

As I went to get dressed I thought about Stosh... and Rosie, and quickly put them out of my mind. I had other things to think about.

Chapter 56

THE CALL FROM HOWIE CAME A LITTLE AFTER ELEVEN. THE grave would be dug up this afternoon. The day seemed to go by in slow motion. There was little to think about, but I kept going over it. Once it was set in motion it would gain a life of its own that I had no control over. I could only hope that I had given it enough thought to go as planned. Even close to the plan would be acceptable.

***

I GOT TO THE CEMETERY AT SEVEN. I drove down the path and then, before I got to the chain, turned left onto an overgrown two-track and drove as far into the woods as I could, to a spot where my car couldn't be seen from the main path. Before I got out of the car I rubbed mosquito repellant on my exposed skin. Then I got out and sprayed it on my pants and jacket. I walked back to the path and up to the cemetery. My Taurus was in the shoulder holster with my black jacket over that. The night would get chilly, and I had no idea how long I'd be out there.

Short of the cemetery, I stepped into the tree line and walked slowly into the woods and then toward the clearing. I stopped a foot from the edge and scanned the cemetery. No one was there. I walked to the uncovered 1914 grave and looked down at a pine box. I felt terrible about being a part of disturbing the grave and apologized to the person who belonged to the name Jenkins. That McElroy was willing to use a grave this way was awful.

I made my way back to the trees to the big oak at the start of my hidden path. That gave me a view of the path coming into the clearing.

Watching the setting sun gave me something to do for ten minutes. It was just above the treetops, and shadows were scattered across the graves. As the orange ball melted into the tops of the trees, the light scattering through the leaves reminded me of the fireflies in the field. When there was just the tip of the orb left, an orange line pancaked across the treetops. By the time the sun had totally set into the trees the light in the clearing had dropped significantly, and the cemetery took on an eerie feel. But it would be another two hours until it was truly dark.

To pass the time, I counted how many different bird calls I heard. I got up to eight before the music stopped and gave way to crickets. It was then that I remembered to turn off the ringer on my phone. It hardly ever rang, but this wouldn't be a good time. Every couple of minutes I heard a car on the road, but otherwise it was quiet and peaceful. Not quite as peaceful as the mountains, but they had their own kind of peace you wouldn't find anywhere else.

I checked my watch more often as time went by. Toward ten I was surprised that only five minutes had passed. As I began to wonder, I saw something move at the end of the path into the cemetery. I looked again at my watch… ten thirty. It was a person, but I didn't make out McElroy until he got out in the center of the cemetery. He was walking toward the uncovered grave, carrying a shovel and a satchel. I was surprised that I hadn't heard a car.

He jumped into the hole with the shovel, and I heard scraping sounds. He was uncovering the last of the dirt from the coffin. After ten minutes, he threw the shovel out of the hole and climbed back out. He threw the satchel in and jumped in after it. I quietly exited the trees and started toward the grave. About twenty feet away I stopped and knelt on one knee and waited. I glanced back at the spot where my path was.

It was less than five minutes before the satchel landed on the grass next to the grave and McElroy climbed back out again. As he bent to pick up the satchel, the night turned to day as floodlights lit up the cemetery, and a voice over a bullhorn said, "DEA and FBI. Raise your hands."

McElroy just froze.

"I said raise your hands!" the voice yelled.

As McElroy started to raise his hands, the lights suddenly went out, and the voice yelled, "What the hell! Get that light back on!"

I ran to McElroy who was standing still with his arms half raised and yelled, "Follow me!"

He lowered his arms but didn't move.

I grabbed his shoulder holster and pulled. "Hey! Let's go!" I started running toward where I thought the oak tree was. Twenty feet from the trees I looked back over my shoulder. McElroy wasn't far behind. The voice on the bullhorn was still yelling about the lights. When we reached the edge of the trees I turned and told him we were going into the woods and to stay close or he'd lose me. We were only a few feet from the oak tree. I walked over to it and headed into the pitch-black darkness.

Every twenty steps or so I stopped to make sure McElroy was with me. He was. It was so dark I could barely see a few feet in front of me. I was relying on my memory to get us through the trees. But I wasn't struggling through underbrush, so I had hope that we were on the path. At one stop I looked back and saw light filtering through the trees, and I heard a very angry muffled voice on the bullhorn. At the next stop McElroy started to ask something. I told him we'd talk when we were out the other side. There was a chill in the air, but I had worked up a sweat. Ten minutes later—it seemed like an hour—I stepped out of the trees and into the field behind the facility. I was breathing hard, but McElroy was breathing harder.

He started to run across the field, but after about fifty feet he doubled over and was gasping for air. I came up to him and waited. As he stood, I said, "We don't have to hurry. They'll never find their way through the woods in the dark."

"But they'll be after me. I've got to get away from here."

"No, they won't. They couldn't have seen you from that far away. All they know is someone was there. They don't know who. As long as we get to the facility, we'll be okay. Let's go." We walked as quickly as he could handle.

Halfway across I asked if he had a key. I suspected he did.

"Yes. I…" He let that thought drift away.

"Where's your car?" I asked.

"In the lot in front. I walked over to the cemetery."

"Good. We can drive back there."

"What? We can't go back there!"

"Sure we can. Again, they don't know who we were."

I again caught a whiff of skunk and crossed my fingers. As we neared one of the wings, he said, "I've got questions."

"So do I. Let's get inside."

After opening a door, we walked into a hallway and he said, "There's a head down the hall. You need it?"

"Nope."

He pointed to a room on the left. "Meet you in there." Ten minutes later we were sitting in what looked like a conference room. There were two couches, four chairs, and a desk.

He rested his hands on his knees and leaned forward. "You saved my ass."

"Hey. Isn't that what teammates do?"

He nodded. "Nevertheless, I owe you one."

We sat for a couple of minutes, and I watched as the arrogant look slowly came back to his face. He looked up at me and asked, "How did they know I was there?"

I smiled. "That's easy… you have a leak."

He thought about that as he leaned back on the couch.

"And why were *you* there?"

I started to answer and heard a loud noise like chains being dragged across grating. The startled look on my face made him laugh.

"Boiler plant. This is an old place. So why?"

"That's easy too. I've been there almost every day or night since this thing started."

"And what thing would that be?"

"I told you I was hired by the aunt of Rentel... Susan Janice. She wanted me to look into what had happened to him. She received a phone call telling her she would find answers at a cemetery... this one."

"Answers to what?"

"Didn't know at the time, but I figured it had something to do with Rentel. Now it looks like it has to do with your stashing drugs in a coffin."

He stared at me before asking who the caller was.

I shook my head. "No clue. But, again, you've got a leak."

"And what does this aunt have to say now?"

"Nothing. She was supposed to call me after I looked at the cemetery, but she never did. She disappeared."

"That's odd," he said with a look that made me think he didn't believe what he had just said.

"Maybe not that odd. You said you owed me one. How about you tell me where she is."

He laughed. "And what makes you think I know?"

I smiled. "Makes sense. Why else would she disappear? You had Rentel. Maybe he said something about his aunt. Maybe you made some good guesses, or maybe you had Darny pay her a visit and she said something about the cemetery. Either way, she was a liability. So Darny does what he does best, and she disappears."

We stared at each other for a good twenty seconds, him trying to decide and me waiting.

I finally said, "So, you wanna even the score?"

Chapter 57

HE LED ME DOWN A SET OF IRON-GRATED STAIRS. A SINGLE bare light bulb shone at the bottom. He flicked a switch and opened a rusty door that screeched as he pulled it. We stepped into a damp, cool, musty-smelling basement filled with machinery that looked like it was a hundred years old, which it probably was. I paused for a bit and let my eyes adapt to the dim lighting.

"You're in the belly of the beast, Manning. It's a maze down here. Tunnels link all the wings upstairs." He pointed to the left. "Head down that way."

There were boilers and pumps and electric boxes and pipes running in every direction. I was walking on a grated, steel cat-walk at floor level that was barely wide enough for one person. I had to watch where I stepped to stay on the grating. On either side was a concrete channel. The one on the left had a bit of water in it. After a few steps the chain noise started again, only much louder. I figured it was only a matter of time before one of the boilers blew up, and I walked a little faster. When we reached a bend in the catwalk, I realized this would be a perfect spot to get rid of someone, if someone had a mind to do that. And with McElroy's track record, I wondered if that someone would be me. But even though McElroy was behind me I felt somewhat secure with my gun under my shoulder. And he hadn't seemed concerned about whether I was carrying or not. I would think he had assumed I was, and he had let me keep the gun.

Another rusty door ahead offered escape from the noise. I stepped out into warmer, fresher air and a stairway heading up. I assumed McElroy was behind me and started the climb. I held the door for him as I stepped out into a hallway that was a twin of the last one except in another wing of the facility. McElroy pointed to the left.

As I turned, I saw a door open to the right, and Darny came out looking pleased with himself. The door had a number six over the top. When he saw me, his pleased look turned into a sneer. He stopped and waited for me to follow McElroy who led us to room three. We stepped into the room, and he turned on a lamp. I walked up to the bed and looked at the woman lying there, asleep with a white sheet pulled up under her chin.

"This who you're worried about?" asked McElroy. "This the aunt?"

"Never met her." I looked at her carefully. She did look like the lady in the picture with Gregory. She was breathing normally and looked peaceful. "But if you kidnapped her from apartment 3D at 210 Long in Oak Park then it's her."

"Kidnapped is a pretty harsh word," McElroy said. "That wasn't how it happened."

"What would *you* call it?"

He didn't answer.

"And how did you even know about her?" I asked.

McElroy laughed. "She called Walker and started asking questions. Mrs. Starley, Quark's secretary, said she'd look into it and get back to her if she gave her number. She did. With that we got the address."

I nodded. So Starley was the contact at Walker. "Okay, so how did it happen if it wasn't kidnapping?"

He thought for a few seconds and then told Darny to tell me.

"Why should we tell this guy anything?" Darny asked. Evidently he didn't remember I was on the team.

"Because I told you to," McElroy said sternly. Looked like Darny was the same handful as when he was with the FBI.

"Huh," Darny huffed. "I knocked on her door and told her I was with the FBI. Showed her my ID. Told her I had some information about Rentel, and she needed to come with me and look at some pictures."

"And she went with you willingly?"

"Yup."

"And how did she end up in this bed?"

"Gave her some coffee with a knockout drug in it. Easy." He looked pleased with himself. Then he added, "Not like that other one who punched me and kicked me in the shin and spit on me."

"What other one?" I asked.

Darny looked at McElroy for permission. McElroy nodded.

"Real feisty, but real dirty. Looked like she crawled out of a dumpster."

I caught my breath.

"Put up a real fight. Had to slug her to put her out." He held up his hand and showed me a cut. "Cut my hand on her glasses. Then I ripped them off and smashed 'em with my boot." He grinned. "I'm gonna have some fun with *that* one."

I turned to McElroy. "What are you running here? What's the story with the other one?" My stomach was turning.

"Doesn't matter," McElroy said. "You've got what you want. This woman is fine. We're even."

"You keep her drugged?"

"Both of them. Wake up enough to eat and then back to sleep. Drugs are in the food."

"What are you going to do with her?"

"Don't know. That's not up to me."

"Who's it up to?"

He glared at me. "Saving my ass only goes so far." He nodded at Darny who turned and left the room.

"We're done here," McElroy said. "Let's get back to the cemetery." He turned off the light and waited for me to leave the room. But in that split second I made a decision.

"One more thing. I don't know about this deal."

"What do you mean?"

"I'm in on the drugs. But kidnapping and who knows what else is another thing."

He laughed. "Like I said, you use some pretty harsh words."

"Yeah? What's going to happen to Susan? She knows more than you want her to know or she'd be sleeping in her own bed."

"Remains to be seen."

I took a deep breath. "I saw Sergeant Malone's body after they pulled him out of that garbage truck."

He angrily turned toward me. "What are you saying? I had something to do with that?"

"Did you?"

"Of course not. He was one of my own."

"So who did it?"

"No leads yet. We're investigating."

"Seems like something Darny would do," I said.

He turned toward me. "Hey, Darny is a bit hard to control, but he's not a murderer. He worked for the FBI for Chrissake."

"He was fired by the FBI. And he threatened me in my office."

"But you're still here to talk about it."

Maybe only because I have an office manager with a shotgun, I thought.

"The guy's a loose cannon," I said. "To pull something off, you involve as few people as possible. Just yourself is optimal. And if you have to involve others you sure don't want someone who is a loose cannon."

He sighed. "Sometimes you have no choice."

"What does that mean?"

"You have no idea. You're right about Darny. I have little control over him because I'm not the one calling the shots."

"Who is?"

He just stared at me. His look was part fed up and part helpless. McElroy wasn't dumb. He knew the risk involved with Darny. But for some reason someone thought Darny was worth the risk. My guess was he not only was willing to do the dirty work… he enjoyed it. McElroy was stuck. If he wanted the money, he had to put up with Darny. I almost felt sorry for him. I needed to find out who it was who thought Darny worth the risk.

I walked to the door, but I wasn't leaving. "I've got to see the other woman."

"You've used up your favor," he said disgustedly.

"Then I'm out," I said as I reached inside my jacket with my right hand.

His eyes followed my arm. "What do you care? It's just some street woman." When I didn't move, he continued. "She's fine. Just like your aunt."

"Show me."

He sighed and shook his head.

I wanted to know that the other woman was okay, but mostly I wanted to know if it was Rosie. If she wasn't okay, this would end right here. And *if* she wasn't, and it *was* Rosie, Darny would be wishing he were dead.

As we left the room I glanced in an open door on my left. It was small, just enough room for a sink and a toilet. We walked to room six.

In the dim light from the hall I could see shadows of features. The woman sure didn't look like Rosie. But as my eyes adjusted, she did look like the woman who had stopped me at Rosie's apartment. Just like Susan, she was breathing slowly and looked to be sleeping peacefully. The only difference was a scratch on her right temple where Darny had ripped the glasses off.

"Satisfied?" McElroy asked.

I wasn't anywhere near satisfied. I would rather have pulled out my gun and shot him. But anything I would have said may have led to just that.

"How long has she been here?" I asked, still looking at her.

"You ask too many questions."

I turned to him, wondering how many more rooms were occupied. The place was a prison. Angry and trying to control myself, I said, "Look. This isn't just about you stealing a few kilos every once in a while. I've been working on a connection for massive amounts of both drugs and money. But, as you pointed out, I don't have the money. I need a backer with deep pockets. That's why I've been watching this place. You're not in this alone. And if there's somebody with money, maybe we can do business. But I'm not getting involved with some chicken-shit, sloppy operation that kidnaps people and who knows what else. It's stupidity like that that gets you arrested. Capone went to prison for tax evasion."

His mouth was partly open, and he had that deer in the headlights look.

"I've seen the inside of jails," I said. "Not something I'm interested in." I turned and walked out of the room.

***

HE CAUGHT UP TO ME and walked alongside me back to the hub. McElroy was a few inches shorter than me and carried more than a few extra pounds. As we walked, I counted the rooms. Room one was the last door on my right. I wondered if there was anything more I could be doing. I hated to leave Rosie in that room. But there was McElroy, and Darny was lurking somewhere… and who knows who else. As I thought about Rosie, I felt sick and hoped I'd make it to the car without throwing up.

As we walked, I checked my watch. It was a quarter to twelve. I needed to call Stosh, but I was stuck with McElroy for at least a half hour. My only solace was that Rosie and Susan, while drugged, didn't seem to be in distress. But I didn't like the look on Darny's face when he had come out of room six. There was nothing but meanness in his cold eyes.

As we walked across the gravel to his car, McElroy said, "So you weren't out to cut in on my little deal?"

I laughed. "That wouldn't be worth being eaten alive by mosquitoes every night."

Chapter 58

AS MCELROY PULLED OFF OF THE GRAVEL PARKING AREA ONTO the blacktop of the drive, he asked, "How did you know about the drugs?"

"Ah, if I gave away all my secrets you wouldn't need me. I know about your operation—*how* is my business. That gives me some insurance that you won't double-cross me."

"Who's your connection?"

"Now who's asking too many questions?"

He didn't respond.

***

THERE WERE SIX BLACK SEDANS and a van in the road to the cemetery. All of them had arrays of antennas. McElroy stopped a few feet from the last car. A man in jeans and a jacket and a ball cap was leaning against the door of the first car. He walked toward us.

McElroy had his shield out as we met the agent. "Chief Detective McElroy, Chicago Police."

The agent looked at it and nodded. Then he glanced at me.

"With me," McElroy said.

"Your business here?"

"We got a tip something was going down with a drug case we're working."

The agent stared at him for a few seconds and then motioned us past. As I walked past him, I felt a sting on my neck and slapped at it. Evidently my mosquito repellant had worn off. Through the dark tunnel of trees on the other side of the chain I could see light and hear voices. From the end of the path, I saw a group of men near the open grave. We walked toward them.

McElroy again showed his shield and asked who was in charge. The man he was talking to said *he* was and identified himself as Agent Collins with the DEA. When he looked at me, McElroy again said I was with him, and the agent let it go at that. McElroy explained about his case, and Collins filled him on their involvement. As he was talking, Thward walked to where we were standing.

"Thward," said McElroy.

"McElroy. What brings you here?"

He explained again and suggested we walk over to the grave.

As McElroy started to walk, I touched his arm and said, "I've had a long day. You've got this under control, right?"

"Yup. I'll be in touch."

I gave him a two-finger salute and walked away from the light.

The Mustang was a welcome refuge from the mosquitoes. Why they were attracted to me with that crowd back at the grave was beyond me. Maybe Howie was right… some people just attract them. I started the car and dialed Stosh.

A groggy voice answered. "Powolski."

"Put the coffee on. I'll be there in an hour." I hung up before he had a chance to argue.

I only passed two cars on Lake Street before I got to 59 and made it to Stosh's house in fifty minutes. The lights were on.

***

I LET MYSELF IN. Stosh was sitting at the kitchen table with a mug of coffee in front of him. The back door was open. He pointed at the pot on the counter. I filled a mug and sat opposite him. He just looked at me as I told him about McElroy and the cemetery.

"I thought you were going to let me know if you lost track of Rosie," I said.

He took a sip. "And what makes you think I lost track of her?"

I just glared at him.

As he put the mug down, he sighed and said, "Okay. What do you know that I don't?"

"I know that she ended up in the hands of Darny who ripped off her glasses and smashed them with his boot. And I know she was drugged. Now it's your turn."

He got up and refilled his mug and closed the back door before coming back to the table. While he was up I set an envelope with Chester's affidavit on the table. He sat down and read it and nodded. Then he started to explain.

"About a year ago, DEA offered to train officers to help control the drug situation. We asked for volunteers. While Rosie and Vasquez were out in California, the department learned of something going on over in the Fourth. Arrests that involved coerced confessions, mostly drug-related. A quiet investigation was started. The latest case is Rentel. Planted evidence and arm-twisting... you called it a goon squad. Rentel wasn't the first to disappear. There are two others that we know of."

He started to say something but stopped and drank some coffee.

"And you didn't say anything about all this when I brought it up?"

He was looking at the mug. I knew what he was wrestling with wasn't easy.

He shook his head. "Some things are just police business, kid. And it's an ongoing investigation. These things take time. You..."

I figured he was going to give me the same old lecture about the choices I had made. But this time he let it go. He knew I knew.

"So how did Rosie end up missing?"

He looked like he was still thinking about police business. Then his face changed, and he continued.

A team put together by the feds had been looking into vague allegations of coercion in the fourth precinct. They didn't know how far it went or how high it went. The only thing they did know was that something was going on in the Fourth. And they weren't getting very far until I came along with my *wild theory* about the drugs. That had coincided with Rosie and Vasquez training in California, and the powers-that-be made the decision to use them to get inside the Fourth. Turned out that was easy.

The Fourth was cooperating with DEA on a drug sting on the streets of the west side. Rosie and Velasquez set themselves up on the street as drug addict and pusher and wandered into the trap. The plan was for them to stay together, but they got separated, my guess was by Darny. Velasquez went through the system, but Rosie just disappeared. And very shortly after they were arrested, they lost the signal from her glasses. I knew Rosie had kicked Darny in the shins, and he had ripped off her glasses and punched her. Not exactly by the book. So to cover that up, or to get his revenge, Rosie had disappeared and ended up at Walker in room number six. No one cared about a street person, especially one with an armful of needle marks.

I thought while sipping my coffee.

"You don't seem too concerned," Stosh said.

"Just trying to put it all together."

"I mean about Rosie being missing."

I set my mug down. "I *am* concerned. And I'd be even more concerned if I didn't know where she was."

The look on his face made being up at two in the morning worthwhile.

"You wanna repeat that?" he said.

"No." I told him about my night at Walker.

He listened quietly, and I could see the wheels turning.

I finished, and he said, "So we go in first thing in the morning and get her and the aunt and whoever the hell else out of there."

Most of me agreed, and we talked about it for twenty minutes. I would have loved to go in with the cavalry and arrest everybody in sight. But that wouldn't be McElroy and probably not Darny. And he was the one I wanted most. Starley was involved, but maybe someone else was too. And we wouldn't find out who by storming the place. And we wouldn't find out who was running this show. The big plus was getting Rosie and Susan out of there. I asked him to give me a day. He asked what good that would do.

"I have an appointment with Thward in the morning. He has a man on site. We'll give him a heads up about Rosie and Susan, and I'll step up my timeline."

"What timeline is that?"

I smiled. "You don't want to know."

He shook his head. "Your plan has a problem."

"It does? You don't even know what my plan is."

"Doesn't matter."

"So what's the problem?"

"You're emotionally involved. The fact that it's Rosie will influence your judgment."

"I disagree. I've worked with Rosie many times, and things turned out okay."

He shook his head. "Worked with. This time she's the victim. And even if things turned out okay, they didn't always go so well."

I agreed. "I have a question." When he didn't ask, I continued. "She's supposed to be an addict. When she comes out of whatever drugs they have her on they'll expect her to act like one."

He waved his hand. "Not a problem. That course she took covered everything."

I nodded and glanced at my watch. "Okay to sleep here?"

"Sure. You know where everything is." He got up and headed for the bedroom, putting his hand on my shoulder as he walked by.

After the first time a call had taken Stosh and I away from our Gin game and we got back at four in the morning, I had left a change of clothes and toiletries in the second bedroom. I had used it twice. I was asleep before my head hit the pillow.

Chapter 59

WEDNESDAY MORNING TRAFFIC WAS BAD DUE TO HEAVY RAIN, and I was a few minutes late for my meeting with Thward. Peggy stopped typing and welcomed me with a big smile.

"Still enjoying the clean air?" I asked.

"Every day… thanks to you."

"I'm glad. He free?"

"Go on in." She announced me over the intercom and asked if I wanted coffee. I didn't.

Thward stood and shook my hand with a grin. "Well, that was a fun night."

"Except for the mosquitoes." The rain had stopped, and the window was open. I could hear the sounds of traffic from the street five floors below.

He laughed. "I would have loved to see the look on his face when the lights went on. Your plan went perfectly."

"Thanks." I sat. "But things got a bit more complicated over at Walker."

His smile faded as I told him about Susan and Rosie.

"Well, at least you found them."

I nodded.

He keyed the intercom and asked Mrs. Mitchell to get ahold of Hayes, his man at Walker. I asked how he happened to find an agent who could drive a tractor.

"Grew up on a farm," he said.

"How do you contact him?"

"He has a portable phone. Pretty amazing… fits in his pocket."

I reached in mine and pulled out my phone. "Like this?"

He looked surprised. "I heard they were coming out for the public but didn't know they were out yet."

"They're not. I've got a connection at Motorola. Can I get Hayes's number?"

"Sure. Get it from Mrs. Mitchell on your way out." He drummed the fingers of his left hand on his desk. Nervous habit.

"You quit smoking?"

He laughed. "About twenty times. After you made me aware of the conditions in the office, I was disgusted by how bad it was. I can't believe I never noticed. I felt so bad for Mrs. Mitchell. Best deal I ever made, on both ends."

I reached in my inside jacket pocket and pulled out an envelope that I handed to Thward. It was a copy of Chester's affidavit. My copy was still in the pocket.

The intercom buzzed, and Peggy said, "Hayes on line two."

I listened to Thward's side of the conversation as he explained the situation to Hayes, and I asked if I could talk to him. I told him Susan and Rosie were in rooms three and six of the south wing and asked if he'd keep an eye on them. I also told him about the tunnels that connected the wings. When we were done, I gave him my phone number. I handed the phone back to Thward, and they talked for another minute.

After he hung up, Thward took a sip of coffee and listened as I told him what Stosh had told me. "I knew about the sting, but I didn't know about the two undercover cops. That changes things."

"I didn't like the look on Darny's face," I said. "Do you think Rosie is in danger?"

"I wouldn't rule it out, but hopefully McElroy has some control over him. And Hayes is a good man." He sighed, and I could see in his eyes that he had made a decision. "Something like that was why Darny was fired. A man spit on him during an arrest, and Darny beat him within an inch of his life."

"He wasn't charged?"

"It was a street person. We took care of all his hospital bills, but the day before he was supposed to be discharged he just disappeared."

I raised my eyebrows. "Another disappeared? You think Darny had something to do with it?"

"I wouldn't doubt it, but we never found anything. But he'll never work in law enforcement again."

"Except for whatever he's doing with McElroy."

"Yeah. If this plan of yours doesn't work, I'll put an end to that, and this time he'll end up behind bars."

He pushed the intercom again and asked Mrs. Mitchell to bring in the paperwork. She set three sheets of paper on the desk in front of him and looked at me with a smile. Thward took a few minutes to read the document and handed it to me.

I took it and said, "Three pages?"

He laughed. "You're walking out of here with evidence. And if you're wondering… that's me way out on that limb so far you can hardly see me." He handed me a pen. "Sign your life away."

I did.

He slid it in front of Peggy. "Mrs. Mitchell, please sign as a witness."

She did, and he signed below her. He thanked her and she left.

Thward opened the safe in the corner and took out a packet about three times the size of a pack of cigarettes. It was wrapped in blue cellophane. He set it on the edge of the desk.

"It's less than a half kilo. Street value of around twenty grand."

"Quality?"

"The lab went through the whole stash and picked out the best. Not the best I've ever seen, but pretty high quality. If they test it, they'll be satisfied."

Twenty grand. I played with my second thoughts.

"Spencer, you sure McElroy is buying your crossing over to the bad side?"

"I've thought about it. Pretty sure. He's the one who brought up my dire financial situation. And it's not hard for someone who has already gone over to the bad side to believe someone else would. And I'm not even a cop."

He sat. "I hope so. That's a weak link in your chain. Do you have a time set up?"

"Not yet. Gonna call McElroy after I leave here and tell him my contact has another buyer and we have to move tonight."

"Okay. Let me know."

"Will do."

He picked up a briefcase, set it on the desk, and snapped it open. The inside had a foam liner with a cutout the size of the packet.

"Is the coke marked?" I asked.

"Yup. Infrared stamp on the wrapper."

He closed the case and pushed it across the desk to me. I nodded, picked it up, and started for the door.

"Don't get stopped for speeding," he said.

"No kidding." I turned to leave.

"Hey," he said, "did you see Jetter out at Walker?"

"Nope."

"Well, keep an eye out. Where there's Darny there's Jetter. He's not as nuts, but it doesn't take much to pull a trigger."

"Got it."

I stopped at Peggy's desk on my way out and programmed Hayes's number into my speed dial list.

***

WHEN I GOT TO THE CAR, I called McElroy. I told him my contact had called, and if we didn't make a move tonight he'd go elsewhere. He said he wouldn't be pushed around. I reminded him the feds had all his drugs. There was a long pause before he asked if I had a sample. I told him I did and reminded him that all the players had to be there or there was no deal. He wasn't happy but said he'd call me back. Twenty minutes later, he did. We were on for eight. I told him he owed me some money. He said he'd have it tonight.

Thward had mentioned the weak link in my chain. As I drove, I found myself wishing that was the only one… because I had thought of several more.

I got back to the office a little before noon and went to the deli for sandwiches after locking the briefcase in the safe. Carol and I ate at the table in the front office and took turns tossing food to Watson. I told her as much as I could about the case and knew she was dying to ask questions. But she also knew I had told her all I could. She never asked what was in the briefcase.

Unfortunately, I had nothing on the schedule for the afternoon. That left me time to think about all the things that could go wrong.

Chapter 60

ALL THE WORLD'S A STAGE, AND WE ALL HAVE PARTS TO PLAY. Some are consciously chosen, some aren't. I had created a character, and all I had to do was stay in character. It really was the same as the games I used to play with my friends... cops and robbers, pirates, soldiers. Well, except for the real bodies and the cocaine.

It was dusk as I crossed the river and turned south on 31. As I drove, I had watched the sun filter through pastel-colored clouds as it set behind the trees. I pulled into the drive and parked on the gravel. Four other cars were parked in the lot. I sat and looked at the building for a couple of minutes, wondering how a health facility could be so unhealthy.

I pulled on my shoulder holster, tucked the Taurus under my arm, and put on a light jacket. I got out and started toward the trunk and then, as an afterthought, went back for my phone and slipped it into the front pocket of my jeans. I popped the trunk and took out the briefcase. As I walked toward the building, I wondered if I looked like a guy carrying twenty grand worth of cocaine. And I thought about the people who had disappeared and the two who had died. For what?

On that brief walk, I went over the plan. As much as Thward was worried about it, the tough hurdle was already cleared. McElroy had bought my act. To him, the right amount of money would turn Mother Theresa. I felt confident that when I left here it would all be over. And I felt confident that Agent Hayes was watching over Rosie. But I still couldn't stop worrying about her.

McElroy was waiting for me and unlocked the front door. He glanced at the briefcase but didn't say anything. We went through the inner doors and down the middle hallway toward Quark's office. My anxiety rose as I wondered who would be waiting for us. I hoped there would be someone besides Mrs. Starley, like Quark or Bridgewater, or both. But there also had to be somebody even bigger. I hoped that would be Lansing. I wanted him bad.

Near the end of the hall, McElroy said, "Next door on your right." He held out his hand. "You first."

There was a large, wooden, rectangular table in the middle of the room surrounded by cushioned chairs with red fabric. Five people were in the room. Two of them looked surprised to see me. Evidently McElroy had kept me a secret. A bar was laid out on a small credenza on the back wall. Two people were at the bar mixing drinks, Quark and his secretary, Mrs. Starley. Darny and Jetter were sitting on red, cushioned chairs next to the bar. Darny didn't look surprised... he looked happy. Jetter looked like a mannequin. Nothing on his face moved. The fifth person was seated at the table on the side facing the door, sipping his drink... Rodney Lansing. There really was a Santa Claus. Even if I didn't know what he looked like, I could have picked him out. Ben's description of pompous and sanctimonious was written all over him. If he had been any more full of himself he would have burst. Money and power had made the man.

McElroy introduced me, saying he understood some there already had met me.

Lansing raised his drink to me. "Welcome to the party, Manning."

I nodded. The other three glanced at me and said nothing. McElroy pointed to a chair, and I sat across from Lansing. I kept the briefcase on my lap.

"What's your poison, Manning?" Lansing asked.

"I'm good."

He frowned. "Can't trust a man who doesn't drink." His speech was a bit slurred.

McElroy sat next to me. I watched the two at the bar and thought about the team. It made sense. Quark and Starley were the connections to Walker. They needed someone who had access. Lansing was the money man... or at least his wife was, whether she knew it or not. I already knew about Darny and Jetter.

I thought about what was going on at Walker. The facility was failing, and there didn't seem to be any government oversight. Somehow Lansing had discovered it and got Quark a job. And McElroy somehow had joined in. But joined in what? The cemetery was being used to stash drugs and maybe a body or two. And because the facility wasn't much used, rooms could be used to hide people they needed to secrete. And it was all out in the middle of nowhere where nobody would be paying attention to comings and goings. If Lansing had formed the goon squad to intimidate people and then needed a place to cover when his goons went too far, this place was perfect. Drugged patients were normal. And bodies were buried in cemeteries.

I looked at each person, trying to decide who was in charge. It certainly wasn't Darny or Jetter or McElroy, although McElroy liked to act like he was. And Quark had fallen into the job. That left Lansing and Starley, and I didn't think Lansing was capable of being in charge of anything. Without his wife's money to buy him a position, nobody would have ever heard of him. That left Mrs. Starley, and I remembered when Darny had failed to take account of a woman. So, who was in charge? Or maybe there was nothing to be in charge *of*. Maybe what I had stumbled upon wasn't a well-organized outfit but a jumble of misfits who were using Walker for whatever happened to come along. Or maybe there was someone else.

Quark and Starley were sitting next to Lansing. Quark looked smug, a flunky who thought he had some power. The moustache was still trying to get a start. Starley looked calm and strong. Lansing looked a little sleepy. I wondered how many drinks he had already had. Darny looked like the alpha dog that was waiting for his master to unleash him. I knew he would love to get back at me for the incident in the office. But now that we were on the same team... And Jetter was obediently waiting to be told what to do.

I didn't know where all this was going. But I did know that when they all walked out the front door their next destination would be jail.

Lansing got up to pour another drink. He added more ice to his glass, filled it with Crown Royal, and returned to the table.

After another couple of minutes of silence, I said, "So, I assume McElroy explained the deal to you all."

"Sure," Lansing said.

"And?"

"And," McElroy said, "we'll discuss it when we're all here."

Now it made a bit more sense. None of these people seemed like leaders because they weren't. "Who's missing?" I asked.

McElroy looked at his watch. "We'll give him ten more minutes. He said he'd be here by eight thirty."

I took that to mean I'd find out who it was when he walked in the door. They talked among themselves, Starley and Quark got up for another drink, and eight thirty came and went.

McElroy looked at his watch again and said, "Okay, enough waiting. I've told you all the offer. Manning here has a connection for a large amount of high-quality cocaine and needs money. We have money. Does anyone have any questions?"

"You mean *I* have money," Lansing said. "But this all sounds too good to be true."

I spread my hands, palms up. "I have no trouble walking out of here. There are other possibilities."

"Why us?" Quark asked.

"Because I found out what McElroy was doing and what was going on here, and it seemed like a good match. And why are *you* interested?"

Lansing laughed. "Why not? What McElroy has going on here is small peanuts. Bigger is better."

And there it was... the flip side of the arrogance coin—greed.

Lansing squinted his eyes and looked doubtful. "How do we know the stuff is as good as McElroy says?"

"I brought a sample. Take a look." I popped the latches on the briefcase and lifted out the packet. As I handed it to McElroy, the door opened.

"Sorry I'm late," a voice said. A voice that I recognized. A voice that instantly turned my hands clammy and made me start to sweat. "Meeting with the mayor I couldn't get out of."

So far he was looking at my back. I didn't want to think about what would happen when he saw my face. But I didn't have long to not think about it. Sheriff Grimes walked to the bar, poured a shot of Crown Royal, and tossed it back. He poured another and turned.

"That hits the spot. Now we can—"

His jaw dropped when he saw me. I tried to look confident, but I felt anything but.

"What the hell is *he* doing here?" Grimes asked.

"He's our man," McElroy said with a smile. He seemed happy that Grimes was shocked, like he finally knew something Grimes didn't.

"Our man? This is the guy you're going to pull off this big deal with?"

McElroy still looked smug. The others in the room looked confused. Except for Darny… he looked hopeful, like a pit bull straining to break its leash. Grimes and I were the only two in the room who knew what was going on, and I considered trying to make him believe that my talk was the act and that this was the real me. But I didn't hold out much hope. McElroy yes… Grimes no.

"You damn fool," Grimes said, holding the drink in his left hand and pointing at McElroy with his right. "You told me you vetted this guy."

McElroy had lost the smile and was starting to look worried.

"I did. He's broke. If it wasn't for his parents' house he'd be out on the street. I—"

Grimes slammed down the glass and splashed good whiskey on the table. "Broke my ass! He's being fed with the silver spoon those parents left him."

McElroy's jaw was set hard, and I could see the muscles working. The smile had been replaced by anger, but I wasn't sure if it was directed at me or Grimes. Until Grimes walked in, he was the boss in the room. Now he was on the edge of being the goat. He tried to defend himself.

"He came here with product." He held up the packet. "He came here to do this deal. It'll make all of us—"

"You're an idiot, McElroy. The only reason he's here is to put all of us in jail."

McElroy tried to respond, but Grimes held up his hand. He reached inside his jacket, pulled out his gun, and stared hard at McElroy. "If you say one more word, I'm going to shoot you." He aimed the gun at me and smiled. "I was at a meeting a few weeks ago where this guy gave a speech about doing anything he needed to do to put criminals in jail. He was very convincing, and I'm guessing that includes holding up a big white carrot in front of an idiot like you."

I looked around the room. McElroy had lost all of his cockiness. Except for Darny who still looked like that pit bull and Jetter who still looked like a mannequin, the rest looked worried. This had just gone from a sweet deal that seemed too good to be true, to a sweet deal that *was* too good to be true. And a jail cell was staring them in the face.

McElroy took out a knife and cut the packet. He wet his finger and tasted it. A little confidence came back as he looked at Grimes with a little hope in his eyes. "This is real. Where would he get it?"

"Doesn't matter," Grimes said. "He did. He's a lot better at his job than you, but not as good as me." He shook his head. "I almost turned down the invite to that dinner. If I had, we'd all be wearing orange."

Lansing downed his drink and said, "So whadda we do?"

"We find out who else is in on this."

McElroy looked from me to Grimes. "You think he'll talk?"

"Nope."

"Then what?"

Grimes smiled. "He has a few soft spots. One is kids. The other is women. And he hates to see anyone taken advantage of... or hurt. You still have those women here?"

Now Darny stood. That was his cue. "We sure do," he said with a smile. Jetter stood next to him.

Grimes returned the smile. "Excellent. Darny, you and McElroy take Manning over and show him what happens to someone if he doesn't talk."

"Which woman, boss?" Darny asked.

"Pick one."

I knew which one it would be. Darny didn't like being spit on. He had a score to settle with Rosie, and he had another to settle with me. And he would enjoy both.

"Stand up Manning, and back away from the table," Grimes said, his gun still aimed at me.

I did.

"Pull open your jacket. McElroy get his gun."

McElroy pulled out my Taurus.

"Now pull up your pant legs."

I did.

"Okay, he's clean. Take him through the tunnel."

"What about the coke?" Lansing asked.

Without taking his eyes off me, Grimes said, "You put it back in the briefcase and walk out the front door with it. Find a safe place while we figure all this out." He turned to McElroy. "We had a perfect setup here until you came along with your damned drug retirement plan. I have no idea why I listened to you. Okay, get going."

"What about me, boss?" Jetter asked.

"Come with me."

Darny walked to me, grabbed me by the shoulders, and pushed me toward the door. McElroy followed. I thought about the people who had told me to start carrying a gun and how much good it did me. But I did have one hope, and I put together a plan.

Chapter 61

MCELROY OPENED THE DOOR TO THE BASEMENT STAIRS, AND Darny pushed me in. My plan depended on who led the way. It needed to be me. So far so good as I walked slowly down the dimly lit stairwell. Darny followed me and told me to open the basement door. It screeched again as I pulled it open.

"Get going smart guy," Darny said. "Not much of a bigshot now, are you? Not one woman with a shotgun within miles." He laughed like a crazy person.

I stepped onto the grated catwalk that led across the room between the boilers. The plan also depended on the boilers not being on. They weren't. I walked quickly to get farther ahead of Darny. With him behind me and walking carefully in the dim light, he wouldn't be able to see what I was doing. I slowly reached into my pants pocket and pulled out my phone. I pulled up my saved numbers and was about to dial Hayes when I noticed I didn't have a signal. I hadn't considered that. I kept glancing at the phone and started talking to Darny.

"Where are we going?"

"None of your business. Just keep walking."

"Look, maybe we can make some kind of deal here."

That's when the boilers started rattling. The noise continued as I reached the end of the catwalk and stepped onto the concrete platform in front of the door to the stairway of the south wing. Halfway up the stairs I noticed the phone signal was back. Holding the phone in front of me at my waist, I dialed Hayes and hoped he answered as I started talking again to Darny.

"So Darny, you didn't answer about making a deal."

He laughed. "You're in no position to deal, wise guy. You're going to sing like a bird when you see what I'm gonna do to that bitch who spit on me."

"So we're going to room six, huh. And you and McElroy think you'll get away with this?"

As I climbed the last few stairs, I slid my phone back into my pocket and opened the door that led into the hallway. I left the phone on but didn't know if Hayes would be able to hear, or even had answered in the first place. As Darny stepped into the hall he waved his gun in the direction of room six. He told McElroy to go in and turn on the lamp. I kept talking.

***

ROSIE WAS LYING UNDER A WHITE BLANKET. Her right arm was at her side outside the blanket, her fingers resting flat on the mattress.

"Okay, we're here," I said. "Room six. Now what? You've got me and a woman who's asleep."

I really wanted to wipe the sinister smile off Darny's face as he said, "Oh, she won't be asleep for long." He took a step toward Rosie.

"Now, wait a minute," said McElroy, looking a bit nervous. His gun wasn't quite steady. "Give him a chance to talk. Maybe we don't need to do this."

Darny turned on McElroy. It might have been my chance, but McElroy still had his gun pointed at *me*.

"I never been able to figure why you're in this deal," snarled Darny. "*We* don't need to do anything. Grimes'd be better off with you scrubbing floors in this joint." He pulled his gun and pointed it at me. "Okay, wise guy. Here's your chance to spill." He waved the gun back and forth. "Otherwise, this baby gets put away." His eyes lit up. "You ever seen somebody's ear get pulled off? Makes a nice snapping sound."

I figured that was a rhetorical question. I also figured I'd better start talking... about something.

"Okay." I held both hands up in front of me. "No need to get crazy. What is it you want to know?"

I thought I heard a sound like a motor running, but then the heat kicked on with a rumble from the basement.

"Quit stalling," Darny said. "You heard Grimes. Who's in this with you?"

I slowly lowered my hands and glanced past Darny at the bed. Rosie's right hand was still on the mattress, but her fingers were no longer resting casually. They were arranged in twos with the thumb spread apart in the Vulcan salute. I felt my heart skip a beat and started to think. Darny and McElroy still had the guns, but the odds were more even, and Rosie wasn't about to let Darny tear her ear off. But I wondered how much strength she had left.

Darny took two steps toward the bed and said, "You got ten seconds, wise guy."

I let the time run out, and as he started to holster the gun, I said, "There's more people in on this than I can remember. Right now, there's officers and agents from four agencies that have this place surrounded. If you give me the guns, I'll guarantee you some kind of deal."

"Ha ha ha! That's the best you can come up with, wise guy? You ain't in no position to be making deals. And I ain't so sure about the ear." He reached in his pocket with his left hand and pulled out a jackknife. "Maybe I'll use this. I could carve nice little outlines around these tats she's got." He grinned at me. "And *then* I'll rip her ear off."

In a scared voice, McElroy said, "Come on, Manning. Spill it, This doesn't need to happen." He obviously wasn't a part of the goon squad.

I turned to McElroy. "Why don't you take a walk out into the lobby and see what's going on? What do you got to lose?"

McElroy looked like he was willing to do that, but Darny stopped him.

"You walk toward that door, you won't make it to the hall."

McElroy looked at me with eyes pleading for me to come up with something to stop Darny. But I knew nothing I said was going to matter. Darny had his mind set on revenge.

"I'm telling you—"

"And I'm telling you," Darny said. "No more talking." He waved his gun to my left. "Back against the wall."

I stepped back and moved as close to McElroy as I dared. I wanted to be able to take him out if Rosie was able to fight off Darny. But my hopes dropped when Darny stood at the side of the bed and poked his gun into Rosie's stomach. If she moved, he'd pull the trigger.

"Now the fun starts," he said. "Keep that wise guy covered, McElroy."

He reached out with the knife in his left hand, licked his lips like a kid waiting for an ice cream cone, and touched Rosie's neck with the point of the knife. That's when it happened.

There was a huge crash as the window and the wall around it exploded in, and the bucket of a backhoe smashed into the room. Debris covered the foot of the bed, and wood and glass and bars and plaster showered Darny. McElroy froze as I grabbed his gun, and Rosie jumped out of bed. I swung the butt as hard as I could at the back of McElroy's head, and he collapsed in a heap. I turned to help Rosie with Darny, but she didn't need it.

I turned just in time to see her right foot making contact between Darny's legs. I don't know how he managed to hang onto the gun, but he dropped the knife and doubled over with his left hand uselessly trying to give himself some comfort. But if he got any comfort, it didn't last long. As Darny bent over, Rosie smashed her knee into his face. Now he dropped the gun and held his nose as blood streamed out between his fingers.

Rosie picked up the gun and said, "Give me one good reason why I shouldn't shoot this bastard."

"Because you wear that blue uniform," I said.

"I said a *good* reason," she snarled between gritted teeth. I'd never seen her so angry.

"Because that would put him out of his misery?"

She smiled. "Yeah, that works." She reached out and pushed him backward as she caught her right foot behind his leg, and he fell hard to the floor.

A face and a hand appeared in the window next to the bucket. The hand was holding a gun. "You okay in there?"

"Under control," I said, trying to get enough breath to stop gasping. "Hayes, I assume."

"At your service."

"Nice timing."

"Had nothing to do with timing. Just figured I needed to do something as soon as I could when I heard your call. I was in the barn, so I got old Bess here and started toward the wing. I was coming across the field when I saw the light come on. I just kept coming and hoped for the best. And I let Thward know you're in this room."

I laughed. "Nice work, I bet this is the first time an agent used a backhoe as a weapon."

"Be my bet too."

"If you can stay for a few minutes, just help us cover these two."

"My pleasure."

"Rosie are you okay?" I asked.

"Never better."

"Are your feet okay?"

"Sure."

"Get back on the bed up by the pillow. You're stepping in glass." She had to be cut, but adrenalin was overcoming the pain.

I went over to McElroy and pushed him with my foot. He rolled over on his side and opened his eyes.

"Stand up McElroy," I said.

With his left hand on the wall, he slowly got to his feet.

"There will be more charges than I can even think of, but for the moment, both of you are under arrest for the murder of Martin Rentel."

Between his fingers, Darny said, "You can't arrest anybody. You're just a PI."

Rosie, in a white hospital gown, walked up to him. "Let me introduce myself. Detective Lonnigan, Chicago police."

He looked up at her and said, "Yeah, let's see your ID." I don't know how he managed to laugh, but he did.

"How about this one?" said Hayes, holding out his badge. "Special Agent Hayes, FBI."

Darny changed his tune as he squeezed his nose, trying to stop the bleeding. "You gotta get me an ambulance."

"Yeah, we'll get right on that," I said.

Chapter 62

MCELROY HAD COME TO AND WAS LOOKING AT ME WITH A slight smile.

"Did you say Rentel?"

"I did."

"Martin Rentel?"

"Yup."

The smile turned into a laugh. "Think again, Manning. You got drugs. I'll give you that, but you don't have murder. I already told you, we found Yancy's service gun next to Rentel's body. We just need to find him."

My smile confused him. "I can help with that. I reached into my pocket, snapped open the affidavit, and handed it to him.

As he read it, his smile disappeared. "Oh, hell." He crumpled it and threw it on the floor.

"What is it?" Darny asked.

McElroy shook his head. "You don't want to know."

A voice from the hall yelled, "FBI! What's the status inside the room?"

Hayes responded. "FBI Hayes. Two suspects on the floor, unarmed. The situation is under control. I'm outside the room. One Chicago detective with a gun inside the room. One private investigator with a gun inside the room."

"Outside the room?"

"Yup. Just take my word for it."

There was a slight pause. "Okay, we're coming in."

One agent in full body gear with an automatic rifle came slowly into the room followed by two more. Rosie and I set our guns down and raised our hands.

The lead agent looked over the room, lingering on the portion of the wall that wasn't there. "Where's the detective?" he asked.

Rosie laughed. "That would be me. Long story."

The agent radioed to command that the situation in room six was secured.

I heard Hayes on his phone asking for an ambulance.

As the agents cuffed Darny and McElroy, I asked Hayes about the ambulance. I didn't care about Darny, but I knew Rosie needed attention.

He said it was already there, and the paramedics were on their way in.

I told the lead agent there was at least one other person, a woman patient who was probably drugged and asleep, in room three but that all the rooms should be checked. He nodded to one of the other agents who asked for backup and left the room.

I went over to the bed and sat next to Rosie. I put my arm around her and asked if she was okay.

She put her hand on my leg and said, "There were some moments, but good now thanks to my knight in shining armor."

I pulled her closer.

She looked up at me and smiled. "But I've got lots of questions."

"Me too."

The paramedics came in and got Rosie and Darny onto gurneys. As a paramedic rolled Rosie out, she turned her head to me and said, "Get me some clothes, preferably that don't smell like garbage." If the paramedic wondered, he didn't ask. I was the last one out of the room. As I turned to leave, Hayes said, "If you don't need me anymore, I'll get back to the plowing."

I laughed. "You do that. Thanks, Hayes. That was an amazing example of how to improvise in the field. I bet that's not in the training manual."

He laughed. "My pleasure, Manning."

As I turned into the hall, I heard the ripping of more wall coming apart as Hayes pulled out the bucket. I'd forever look at backhoes in a different light.

***

AS I PASSED ROOM THREE, I GLANCED IN. There was a paramedic with Susan. I asked how she was. He told me she wasn't waking up, but her vital signs were good. I thanked him and gave a sigh of relief. I looked back down the hall and saw two agents going in and out of rooms.

The parking lot was crowded. I stood inside the front doors and took in the scene. A lot of black sedans and red lights and a coms truck. Two of the police cars were from Elgin. I needed to check in with Thward, but I had two calls to make first.

Stosh answered on the first ring. "Is she okay?"

"She is. Some cuts on her feet, but other than that she's alert and gave some bit of payback to Darny."

"Is she drugged?"

I watched two black cars leave and imagined there were discussions going on about jurisdiction.

"Funny thing about that. Didn't seem to be."

"How do you explain that if they were keeping her drugged?"

"I can't, but it's on my list of questions."

"Okay, let's talk tomorrow. Good job, kid."

I glanced at my watch after I disconnected. It was already tomorrow by two minutes. I dialed the next number, and it took Chester two rings to answer. I filled him in on the highlights and told him to let our guest know he could go home. I promised the whole story over breakfast.

As I started toward the door, I thought of one more call. A sleepy sounding Maggie Park answered on the sixth ring.

"Maggie, this is Spencer Manning."

There was a five second pause as she remembered who I was.

"Yes?"

"I have some work for you."

Another pause. "Work? I start work at eight. You're a little early."

"I know, but I thought you'd want to know before you hear it on the news. I have a significant case for you to prosecute."

She sighed. "I don't decide what cases to prosecute. AG Lansing does, so—"

"Well, funny story about that."

Chapter 63

THURSDAY WAS RAINY AND COLD, A PERFECT MORNING TO sleep in. A front had come through during the night. So it was a late breakfast when Jerry and Chester got the details. I was awakened around ten by noise in the kitchen. I was pretty sure it was an anxious Jerry banging pots on purpose. When I shuffled into the kitchen, I told them I was going to throw a dinner Friday night, and they would get the whole story then. Despite what McElroy thought of my financial woes, dinner was on me. But Jerry was having none of that. His patience had run out. Chester said it didn't matter to him one way or the other, but he wasn't turning down a free meal.

Over eggs and bacon, I told as much as I knew. There were questions that would be answered at the dinner and others that would take some time. But all Jerry cared about was his freedom. He turned down my dinner invitation. He was planning on heading to the bar and spending as much time there as it took to forget all this.

Carol called while we were talking over coffee. A very anxious and belligerent Lt. Santone had called and wanted to talk to me ASAP. I'd get to him and a list of others. I helped clean up, and when eleven o'clock rolled by I called McGoon's and reserved the private room for Friday night at seven.

I put the clothes Rosie kept at the house in an overnight bag and drove to All Saints Hospital in Elgin. She was waiting for the doctor to show up and release her. Except for the scabbed cut on her temple, various cuts on her feet, and a bruise on her knee, she was none the worse for wear. Her spirits couldn't have been better. I knew that feeling of having taken down a suspect. Kinda like Superman in his cape, but she had done it in a hospital gown.

While Rosie was getting dressed, I told her I wanted to check on Susan and would be back shortly. I checked at the nurse station and found Susan's room, down at the end of the same hall. She was asleep but looked okay. I went back to the station, and a nurse told me she had been drugged and they were letting that wear off. Other than that she was fine.

After completing the paperwork, I drove Rosie home, and we took turns telling our stories, stories to tell the grandkids.

***

I GOT TO THE OFFICE AT ONE FIFTEEN and stopped first at the deli. Carol was dying to hear what was behind what she was hearing on the news. I gave her the big picture and told her she'd hear the rest at dinner tomorrow if she could make it. She could.

My first call was to Thward. He hadn't left the property until a little after four. They found two more people being held against their will in the south wing. Both were male, and both had extensive bruises. There were also three Walker patients in the north wing who were transferred to All Saints for observation. Two orderlies were questioned and released. They cared for the people in the south wing but had no knowledge of what was going on. And there was one old man who had no ID who wasn't talking. He was also taken to the hospital. Thward was talking with the state and Elgin about digging up graves.

I asked him what was going to happen to the old man. They were checking records at Walker, but if they couldn't ID him, he'd become a ward of the state. He'd pretty much already been a ward of the state, but the job at the front desk had given him some value. I couldn't imagine wherever the state would send him would be good. He'd be fed and housed, but that would be it. I thought there must be something I could do. I invited Thward to the dinner. He'd be there.

Next call was to Door County. I talked with Maxine and Aunt Rose for ten minutes and gave them the short story. Barker could take his family home. Maxine laughed and said his kids wouldn't be happy about that. That was confirmed by Barker. They were having a great time. So was he.

I called Ben and left a message. McGoon's at seven in the private room.

My last call was to Santone. He was not happy. Blindsiding him in his backyard wasn't a good way to make friends. He wanted the whole story. I told him I didn't have time, but if he wanted a free dinner...

I spent the rest of the day tying up as many loose ends as I could and offering a few more invites to dinner, which I was very much looking forward to. It was going to be a momentous evening for more reasons than one.

Chapter 64

ROSIE AND I WALKED INTO MCGOON'S AT TEN TO SEVEN. Ben and Thward were already in the room with drinks in hand. I knew one person was going to be late. By ten after, everyone else was there—Stosh, Chester, Ben, Carol, Thward, Lt. Santone, and Susan and Gregory Janice. I had them all be seated and made introductions that included a brief description of their role in the adventure. Only Rosie and I had all the pieces of the puzzle, which made for a feeling of wonder in the room. But they'd all have to wait.

I told them I'd explain it all and take questions after dinner and that I was waiting for one more person. They all glanced at the empty chair. Jane and a waiter I hadn't seen before came into the room. She looked at me with raised eyebrows, and I smiled and nodded.

"Jane and friend will take your orders. Order anything on the menu, and please refresh your drinks."

If I was killing them with anticipation, they'd at least be well fed.

***

WELL FED THEY WERE. And as Jane was taking dessert and drink orders my last guest walked in. I saw her coming and met her at the door. I showed her to her seat and introduced her to Stosh on her left and Lt. Santone on her right. As Jane left the room and closed the doors, I stood and raised my bottle of Guinness.

"Thank you all for coming. You all have been a part of one of the strangest cases I've ever worked. All of you had a hand in its success. I'm going to briefly walk through what happened and then open it up for questions. We're going to start with the key to the puzzle, Vicki Gable. You're on, ma'am."

Vicki took a drink of water and then nervously stood. She cleared her throat and said, "If you know Martin Rentel, you'll find answers at the cemetery at the Walker State Mental Health Facility."

"That's the voice!" Susan shouted. "That's the lady on the phone!"

Vicki looked at me with wide eyes, and I smiled and nodded. Perfect.

"She indeed is," I said. "About five weeks ago Susan got that mystery phone call from Vicki who basically *is* the records department for the fourth precinct station. She overheard part of a conversation between Darny and Jetter—I'll come back to them. Darny said maybe they could use the cemetery for Rentel too."

I told as much of the story as I could remember and twenty minutes later opened it up for questions. While I was talking, I couldn't miss Santone's look of increasing dismay. He was the first to respond.

As he shook his head, Santone said, "This sounds like a plot out of a bad B movie. You really expect us to buy all this?"

I didn't have to answer.

Thward laughed and said, "If you combine stupidity with greed and arrogance anything can happen. One of the biggest mistakes we can make is thinking criminals are smart."

"You said it," chimed in Stosh.

Santone was still shaking his head. "A goon squad? Planted evidence? Graves used to stash cocaine? Who is this Darny and Jetter?"

I took a long drink of Guinness and said, "The guys who walked into my office after my second visit to Walker, showed me their FBI credentials, and told me I was interfering with an investigation. The guys who showed up at Susan's door and showed their FBI credentials and told her they had information on Rentel and she needed to go with them and look at some pictures. The guys who were fired by Special Agent Thward of the FBI about a year ago."

Santone shook his head. "Are you saying these two guys impersonated FBI agents and were abusing suspects?"

Thward chimed in. "That's exactly what he's saying."

Santone shook his head and downed half his drink.

"What charges have been filed?" Gregory asked.

"I'll take that," Thward said. "The FBI has taken the lead on this. It's complicated, but we'll hand off to the appropriate jurisdictions when we get it all straightened out."

"Will someone be charged for Rentel's murder?"

"Yes. Probably multiple."

"And how are all these people connected? It's a pretty odd bunch."

"I was wondering the same thing," I said. "That's what made it so hard to figure out. Trying to put everything together just didn't make sense. I've listened to most of the interviews. Lansing and Grimes aren't talking, and Quark doesn't know much. He was happy to do what he was told and take the money. But McElroy won't shut up. He's not going down alone.

"Lansing and Grimes had a shared interest, Lansing to get re-elected and Grimes to get the chief of police job. The path to both of those was more convictions. We don't know why yet, maybe he found out about his drug skimming and held that over him, but Grimes approached McElroy and proposed the methods to get convictions."

"Why would he get convictions that would make the police and Chief Swalee look good?" Santone asked.

"My educated guess is he was planning on getting the results and then letting the media know it was because of his help, not anything Swalee did, that they got results. That would have swayed public opinion against Swalee and in favor of Grimes. People in this city want their neighborhoods cleaned up.

"Grimes brought in Darny and Jetter. Those two have a long history of misconduct, so I'm guessing sometime after Thward let them go they pulled something that landed them in front of Grimes and he gave them a choice... goon squad or jail."

"And McElroy went along with that?" Santone asked.

"He really had no choice. But from what I saw the other night in Rosie's room, I don't think he agreed with the... methods. He was almost begging me to talk so Darny wouldn't hurt Rosie."

"And how does Walker connect?"

"Lansing certainly knew about Walker and saw an opportunity. It was perfect. A place that was almost empty that nobody paid attention to, and with Quark there he could control things. A grave is a perfect spot to hide anything. Especially a body."

"Do you think there are bodies out there?" Gregory asked.

"It's a good bet," I said. "There's the missing doctor and Rentel wasn't the only suspect to disappear."

"What happened with the doctor?"

"I'm guessing same as Malone. He saw or heard something he shouldn't have."

Jane came in and took another drink order.

"How did you tie the drugs to the cemetery?" Susan asked.

"Remember what Darny said… maybe they could use the cemetery for Rentel *too*. So what else was it being used for? I just started poking around and putting two and two together."

"Who killed Malone?" Gregory asked.

I shrugged. "Don't know, but all this will keep lots of people busy for a while. My guess is Darny. That's one nasty piece of work."

"So you lied to me," Santone said. "You did know about the gun."

I laughed. "Semantics. You asked if I had a hunch. I didn't. I knew."

He shook his head in defeat and took a drink.

After a ten second lull, I asked if there were any more questions. Three hands went up, and I nodded at Ben.

"This isn't a critical part of the picture, but just to satisfy my curiosity. Rosie, if they were drugging you and Susan, how were you able to attack Darny?"

She and I looked at each other and laughed. That was the first question I had asked her after we left the hospital.

"Darny had knocked me out when he grabbed my glasses. I woke up in that room. The door was locked and there were bars on the window. I wasn't getting out of there. And there was a tray of food on the table next to the bed, eggs and hash browns. I figured whoever put me there would want me subdued, and the best way to do that was to put something in the food. So I flushed it and the orange juice down the toilet. Less than an hour later, an orderly came in and took the tray. I pretended I was asleep.

"He came back with what I assumed was lunch. Darny was with him. He poked me in the shoulder. When I didn't react, they left."

"How many days did you do that?" Ben asked.

"I kept track of the meals by making scratches on the door frame with the fork. It was five days."

When Ben started to say something, she put her hand up. "Don't ask. I was starved. But I had water from the sink in the bathroom."

"Did Darny always come in?" Ben asked.

"Darny or who I assume was Jetter."

"You couldn't have gone much longer."

"Nope. I had decided that was my last day. I was going to have to use the fork and put up a fight that I'd probably lose. Then my white knight arrived." She turned to me with a smile.

"And you had enough strength left to attack Darny?" Ben asked.

She nodded. "Hate and adrenalin are a good team."

He raised his glass to her.

There were no more questions. I thanked them all for coming and told them to stay and finish their drinks.

I gave Rosie a kiss on the cheek and told her there were a few things I needed to take care of and then asked if she would be interested in a walk on the beach. She would.

Chapter 65

THERE WERE A FEW PEOPLE I NEEDED TO TALK TO BEFORE WE left. The first was Vicki.

"Couldn't have done this without you, Vicki."

"More than happy to help, Spencer. It was fun!"

"Well, you stuck your neck out. My sincere thanks, and I still owe you a steak."

"I'll hold you to that."

Then I walked over to Ben and told him to pack for Door County.

"Right. I'll believe it when we pull into Moonlight Bay."

We both laughed.

Susan and Gregory came up to me. She wanted to say something, but tears came instead.

"You're welcome," I said with a smile.

She gave me a hug as Rosie walked up and stood next to me.

Gregory shook my hand and asked how much he owed me.

"Your mother just paid me," I said.

He started to protest, but Rosie assured him that was my usual fee. He thanked me profusely.

They walked away, and I told Rosie I had one more thing to do and would be right with her.

Carol was talking to Stosh.

As I walked toward them, he turned and said, "Nice job, kid. All's well that ends well. No hard feelings?"

I smiled. "See you tomorrow."

"Whadda you want for lunch?"

"Surprise me."

He left us and headed toward Thward.

"So, my dear Carol, many thanks for your part in all of this."

"All part of the job, Spencer. But I now have a reputation as the lady with the shotgun."

I laughed. "Not a bad thing. But that's not all you have."

She looked confused.

I pulled an envelope out of my pocket and handed it to her.

"What's this?"

"Open it."

Her eyes opened bigger as she read it.

"This is a deed to the office building," she said.

"It is."

She looked at me with her mouth open. "My name is on it."

I nodded and said, "It is."

"Spencer." She looked down at the deed. "You're giving me the building?"

"Under one condition."

Now she looked wary. "What's that?"

"That you don't raise my rent."

She started to cry and haltingly said, "I think we can agree on that. I don't know what to say."

"No need to say anything."

She gave me a bigger hug than Susan had.

"I don't know anything about being a landlord."

"When I get back from Door, we'll sit down and go over the legal stuff."

She stood on her toes and gave me a kiss on the cheek.

Chapter 66

ROSIE AND I HAD SPENT SEVERAL EVENINGS SITTING ON limestone boulders looking out at Lake Michigan and the twinkling lights of sailboats and lakers. We played a game of trying to figure out what kind of ship we were looking at from the lights. A couple of times we had watched a blood-red moon magically rise out of the water. Some of those times had been sad, some had been happy. Tonight was going to be joyous.

We held hands and talked a bit more about the case. When we were both quiet for a couple of minutes, I reached into my pocket and handed her a tiny box.

She looked at me, eyes wide, and took the box.

"Is this what I think it is?" she asked.

I smiled. "Well, open it and see."

She held it for a bit before opening it, then carefully lifted the cover.

"Oh, Spencer, it's beautiful," she said with tears in her eyes.

"It's my mother's engagement ring."

She opened her mouth, but no words came out.

"Do you like it?"

"Your mother's... it's wonderful." She took out the ring and looked at it in the moonlight. "Does this mean what I think it means?"

I nodded. "Yes. I've been a fool. All this time. But when I thought I was going to lose you... I can't tell you how awful I felt walking away from that place knowing you were in that room with that maniac."

Her bottom lip quivered as she took a deep breath.

I watched as she continued to turn the ring.

"So?" I asked.

She took another deep breath and turned to face me.

"Spencer, I've had so many hopes… it's been so long. I've dreamed of this day."

My stomach dropped when she paused. I waited with dread for her to continue.

She bit her lower lip. "A year ago, even six months… But I've taken a new path with this new job. It's given me a sense of purpose, a direction I've been looking for."

I started to say something, but she stopped me.

"I knew it was dangerous. I just got confirmation of that. But for now, it's what I want to do, and it wouldn't be fair to… to… say yes."

"But Rosie. I know what life is like for a cop. I do things that are just as risky."

She laughed. "Now there's a formula for a successful marriage… two people who are never sure if they'll see each other again when they say *have a nice day, honey*."

"I guess I thought the way we feel about each other could overcome that."

She took both my hands in hers. "And we'll always feel that way. I cherish our relationship, and I always will. And who knows what's going to happen. Six months ago, I had no idea I'd be part of this new team. A year from now may be completely different."

I had no idea what to say, so I said nothing.

Rosie took my hand again and said softly, "Spencer, I waited, patiently. This came along and I had to decide. It would have been different if…"

I nodded. "Yeah, if."

We watched the lights for a few minutes before she said, "Spencer, I have a question."

"Yeah?"

"Look at me."

I turned.

"You said you thought you were going to lose me. If what happened at Walker hadn't happened would you still have given me the ring?"

Staring at the lake, I knew I should have wondered that myself. But I was too caught up in what was going on.

When I didn't answer, she said, "Go back a week. Nothing's changed. I loved you then, and I love you now." She paused. "And I know you love me." She paused again. "And that's not going to change." She held up the ring. "Maybe there will come a day."

"Tomorrow?"

She smiled.

After a minute, I pointed out over the water, toward the northeast. "I think that's a laker."

She put her arm around me, and I put my arm around her.

Chapter 67

WHEN I WAS A KID, I ALWAYS LOOKED FORWARD TO SATURDAY mornings. Cartoons and westerns on TV, and a peanut butter and jelly sandwich and Mom's chocolate chip cookies for lunch. But I wasn't a kid anymore. Getting used to an empty house after Mom and Dad had died was hard. It wasn't exactly under the best of circumstances, but having Chester and Jerry there, not being alone, having the house full of the smells of cooking, had been good.

Friday's paper was on the table where they had left it. The Saturday paper would be out on the driveway. I had gotten used to it being on the table when I woke up. I had left a chess game I was having with Dad on the board in the living room... until Chester asked if I wanted to play. Our last game was still there... it was his turn. Maybe I'd put it away.

I got the paper and sat with it and a bowl of cereal on the deck. The sun had ushered in a warm southwest wind. The story was off of page one, but there were more stories about what had happened at Walker, and they were missing a lot of the details. I tossed the paper at a table and missed. It fell to the decking. Mom's crocuses were in bloom along with other plants that I didn't know the names of, every spring a reminder of her. As I watched the clouds and soaked in the warmth of the sun, I decided it was a nice day for a drive. There was someone I wanted to see.

***

IT WAS FIVE AFTER ONE when I pulled into the unmarked gravel road. I parked and walked up the path to the cemetery. Except for the dug-up grave, it looked the same, but what a change there had been. Avery Wren sat cross-legged in front of the same grave with his rifle cradled in his left arm and his black Lab stretched out on his stomach next to him. I approached from the north so he'd see me coming. He nodded at me as I got close. I sat on the other side of the dog.

"Hello, Avery."

"Hello."

"Beautiful day."

"Mmm." He was quiet for a minute and then said, "Something happened here."

"Yes, it did."

"There were voices."

"Yes."

He didn't ask me how I knew and didn't ask questions. And he just ignored the open grave. It seemed like he didn't want to know what had happened. Maybe it was the realm of ghosts he didn't want to interfere with.

We sat for a good ten minutes just listening to nature. The birds called, and the wind whispered through the trees.

As a squirrel darted between two markers, I asked him about his brother.

"Avery, you said you think your brother is in this cemetery."

He didn't answer, but his expression changed a bit... wistful.

"You know, there have been people living at the facility. Maybe your brother is still alive."

His eyes narrowed, and he took a deep breath. "Possible."

We sat for another minute.

"They're probably going to close the facility."

He nodded.

"There's a man who's been working there longer than anyone can remember. He's the greeter at the front desk."

He didn't respond.

"He doesn't talk, and I'd guess he's about your age."

His eyes narrowed again, and he looked thoughtful.

"Did your brother have a scar on his left wrist?"

He slowly shook his head. "Nope."

I had thought that would clinch it. It didn't, but it didn't disprove anything either. He could have been cut since they last saw each other.

"I've been wondering, Avery." The squirrel darted to another marker and pawed at the grass. "If this place closes, that man is going to need someplace to stay. They don't even know who he is, much less if he has a family. Now I don't know if he's your brother or not. Maybe he isn't, but maybe he is. Either way, maybe you two could be brothers in spirit if not in blood."

He took another deep breath. We sat for another couple of minutes before the Lab lifted his head and set his chin on my lap. Avery reached out and scratched behind the Lab's ear.

"Maybe we could," he said. "If you could see to that, I'd be obliged."

We sat quietly for another ten minutes or so. Then I got up and stretched. So did the Lab. I reached down and rubbed the dog's head and then reached out and squeezed Avery's shoulder.

When I got to the edge of the clearing, I looked back at the place where this had all started. There was a lot that had gone wrong here, but right now, as I looked out over the graves in the quiet of a warm spring day, there was just a man and his dog… and whatever peace he had found in that cemetery.

If you liked this book, please post a review on Amazon.com.

To learn more about Rick Polad and his books
go to rickpolad.com
and click on Contact Us

Acknowledgements

This book would not exist without the help and support of several special people. To my readers and most special people Mike Polad and Carol Deleskiewicz, thanks for your valuable edits and input. Any remaining errors are the property of the author.

Special thanks to my publisher, Gary Lindberg, for his ongoing support and expertise.

And, as always, to all my friends and readers who have asked for more Spencer, my undying thanks.

About the Author

Rick Polad worked as a geologist, taught Earth Science and Astronomy at a junior college for twenty-nine years, and volunteered with the Coast Guard Auxiliary on Lake Michigan. Rick edited the English version of Living With Nuclei, the memoirs of Japanese physicist Motoharu Kimura, and currently works as chief editor for his publisher, Calumet Editions. Rick also worked at Fermilab, the country's highest energy particle accelerator, and currently volunteers at Microtrace, one of the world's premier forensic chemistry labs. You can find more information on the Spencer Manning mysteries at rickpolad.com.

www.ingramcontent.com/pod-product-compliance
Lightning Source LLC
Chambersburg PA
CBHW032243010726
47494CB00002B/610